About the Author

Shaun R. Coghlan was born in Picton, Ontario, Canada
where his love for reading began at an early age. He now
resides in Belleville, Ontario, Canada with his best friend,
Dozer the Basset Hound.

Those of the Moon
Book One

Shaun R. Coghlan

Those of the Moon
Book One

Olympia Publishers
London

www.olympiapublishers.com
OLYMPIA PAPERBACK EDITION

A CIP catalogue record for this title is
available from the British Library.

ISBN: 978-1-78830-989-9

This is a work of fiction.
Names, characters, places and incidents originate from the writer's
imagination. Any resemblance to actual persons, living or dead, is
purely coincidental.

First Published in 2021

Olympia Publishers
Tallis House
2 Tallis Street
London
EC4Y 0AB

Printed in Great Britain

Dedication

I would like to dedicate this book to my family and friends for believing in my dream. I wrote this book during the Covid-19 outbreak so I would also like to thank all the front-line workers as you are the true heroes.

CHAPTER 1
THE LIGHT

Logan sat in an old leather recliner with a bottle of Jameson's on a table he had on the side of the recliner. He felt like the King of the hobos in his chair. He had a small TV on two milk crates which he never used anyways as he spent most of his time reading books, mostly Fantasy fiction. He had not slept in a couple of days which was nothing new for him, between his anxiety and depression he found it hard to sleep. He drank just enough to keep his demons at bay. He got up and headed to the shower. He took the bottle with him, he got in and gave himself a quick washdown. When he got out of the shower he still felt like shit, but he got dressed and ready for his day. He worked as a bartender at a small pub called Murphy's, named after the owner Colin, which was probably the most unoriginal name for an Irish pub Logan could think of. Colin was a good man and knew Logan had a drinking problem but if the work was done and the guests where happy he left Logan to his own devices. His only rule was Logan had to be sober until the bar was closed. Logan was fine with this as Colin did not mind him having a few after the bar was closed, sometimes he even joined him. Logan himself was a loner, besides Colin he really did not talk to anybody other than the customers as he had little choice. The only other person in his life was a nurse named Sarah who he loved more than anything. Logan had met her after a rough night at work when a patron had broken a beer bottle over his head. He smiled and remembered what his mother had always said to him, "It's a good thing you have an Irish head." After a few stitches and some great pain killers he was sent home. The next night Sarah had shown up to the bar, she was the most beautiful woman he had ever seen. She had long red hair, emerald, green eyes, a nice figure and the cutest freckles across her nose. That was the best night of his life, they talked all night as the bar was dead. They stayed at the bar until the sun came up. But like all good things the night had to end, and Sarah had to get some sleep for her night shift and Logan himself could use some sleep. He walked home happier than he had been in a long time. They dated on and off but because of Logan's drinking she left. She still called from time to time to say hi and to see if he was still alive. But lately the calls became fewer and fewer, I guess we all must move on eventually. After all his reminiscing he looked up and noticed he was halfway to the pub. He lived in a small town called Barracks which was cleverly named after the small military base that was stationed there. He was glad it was small as he did not really care for people anyways. He started the same way he does every day by taking down the barstools and unlocking the beer fridges and liquor cabinet. He was just about to unlock the front door when he heard a commotion in the back, he knew it was their waitress Jessica coming in or the cook Bill, either way he did not care. The lunch crowd was as slow as it always was every Wednesday, a few regulars sat at the bar bitching about politics and sports. Both things Logan could not care less about. Jessica came up to the end of the bar and smiled at Logan, she had always had a thing for him, she knew his heart belonged to only one woman, but that did not keep her from trying, she was always flirting with him hoping one day he would break. She was a nice woman, blonde hair and blue eyes and she kept in shape. It wasn't her looks or personality, it was simply the fact that he knew he would fuck it up anyways, and as he thought before he would only love one woman and that was Sarah regardless of how she felt for him. Jessica needed a couple of beers for her table and when Logan brought them over, she smiled and asked, "are you still going to play hard to get?"

He smirked and replied, "what do you think?"

She just laughed and looked him up and down and said, "One day you'll be mine."

He smirked and simply replied, "of course I will dear." He turned around, shook his head, smiled and went back to work. The night crowd was a little busier and Logan and Jessica were quite busy, and Bill was bitching about his food sitting in the window. Bill did not handle being busy well, but he was a hell of a cook and he always got it done eventually! He always had great jokes and kept Logan and Jessica laughing, even in the busy times he was funny because of all the swearing and banging around you could hear. Eventually as the bar slowed down and the late-night stragglers slowly started to leave, Logan sent Jessica home and Bill was getting the kitchen cleaned up and getting ready to leave himself. Logan gave his last guest his tab total that he reluctantly paid while bitching that he was not done drinking. Just as Logan started to count his money, he poured himself a shot of whiskey and drank it quickly as he had been waiting for this all day. Bill stuck his head out of the Kitchen and looked at Logan. "Have a good night, asshole!"

Logan laughed and replied, "Good night, dickhead." He poured another shot as he was finishing counting the day's money. He took the money to the floor safe and locked it up. He put the barstools back up on the bar except for one as he planned on drinking for a while before he went home. He sat down with a glass and a bottle of whisky and poured himself a half a glass of it and chugged it down. This went on for about an hour before Logan decided he had had enough and decided to take the garbage out and lock up for the night. He grabbed the three bags of garbage and the bar keys. He set the bags down to lock the door and headed for the dumpster in the alley. When he looked up, he noticed a beautiful full moon. He fished a pack of cigarettes out of his jacket and lit one up leaning up against the dumpster. Out of nowhere, a strong wind began to blow in the alley and Logan could see a bright light slowly getting brighter in the end of the alley. He could not believe what he was seeing and as he was full of liquid courage he slowly walked towards the bright light. By the time he reached the end of the alley the light was so bright he had to shield his eyes. For some reason he felt drawn to the light, he reached his hand slowly towards it, he was worried it would burn his skin, or worse he would lose his whole hand! He got closer and closer, he closed his eyes and reached out and touched the light. As soon as his hand contacted the light it engulfed his entire body with such power it blew him across the alley, he slammed hard against the dumpster and the world went dark.

CHAPTER 2
THOSE OF THE MOON

Hawk woke up to a beautiful morning. He rolled over to see his stunning wife Lilly, he put his arm around her and pulled her in closer to him. She woke slowly and when she saw Hawk's face, she smiled and kissed him on the nose. She did this every morning, and it was Hawks favorite part of his day. They had been married for one year, which for Elves was a heartbeat. Hawk smiled again and asked her how she slept, she replied with the same answer she always did. "If you are here beside me, I always sleep well my love." He knew she would say it, he just loved hearing it. They both had to get up, Hawk was the top Mage and had to make his way to the Tree of Power where he taught older Elves the ways of magic. He was also a historian and was personally responsible for keeping his eye on the different realms, with his focus being on the realm of Earth, which was the closest realm to their realm of Silver Moon. Lilly was a teacher for the younger Elves, she taught the children about the power of the moon and Moonrion their Goddess. The children ran after her, she was so good with them. He smiled; they had no children, but they were trying. Moon Elves only mated on the full moon and he prayed Moonrion would bless them with a child. Which he knew she would. He headed to the Tree of Power, a giant Blackwood tree with stairs spiralling all the way to the top to where the Moon Elves Elder and the most powerful Mage Dark Owl lived, who was the overseer of all the Elves daily lives. He was also Hawk's direct overseer, and he approved all his teachings. He proceeded up the stairs and entered his laboratory, which also acted as his classroom. He was always early as he wanted to be ready for his students who were eager to learn new spells and potions. For Elves, this was the most important part of life, for magic was used in almost all aspects of their lives. Some were naturally better than others while others had to work harder. And not all would become Mages! In fact, it was usually two out of every ten who would earn the title of Mage. The students arrived on time as per usual and once the chatter had subsided, Hawk said hello to his class and started to write on the slate board. Which was titled: Phases of the moon and its direct effects on Elven magic. His star pupil Raven sat at the front of the class as per usual, she was Mage material and Hawk knew this, but he would never tell her this as he did not want her to become arrogant and lose her focus.

After he had written the subject on the board, he asked his first question. The question was an easy one, which is the way he started all his lectures. He asked the class, "What effects do the moon have on our magic?" Raven was the first to have her hand up, as per usual, Hawk smiled and said, "OK, Raven, what is your answer?"

She smiled and answered confidently, "As the moon becomes fuller, our magic becomes stronger."

"That is correct," he smiled as his next question was a bit trickier. He looked at the class and paused for dramatic purposes. He asked his second question, "Now, can a skilled Mage store magic from the full moon to help keep their abilities at a higher level?"

Another student named Orchid put her hand up and was chosen which made Raven roll her eyes. "Yes, she answered some of the stronger Mages can store power from a full moon, but it will still drain eventually.

"Excellent," replied Hawk. He then asked her, "And how do you think this is possible?"

She thought for a moment and answered, "Well, due to their ability to focus their magic better than more novice Mages."

"Excellent!" said Hawk. The class continued like this for most of the day, questions and answers.

At the end of class, they all prayed and thanked Moonrion for their power and for the blessed day that they had. This was a tradition of all Moon Elves since their ancestors came to be. He gave the class an assignment on growing flowers through their Moon magic. It was an easier spell, but he always made even his most gifted students do the basic spells as all spells require focus and control. Which was always the most important part of moon magic, or any magic for that matter.

He dismissed the class and turned to his papers, when he turned back around, he was startled as Raven was standing behind him.

He looked at her and asked, "What can I do for you, Raven?"

She looked at him and asked, "Why do you make me do these basic spells, you know very well I am capable of much more powerful spells!"

Hawk thought for a moment before he answered her question. He looked at her for a moment and answered, "First of all, I am well aware of your abilities. These simple spells help with focus and control and as you all know, these fundamentals are very important in stronger spells, and you will get to the more powerful spells when I feel you are ready. Be patient, for a Mage who tries to move too fast is a danger to themselves and others."

She smiled and walked out of the class without saying anything else. Hawk smiled, she was right, the spell he assigned them was a simple one, but he was a stickler for focus and control. He had seen many a Mage die or kill someone by not having the focus or control on the spell they were casting to let it happen to any of his students. The last part of his day now was going to report to Dark Owl. Who was the only Elf who had the name Dark in front of his name, as all other Elves had Moon in front of theirs, but most of them just used their second name when they spoke on day-to-day things?

He made it to Dark Owl's door and knocked, the response was immediate, "Come in, Hawk." He walked in and bowed out of respect to his Elder who smiled at him. "How were todays lessons?"

"Good," replied Hawk. "The students are coming along nicely!"

The Elder, who had a long beard, which only older Elves could grow, and silver hair which almost all of the Elves had, with the exception of some who had jet black hair, leaned forward. His dark violet eyes were looking at Hawk and he smiled.

"I am pleased with your progression, you're an excellent professor."

Hawk bowed again and thanked his Elder. Dark Owl leaned back in his chair and asked if Raven was still giving him a hard time on her progression.

Hawk smiled. "She is my most gifted student, but she needs to learn patience, she will be a powerful Mage one day, of that I am sure."

Dark Owl laughed and said, "I would hope so, she is my granddaughter and the young always need to learn patience, she will come around."

"Of course, Dark Owl. I still remember my own frustrations as a young novice."

Dark Owl stood up and told Hawk to go home to his wife and enjoy his evening. He thanked him, and he headed down the stairs and walked home which was a decent sized home carved out of a large dark maple tree.

Their evening started as usual, they had dinner and spoke of their day. Lilly laughed upon hearing about Raven giving him a hard time.

Her response was, "Oh Raven, she wants to be Mage so bad being the granddaughter of our Elder." Which was a large burden to carry as she was expected to become one of the best Mages the Elves had.

They cleaned up after dinner and sat by a small fire drinking some Elven wine. They went to bed early that night. The Vision was foggy at first but slowly it became clearer and clearer, Hawk could see a human throwing bags into some sort of metal container. He then lit a cigarette and slowly looked to the right of the alley he was standing in. Hawk then saw a bright light, which he knew was a huge amount of moon power, more than he had ever seen. He then watched in horror as the human slowly moved his hand towards the light.

Finally, he made contact with the light and Hawk watched him fly across the alley and smash into the metal bag holder. He seemed to be unconscious, or maybe dead, hoped Hawk. He woke up covered in sweat from head to toe. He jolted straight up, startling Lilly who looked worried for she knew when this happened that her husband had a Vision. She grabbed his face with both hands and shook him and asked if he was OK.

He did not even answer her question, he quickly put on a tunic and some trousers and flew out the door and ran full tilt to the Tree of Power to see Dark Owl. He must have looked like a lunatic, but he hardly cared, as this was the most troubling thing he had witnessed in his life. He flew up the stairs of the Tree of Power in record time and as he reached the Elders door, he was about to knock but before he even raised his fist, Dark Owl told him to come in. When Hawk first entered, he could barely talk as he was so out of breath. Dark Owl told him to be seated and brought him some Elven wine, finally everything started to slow down, and he caught his breath.

He looks at his elder and spoke. "We have a serious problem!"

"I know," replied Dark Owl, who was looking away from Hawk at the time so he could not see his facial expression. He slowly turned around and his face was full of worry. "I too have seen the human male who seems to have been blessed with our magic." Blessed Hawk frowned. "I have been studying the Earth realm for many years, they are barbarians who destroy everything they touch like a virus. They are constantly at war with each other and are on the verge of destroying their entire planet, which is a polluted cesspool." Dark Owl looked at Hawk and let out a long sigh. "I too, have a hard time understanding this event! But who are we to judge our Goddess, if this has happened it is her doing and although we do not understand it, she must have a reason? I have been feeling evil in our realm, but it still eludes me."

"What?" replied Hawk. "You usually tell me everything!"

Dark Owl responded bluntly. "Like I just said I do not know where or what it is coming from, when I have figured it out, then I will tell you. As of now there is nothing to tell you, but we must figure out what we are going to do with this human."

Hawk looked at the elder with dread, for he knew what was coming next. Dark Owl said nothing for some time then looked at Hawk.

"I need you to go to the Earth realm and find this human, with there being no more magic there he should be easy to track."

Hawk put his face in his hands, he knew the question was coming but it still hit him like a hammer in the chest. Hawk looked at his Elder who looked as upset as he was.

"Lilly will not like this," said Hawk.

"None of our kind will like this!" replied Dark Owl. "But this is what needs to be done."

"When would I leave?" asked Hawk.

"As soon as possible," replied Dark Owl. "We will open a portal secretly tonight. I do not want any panic among our people."

Hawk just shook his head, "I do not know how Earth will affect my powers, and I will need an illusion spell as I will not exactly fit in with the locals."

Dark Owl looked at him, "Do not worry, Moonrion will protect you, and all Realms have a moon, my friend. So, it should help you in your journey. You are our most powerful Mage besides me." Dark Owl smiled trying to lighten the mood a little it did not work.

"I still think this is crazy. Is there any other way?" Hawk asked again.

Dark Owl looked him straight in the eyes and said, "No. Now go and prepare for your journey. I will prepare the necessary requirements to open the portal, pack light all I want is for you to find this human and bring him back to this realm."

"What if he does not want to come here?"

"I am sure you will figure something out," smiled Dark

Owl.

Hawk headed down the stairs slowly thinking how he was going to tell Lilly about his travelling to Earth realm. She did not know much about it, he had told her some things about the humans, none of which were good. He arrived and started to think of the things he was going to need for his trip. He was surprised when the door opened behind him, it was Lilly and she looked terribly upset, she saw him packing and she immediately started to cry. Hawk turned to her and hugged her tightly and stroked her hair, she calmed a little.

"I know you had a vision last night, and it must be bad by the way you took off this morning."

Hawk sighed and held her face in his hands. "You are right, something very strange has happened, and I must go to the Earth realm."

The tears where now replaced with anger. "Are you crazy? You told me they were mindless barbarians obsessed with killing each other." Lilly's face was a light red.

Hawk sighed, "I know what I said and most of it is true, but they are not all bad, and it seems the Goddess Moonrion has chosen to bestow one Human male with our magic."

Lilly could not believe what she was hearing. "You mean a human can use the power of the moon like we can?"

Hawk answered. "It would seem so, and Dark Owl had the same vision."

She used a few curse words Hawk had never heard her say before and asked. "When do you leave?"

"Tonight," Hawk replied. "Dark Owl does not want anyone knowing about this until he feels it is time. So, my task is to go to Earth, find this human and bring him here as quickly as possible! You must keep this to yourself, it is our Elders orders."

She shook her head in understanding. "I have Moon Wind watching the children right now and I will not return to my duties until you return."

Hawk turned quickly to look at her. "No, you need to be with the children or people will start asking questions, I know it will be difficult, but everything needs to look like business as usual. I promise I will not be long; he is the only human with our magic, he will be easy to locate."

"And then what?" asked Lilly.

Hawk sighed. "Then I am to bring him back to our realm."

"What?" said Lilly. "All the Elves here are going to lose their minds."

"Well, that is what I must do, and this must have happened for some reason, and who are we to question our Goddess?"

Lilly looked at him and shook her head. "You're right, just please come back to me safe and sound my love!"

Hawk hugged her tight again and kissed her on the forehead, "I will, it's a quick in and out retrieval."

"I hope so," frowned Lilly.

Hawk had one small bag packed and was ready to meet Dark Owl at the place where the portal would be opened. Night was falling. He kissed his wife once more and walked out the door, he could hear her weeping as he walked towards the portal, which had not been used in over a century. Dark Owl was at the portal already using powerful magic, the wind picked up around it.

The portal slowly started to glow a bright blue colour. He knew not to interrupt Dark Owl as it could be catastrophic as magic this powerful was extremely dangerous in the wrong hands. Finally, Dark Owl slowly looked over and Hawk knew it was time, he walked towards the portal. He hesitated slightly, then walked through, there was a blinding flash of light and the next thing he saw was the alley from his vision. The first thing that hit him was the stench of it, he gagged and threw up. He looked around and thought to himself, this is going to be bad.

CHAPTER 3
FIRST CONTACT

Hawk looked around and got his bearings, he looked at the spot where the human smashed into the metal bag container and he was no longer there. He looked around and decided it was safe to use some magic, he called upon his Elven abilities and a blue light engulfed him. He now looked just like a human in a trench coat and a black suit. He closed his eyes and focused his magic, and he could now feel more magic than he ever had. He was terrified for the first time in many years.

***

Logan slowly opened his eyes, he was still in the alley where he had smashed against the dumpster, he leaned over and threw up. He probably had a concussion from the impact and the alcohol he drank did not help things. He reached to the back of his head and there was a large bump but no blood, which he figured was a good thing. It was early morning, but he had no idea what time it was, he slowly tried to get up, he felt extremely strange, he just thought it was from his concussion. He tried to stretch and was riddled with pain; his shirt had a large burn hole in it. He closed his eyes and thought he was going to pass out again. Something very strange happened next, as he closed his eyes and focused on the pain a powerful wave went through his body and all his pain and dizziness disappeared. He reached to the back of his head and the bump itself was also gone.

A small silver light passed through his fingers and then it was gone. Now he was no doctor, but he was more scared than relieved that all his pain was gone, for anyone would know that what just happened to him was not natural, and what was that silver light that passed through his fingers. He thought about the night before, about the light and flying across the alley, he sat and thought about what his next move should be.

After about five minutes the only thing he could think of was going to see Sarah, she would be pissed as she would be sleeping, and he smelt like a brewery and garbage, but she might be the only person who might believe him and help him. He zipped up his jacket to cover his shirt and started walking towards Sarah's place, which was an apartment on the other side of town.

He started up the street and started thinking about the light again, he had no idea what it had been, he did not believe in aliens but maybe he should start. He noticed the more he moved the better he felt, in fact he had not felt this good in a long time and he knew it had something to do with that light.

He cursed to himself. "You just had to go and fucking touch it didn't you, you couldn't have just ignored it and gone home." But he would later find out he had no idea just how fucked things were going to become.

He made good time getting to Sarah's apartment, he waited until someone walked out of the building as he was afraid to push the buzzer. In all that was happening he had two stupid worries, one that she had another man there or she would not help him. He slipped pass an older man and headed to the third floor. He walked down to apartment 306 and stood at the door for quite some time before he worked up the courage to knock on it. When he finally did, he knocked hard to try and wake her up, and he never did anything halfway.

After a couple minutes he could hear some scuffling and a lot of swearing. One thing about Sarah, she looked like an angel but had the mouth of a sailor.

She got to the door and asked, "Who is it?"

Logan took a deep breath and answered her. "It's me, Logan!"

He heard a "god dammit" and she opened the door with the chain still holding the door half closed. She looked tired and extremely pissed off.

"Logan Coyle, what the fuck do you think you're doing here?"

He looked at her more seriously than he ever had in his life. "I need your help Sarah, something extremely strange has happened to me and I didn't know where else to go."

She looked at him and frowned. "Try the fucking hospital, Logan. I told you we were over; you must move on."

"I am," answered Logan, "but I don't think the hospital can help me. I need to talk to you, please, I am begging you."

Now Sarah had known Logan for a long time, and he had never begged anyone for anything. She sighed and shut the door, removed the chain and opened the door.

Logan went to hug her. She stepped back and said, "You smell like shit, you need to shower." He opened his jacket and she saw that his shirt had a large burn hole through it. "What in the hell happened to your shirt?"

Logan looked at her. It's a long story," he answered.

"Well get in the shower, I think one of your t-shirts is in the top left drawer." Sarah knew this was going to be bad, every time Logan Coyle showed up at her door lately it was never good.

'Oh well,' she thought, 'at least he is sober.'

The hot water hit Logan and it felt so good to get the smell off of him and his muscles started to loosen up even more, he felt so good it actually scared him, seeing how last night he had been drunk and thrown across an alley. He felt no pain and was not hung over at all, he did not even have the shakes. He got out of the shower, dried off and walked into Sarah's room where she had a pair of his boxers and one of his old shirts with the symbol of The Punisher on it. He was a huge comic book nerd. He got dressed and walked into the kitchen where Sarah had made some coffee and was sitting at her kitchen table.

She sighed and asked, "what is this all about, Logan? I just pulled a sixteen-hour shift, so my patience is thin."

He looked at her, he had forgotten just how beautiful she truly was, he wished he could go back in time and right all his wrongs. He sighed and sat down and took a sip of coffee. He looked at her and started to tell her the story exactly the way it had happened, when he finished, he looked at Sarah to see what her response was going to be, it was not good.

She slammed her hand down on the table so hard she almost knocked the small table over. Logan steadied the table, she looked at him like she had so many times when she was beyond pissed. When she finally settled down enough to say anything, she looked at Logan again. "I knew I shouldn't have opened that door! Jesus, Logan. Did you hear anything you just told me, you've finally lost it, between your depression and anxiety and alcoholism, you've lost it."

Logan looked at her. "I've been working on the depression

and anxiety!"

"How?" she said, "by drinking yourself to death? I told you, Logan. I was done with this shit; I will always care about you! You are a good man deep down when you are not drunk, which is almost never, and now you drop a story like this in my lap and expect me just to believe you. You were probably just drunk and passed out in the alley and had a bad dream."

Logan listened to her and could not blame her, he himself did not believe it. He got up from the table and went to get his coat, he thanked her for the clothes and the shower.

She stood up angrily. "Where in the fuck do you think you're going?"

He looked back at her. "Home," he said.

"Like hell," she said. "You are going to the hospital; something is seriously wrong with you."

He smiled. "I've never felt better, thanks."

She looked over at his clothes and looked at the burnt shirt and something made her shudder. Logan was about to reach for the door handle when out of nowhere he dropped to the ground. He felt a power in his body that felt like all of his senses were going berserk, he looked at his hands glowing that same silver colour like they had in the alley, but a hundred times more extreme.

Sarah saw Logan reach for the door handle to leave when he let out an Earth-shattering scream and dropped to the floor, his whole body seemed to luminate a silver light which was getting brighter.

She was terrified. 'How in the hell was this happening?' She could not believe her eyes, it was just like Logan had described it, but she never believed any of it. Yet here, in her apartment, her ex was glowing.

She ran to Logan not knowing what to do. She didn't even know if she could touch him. When he touched the light, it sent him flying across an alley, and she did not wish to have the same experience, so she stayed close to him and tried to talk to him. Logan was not in pain anymore, but he was looking at a world he had never seen before.

Then he saw a man dressed in a trench coat and a suit. He looked like a fifties gangster and he could see he was coming towards Sarah's place and then just as fast as it had hit him it was gone. He was still on the floor looking around, covered in sweat. Sarah was kneeling beside him looking at him in awe, she could not believe what she had just witnessed.

Logan looked up with a serious look, a flash of silver covered his blue eyes for a second. She was terrified, and for the first time in a long time, she did not know what to do. She helped Logan to his feet and looked at him.

He finally spoke. "Something is coming for me!"

***

Hawk was having a little trouble tracking this human as his power was unlike anything he had ever experienced. He felt like his chest was going to explode, the air was so polluted, and everything smelt horrible to him. His observations of Earth realm were accurate, as he watched cars and trucks drive by, ever adding to the already polluted realm. A sadness fell over him as he had such high hopes for humanity when he first started studying them. But after seeing failure after failure, he had given up on them as a doomed species, destroying the Earth and themselves at a rapid rate. He refocussed on his mission, knowing the sooner he got the human, the sooner he could return home. All the magic seemed to be coming from a six-story brick building. He walked towards what seemed to be the front door, he pulled the handle, it seem to be locked somehow, he spoke some Elvish and touched the lock and the door sprung open.

The building seemed to be what humans called an apartment building, which complicated things a little, but the human was here. Hawk started up the stairs and halfway up he was hit with more power than he had ever felt, it almost knocked him down, but being a powerful Mage himself, he was able to steady himself. He continued up to the third floor and was blasted again. He had a flash of a human hunched down and a female beside him. He was stuck against the wall, the blast had him pinned to the wall and this time his magic did nothing. After a few moments of panic the blast was gone and Hawk could move again. He never knew this human was going to be this strong, he was much more cautious walking down the hall and cast a shielding spell in case a blast decided to hit him again. He finally stopped at the apartment, which was 306 in human numerology, he knew he had found the source of the magic.

CHAPTER 4
THE RETURN

It was a beautiful day in the realm of Silver Moon, but the Elder Dark Owl was restless, he still had not told his people about the human for he knew he must do it at the right time. He knew he was running out of time, as Hawk seemed to be making quick progress. He was also concerned about the feeling of evil that had been haunting him every night, he had not had this feeling for over a century, when the final war against Rubia and her minions was won, and she was killed. Many of the people of Silver Moon had died in this terrible war. Since then, they have had peace, all the different species of the realm stayed in their territory and everyone was at peace with what they had. After focusing on the aftermath of the war, they had looked for months for her body and had found nothing. As soon as that thought left his mind, he felt the evil a hundred times stronger. He bowed his head, perhaps they should have looked longer.

***

The ground shook and started to crack near the base of the White Onyx mountains, the sky turned red, and lightning was striking the sand near the mountain, causing glass towers to form. There was a huge explosion from the lower centre of the mountain, white onyx flew for miles. Then with an eerie silence the sky cleared, and the dust settled. Deep within the mountain sat an ancient throne room, and in the centre of it was a Sarcophagus with symbols and Elvish writing on it which started to glow lightly. It slowly got brighter and brighter until finally the lid started to move, and a feminine hand slowly emerged to grab the side of the lid. The hand slid the heavy lid with ease until it eventually fell to the floor shattering into pieces. Slowly a second hand appeared and both hands pulled a female Moon Elf to a sitting position, she looked more like a skeleton than a true elf. She slowly crawled over the side of the sarcophagus, she hit the floor hard, and she coughed up dust and dirt. She knew she must crawl to the entrance of the mountain as she could not absorb any magic in this dark hole. The skeletal figure crawled for hours towards the entrance; it's hands the only thing that resembled a living being. After what seemed like an eternity the skeletal figure reached the entrance made in the mountain.

As soon as the skeleton creature made contact with the light of the moon, the moon itself turned a dark red and a powerful beam struck the skeletal remains. There was a swirl of red and silver surrounding it's body and within a few minutes there stood a beautiful Moon Elf with long silver hair, a perfect complexion as all Elves have, and her eyes were of two colours, one was dark purple, the other a dark red. She now wore a black dress with red straps which left little to the imagination.

Rubia cracked her neck as she had been in that sarcophagus for a century or more, she said something in Elvish and a mirror appeared, she smiled and thought not bad for a woman who's been "dead" for such a long time. She did not stand there for too long for there was much more work to begin.

***

Dark Owl's people took cover from the strange storm of lightning and the large explosion. Mothers covered their children, husbands covered both. Some of the higher Mages cast shielding spells just to make sure no one was hit with anything. Dark Owl knew he had to go and calm his people and tell them what was happening. He made his way down the stairs to the center of their community where every Elf knew to go in times of emergency. Eventually the storm subsided, and the ground shook no more.

All the Elves were already at the meeting place when Dark Owl arrived. Elves were arguing about what was happening, all of which was wrong. Dark Owl cast a spell to enhance the power and sound of his voice.

"Silence!" Everyone jumped at the powerful command. Dark Owl began to speak. He started by telling them about Hawk's mission to Earth realm and the human that seemed to possess great power. The Elves looked terrified for they knew little about humans except that they were violent barbarians.

He continued to speak. "As for what has taken place today, I am not entirely sure as to what is happening, I will call upon you when I know what has occurred here today. I want all of you to go to your homes for tonight. I will hopefully have news for you as quickly as possible."

The Elves had all started towards their homes whispering and muttering different things. Dark Owl turned back towards his domicile, he was almost certain he knew what was happening, he just did not want to admit it. And then halfway up the stairs he turned and saw the moon turn red for a few moments and all his fears were confirmed, for he knew Rubia somehow had returned, and that the Elves time of peace was over.

CHAPTER 5
THE OUTSIDERS

Logan could feel the man in the suit coming down the hall, he told Sarah to hide in her room! Instead, she ran to her room and came back into the living room brandishing a small pistol.

Logan frowned at her. "When the hell did you get a gun?"

"Last year," she answered. "We are not living in the safest of times, Logan, in case you forgot."

He had not and he could not blame her, the world was going to shit. He looked at her again. "Do you actually know how to use that?"

She looked at him and rolled her eyes. "Yes," she said.

"As long as you can come over here and show me what end the bullet comes out of."

"Relax," she said. "I have over a thousand hours at the gun range."

He smiled at her. "Is now really the time for sarcasm?"

She smiled and shrugged her shoulders. The man was now at the door. He was about to knock when Logan shouted through the door.

"Whatever you're here for I recommend you leave pal!" He looked through the eye hole and almost shat himself.

The man in the suit was not a human at all he looked like an Elf from the fantasy books he loved to read. Except his ears were much longer and curled to the back of his head to a fine point.

Hawk could tell his illusion spell was not working against Logan's magic which was going to be interesting.

He spoke through the door. "My name is Moon Hawk. I have come here due to dire circumstances and I need your help, and I can help you, I know what is happening to you please allow me to speak with you I mean you no harm."

Logan did not know what to believe, on the other side of the door was not supposed to exist except in Fantasy books and fairy tales. He looked at Sarah who still had the gun raised, she looked at Logan and her stance suggested she was ready to use the gun if she needed to.

Logan thought for a moment and spoke. "Oh yeah what do you think is happening to me, Mister Hawk?"

Hawk answered quickly. "I know what happened in the alley and how you now have powers you cannot explain is that enough or do you need more before you believe me."

Logan could not believe that this was happening, perhaps he will wake up in bed soon and this will all have been a bad dream, but despite himself he unlocked the door and waved the Elf or whatever he was inside. Logan saw the Elf whereas Sarah still saw a man with a suit on. She still had the pistol pointed at the man.

Hawk smiled. "You'll have no need for your weapon ma'am and besides, it wouldn't work on me."

Sarah looked at him like he was crazy. "How about I fire a round just to put your theory to the test."

Hawk bowed. "If it makes you feel better you could try it, but I am sure your neighbours would call the police and I do not have time for that."

Logan looked at Sarah and told her to lower the weapon, she sighed and did as he asked her. Logan looked at the Elf who had jet black hair and dark purple eyes, he was quite a bit shorter than Logan who was six foot two, he was also quite slender, not in a sickly way just not nearly as broad as a human. His complexion was perfect with a slender noise and a pointed chin. He was quite stunning to look at, Logan had to admit.

Hawk looked at the two humans, he had never been in the same room with one. Logan was taller than him and broader with a square chin and a goatee, which was something only the oldest Elves could grow. His arms were also thicker, and his chest was barrel shaped like a Dwarf. He also had blue eyes that fascinated Hawk. Then there was the female, she was shorter than both of them, she had a pale complexion similar to the Elf, but she had fire red hair which Hawk had only seen in the books he had on humans and again, the human's eyes where a beautiful colour of dark green. By the look she had in her eyes she had a fighting spirit.

Logan finally broke the silence. "Ok, first off, drop the man in the suit look and show Sarah what you truly look like."

Hawk looked at Logan and frowned but did as he had requested, there was a swirl of purple going around Hawk and then Sarah saw what he really was. Her jaw dropped and she took a few steps back, tripping over a chair and falling to the ground, it was a good thing she had safe tied the pistol before she saw him, or it surely would have gone off.

She slowly got off the ground and simply asked, "Are you a fucking Elf? Holy shit, you're not supposed to exist, this is crazy."

Hawk smiled. "Ah yes, I forgot you humans and your colourful language. And to answer your question yes, I am an Elf, a Moon Elf to be precise from the realm of Silver Moon."

Logan looked at Sarah, she was just staring at the elf, she

was a little paler than usual which he did not think was possible.

Logan again broke the silence. "Ok, Moon Hawk of Silver Moon you said you can tell me what is going on with me and help me, so how are you going to do this?"

Hawk looked at Logan for a moment and spoke. "First off, let me again reiterate that I mean neither of you any harm, and you must understand there is going to be much that you will not understand right away but things will make sense in time, I promise!"

Logan looked at him. "OK, so start talking."

Sarah still looking stunned, turned towards the kitchen and started to make some more coffee. Hawk started to explain things to Logan from the light in the tunnel to the ability to heal himself from the impact of the blast, he also explained why he dropped to the floor with a silver light around him.

Logan took another cup of coffee that Sarah had made and paced for a few moments then he looked at the elf. "So, let me get this straight, I have absorbed a large amount of your so-called moon magic and that I can use it to heal myself and the episode on the floor was because you are also a magic user, and it was warning me of your arrival? I thought you meant us no harm so why the warning?"

Hawk looked at him and said, "At the time, Logan, you did not know if I was a threat, so the magic was protecting you and you just didn't know how to control it."

Logan had to admit that this was all starting to make sense. "OK, so how did you get here?"

Hawk answered. "In my realm we opened a portal for me to come and find you so that we could bring you back to our realm to help you learn to control your power!"

Now Sarah interrupted the conversation. "What do you mean take him to your realm he's not going anywhere this is all crazy talk I think it's time to leave, mister whatever the fuck you are."

Logan looked at her for a second and smiled, she did care. Logan scratched his head in frustration he turned and looked at Hawk again.

When he spoke this time there was a hint of anger in his voice. "Ok, and what if I refuse and ask you just to leave?"

Hawk looked at him. "Listen, Logan. I know this must be the most ridiculous thing you have ever heard, but what is happening to you is very real and without our help you could kill someone including Sarah or yourself and I don't think you would want that. I can truly help you but not in this realm."

Logan looked at him, he wanted to grab and choke him for suggesting he could ever hurt Sarah, but he kept it together.

"So basically, you're pretending to give me a choice when I really don't have one!"

Hawk looked at him and frowned, he picked his words carefully. "No, Logan, I am not forcing you to go anywhere nor could I if I tried, your magic is very powerful. What I am asking you is if you will come with me and work together so that you can learn control. It's entirely up to you but heed my warning, you are dangerous right now to yourself and others."

Logan looked at Sarah and she shook her head, no. He asked Hawk how long he had to think about his offer.

Hawk looked at him. "I can open a portal later tonight so in your time you would have ten hours."

Logan sighed and looked at him. "So not much time at all. Ok, Hawk, I will think about your offer only on two conditions, one you tell me everything, no lies, and two Sarah is coming with me!"

Hawk frowned. "Logan I do not know what is happening in my realm right now, it might be dangerous for Sarah and she does not possess any power to protect herself."

Logan looked at him. "Those are the conditions, she can handle herself and if she cannot, I will."

"Fine, Logan. I agree to your terms."

Logan smiled and looked at the Elf. "And now if you will excuse us, Sarah and I have much to discuss."

Hawk bowed and simply replied, "of course."

They went into Sarah's room and closed the door; they had a lot to talk about. Before he could say anything Sarah swung at him to slap him, there was a silver flash and she pulled her hand back, shook it and looked at Logan with something he had never seen in her eyes, a hint of fear. He ran over to her to look at her hand which was red and swollen, he took her hand in his and closed his eyes and tried to relax and within seconds she could see a warm light illuminate from his hand, she felt warmth and when he opened his eyes her hand was back to normal. She saw that flash of silver cross his eyes again, which freaked her out. She was pissed to say the least for being pulled into this without being asked, and she was concerned for Logan, she did not trust this Elf sitting in her kitchen.

"Well?" asked Logan, "What do you think?"

"What do I think! I think you're fucking crazy, have you genuinely thought this through? Some fantasy creature walks through our door, which is not supposed to exist, and you are just going to go on a fun little journey with him. We have no idea what is on the other side of that portal, what else could be real if he is? What if only some of them are like this Hawk and they kill you the second you get there."

Logan thought about it. Sarah had brought up a lot of good points, none of which he had a proper answer for. He sighed and still said nothing. Sarah was only getting more upset.

"Say something, Logan, Jesus Christ! I feel like I am losing my mind, and furthermore how am I just going to leave this "realm," I am a nurse at the hospital, and I would lose my job and this place if I were to leave, that's if we even survive to come back. You heard the elf; he does not even know what is happening in his realm right now! What if we walk into some war or battle or whatever they have there! And what if you start having panic attacks and anxiety again?"

Finally, Logan answered her. "I don't know, Sarah. I have no idea what to do! But you heard Hawk, what if I hurt someone or worse kill them. Look at what just happened to your hand when you tried to slap me! If I had not healed it, you would still be in pain. And I do not think there is a war in their realm, he seemed too calm for someone coming from a warzone. And I am not sure about my anxiety and panic attacks but ever since I have had this magic, I feel better than I have in years so who knows, maybe with this magic they will not be a problem anymore. And you know better than anyone I hate this place and the people in it with the exclusion of you! I have always felt I was here for something more! Now I think I have found it! Most of my life I have felt like an alcoholic loser, a fuck up who no one would miss if I died tomorrow. All my family is gone and now I have an opportunity to go and help something that I did not even think existed. I get to go to a new realm and see things no human has ever seen I want to be more than this." A tear rolled down his cheek.

Sarah looked at him with tears in her eyes. "So, you want

to change to help this thing, but I was never good enough for you to change for, after all these years I have waited to be with you! At least I know where we stand Logan!"

He wiped the tears from her eyes and looked at her, he hated seeing her cry, it broke his heart and soul. He walked towards her to hug her, but she turned away and he knew not to push it any further. When she finally turned around again she looked at him but said nothing, she had stopped crying.

Logan looked at her. "I know I never changed and kept fucking up things with us, but I never felt that I was ever good enough for you. I was hoping you would meet a doctor or someone who could give you a good life like you deserved, and for this I am sorry. But whatever my past sins have been I feel like I can make up for it now!"

Sarah looked at Logan with compassion and worry. "Logan, I never wanted a doctor or anyone else like that, I wanted you! The real you, the one who wasn't always drunk and wallowing in life. I love you more than you will ever know please stay here with me we can work on this we will put the past behind us, a fresh start!"

Logan looked at her, he was happy and angry at the same time. "A few days ago, I had not heard from you in a month or so and now that all this has happened you just want to start over? Oh, and have you forgotten about this strange power I now have that could end up killing me or you or both of us?"

Sarah sighed, "Logan, the reason I did not call is because of how painful it was, I am sorry for that! I miss you every day and I just needed some space to figure things out. I should have told you!"

"Well, you are now so that is something, I guess," he replied. Logan turned away from her thinking, he felt her arms wrap around him. He had missed being this close to her, she smelled like an angel. He turned and took her in his arms and kissed her forehead gently like he used to when they were together. Logan looked down at her and told her he loved her, but he had made up his mind to go and help the Elf and that he wanted her to come with him.

She hugged him tightly and looked into his eyes, she was tearing up again and she simply answered. "And I will be here if you return but I cannot go with you." He was heartbroken, but he understood, she loved being a nurse and she was a damn good one.

"Well, I guess I will tell the Elf that I will leave with him tonight."

Sarah let him go and simply replied. "I guess you should."

Logan walked out of the bedroom and looked at Hawk, whose face was one of hope and worry. Logan looked at him sadly and Hawk's stomach dropped, he was going to say no.

Logan thought for a moment. "I have decided that I will go, but I am doing this more for me than you, I want to learn how to control this power and you seem to be my only choice."

Hawk smiled and asked, "And what of Sarah?"

Logan shook his head, and he did not need to be told the answer as he could tell that her answer had been no. Hawk felt a pang of guilt, for he knew how hard this must be for the human, after all he missed Lilly so much and it had not even been a day yet. Hawk could feel the love the two of them had for each other and he was shocked for he did not know humans could love so deeply.

Logan asked Hawk what he should bring with him, the Elf looked at him and simply replied, "What you're wearing will suffice, and we will provide you with everything else."

Logan thought to himself, 'Well, that is easy enough, I guess.'

"May I bring my cell phone to keep in touch with Sarah?"

Hawk felt guilty again and told Logan that once they crossed realms there would be no contact and that Earth's technology would not work in his realm. He looked at his phone and left it on Sarah's table for safe keeping.

Logan looked at Hawk and simply asked, "Well, what's next, Elf?"

Hawk briefly explained opening the portal and how it would feel going through it. Hawk summed it up as it being slightly painful and disorienting, but he would be fine as their bodies were similar.

"So, when do we leave?" asked Logan.

Hawk looked out the window and told him they would leave at nightfall. Logan picked up his cell phone and called his boss Colin and told him he had to leave town and didn't know when he would be back. He was less than thrilled but being the man Colin was, he told Logan when he came back his job would still be there if he wanted it. Logan thanked him and hung up.

Sarah came out of her bedroom, her eyes where bloodshot and puffy but she had stopped crying. She looked at the Elf and spoke with scary calmness.

"Look, Elf, if anything happens to him magic or no magic, I will find you and string you up by the balls, or whatever Elves have."

Hawk looked taken aback. "I have forgotten the ruthlessness of you humans and if it makes you feel better, we are similar from the waist down to your males."

"Good," she smiled. "Then you understand me."

Hawk suddenly had a pain from the waist down just thinking about it. He knew she could never cross to his realm but the look in her eyes and all the strange things happening, who knows.

Hawk looked at her. "I give you my word. I will do everything in my power to keep him safe."

"Words mean shit to me," she answered bluntly. "Remember you came for his help not the other way around, don't fail me, Elf."

Logan smiled. She had always been a firecracker and she had two black belts in Karate and Taekwondo so she really could take care of herself.

Hawk looked at her and simply replied, "You are correct, actions speak louder than words." Hawk turned his attention back to Logan. "Do you have any more family you would like to contact before we leave?"

Logan looked sad again and said no as they had all passed on; the Elf had forgotten how short humans lived he gave his condolences and Logan just nodded saying nothing else on the matter.

The sun was starting to go down and Logan was getting nervous, he was now second guessing himself. He still could not believe there were other realms, and he was going to see one. And he was worried how the Elves would respond to him.

Hawk was also in deep thought for he too did not know how the other Elves would react, after all he had told them they were basically mindless barbarians, and one of Logan's conditions was that Hawk was not to lie to him, he just prayed his people would keep open minds.

In his small time spent with Logan and Sarah, he had learned there was much more to these humans than he had given them credit for.

Nightfall was quickly approaching, and Hawk let Logan know it was time to go. Logan looked at Sarah and Hawk was the man in the suit again. Sarah hugged Logan so tightly he could barely breathe, she kissed him so hard she cut his lip a little, she apologized and laughed.

Logan smiled. "I will be back once I have this all figured out."

Logan and Hawk headed out the door and made their way down to the street. They walked towards the alley at a quick pace, as the Elf seemed like he was in a hurry. They finally reached the place where all of this had started. Hawk stood directly in the middle of where the light had been, he began to speak in what Logan figured was Elvish. Which made Logan think of the question of where he learned English. The Elf seemed to be in a trance, the alley started to get windy, and Logan felt strange. Just as he was starting to get worried a large blue sphere stood in front of him.

Hawk came out of the trance and looked at Logan. "Are you ready?"

Logan looked over and answered. "No, but let's get this over with."

Just as Hawk was about to step into the portal, they heard a crash behind them. They both turned around and there was Sarah's car, she came running at them full tilt.

Logan looked at her. "What the hell are you doing?"

"Going with you," she answered.

Logan looked at her. "Are you sure?"

"Yes, I am sure!"

Hawk looked at them. "We must go now; the portal will not stay open forever."

Hawk went first, followed by Sarah and then Logan. Just like that the alley was quiet with an abandoned car in it.

CHAPTER 6
CREATION

Rubia was getting restless, every day she was becoming more powerful; however, she knew that there was much to be done before plotting her revenge. She had finally restored her throne room, she now had a proper bed, and her throne looked brand new. She had golden torches to light her new home, which was starting to come together nicely. She had a new mirror and a large collection of provocative dresses, she figured that just a short time ago she had been a hideous skeleton crawling towards the light, she might as well show some skin. She had felt the power of the portal that had been opened by the Elves, and she could guess what they had planned for the human. Which could complicate things for her if they succeed in bringing this human to their realm, his power will rival all the Elves Mages power combined, including their elder Dark Owl. She also knew that this human would need time and training to control his power.

Now that all her creature comforts had been met, it was time to start focusing on rebuilding an army, which she would need to strike her revenge and become the true ruler of Silver Moon. She too had opened a portal of her own to earth but for a different reason, she had used her portal to collect some of Earth's most deadly snakes, she had always been a big fan. Now they had snakes in Silver Moon, but they were harmless.

She had a deep crater in her cave full of the earth's most deadly species from a king cobra to a green anaconda. She looked down at them all crawling over each other and smiled. She thought she would start with choosing which species would be her general. She chose the king cobra. She focused her magic and brought the snake out of the crater and set it into the centre of her throne room. The cobra rose and opened its hood, hissing at her defiantly, she smiled, it seemed she had chosen well.

She closed her eyes focusing her magic upon the snake, a powerful blast struck the reptile. She opened her eyes, and she could see her creation coming to life, the cobra started to twitch and rolled on its back slowly it started to grow arms and legs its body became more upright like its creator and within minutes stood her first Snakara. It now stood on two legs and it also had two muscular arms.

The creature looked around confused. Rubia smiled at the abomination.

It spoke, "What am I and where is this place?"

Rubia looked at the bipedal cobra and smiled again. She answered the creature. "You are in a realm called Silver Moon you are now my new general. I will call you Midra and you will follow my commands."

The large reptile looked at her and bowed. "Yes, my Queen."

Rubia was incredibly happy with her first creation. She would have to give herself some time to replenish her magic as making this army was going to be very taxing. Rubia knew each species she had taken from earth realm and she was thinking of each position she would have for them. Of course, her next transformations were the reticulated python and the green anaconda as her main muscle. She also brought many rattlesnakes for her main army as their rattles would be a perfect way to communicate on the battlefield.

Midra stood beside her throne, his muscular arms crossed, his hood was no longer out as he was calm. They would all call her Queen, she had included obedience in her spell, and she had made them just smart enough to carry out her orders. She also knew they would all need weapons and armour which was not going to be difficult, she had a secret stash from the last war she had started, the only difference this time was she would be victorious.

She was finally ready to change her next two Snakaras she brought the anaconda and python to the center of the throne room and repeated the previous spell and there before her where two very large snake hybrids. They were both confused and hissed at each other.

She calmed them and when they saw her they both bowed and spoke, "Our Queen." She ordered them to stand next to her throne, they obeyed.

She had made these two giants a little less intelligent than the King cobra, after all she did not need any hostility in her ranks, although they were much bigger than her general they lacked his deadly venomous bite. She knew they would follow his every order.

She named the python Malar and the Anaconda Sucuri. She was happy with her nights work. Her first orders, for her three Snakaras were to go to their Barracks which she had ready for her new army. Tomorrow she would finish most of the transformations but for now she had to rest. She headed to her large bed and flopped down with a vicious smile on her face.

She woke the next evening refreshed. She had slept the day away, which did not last long in Silver Moon. She walked to the front of her new cavern and looked to the sky; the moon was full which would make the rest of her creations much easier as the full moon brought the most powerful magic with it. She decided the front of her cavern needed some beautification. She looked at the white onyx and decided she would make two walls on either side to put archers behind. Manipulating the Onyx was an easy task for her.

After she was content with the walls, she went back into her lair to finalize the transformations she had been conducting. Her last special choice was a black mamba, which she planned on using as a spy and assassin as its black scales would be near impossible to see at night. She brought the jet-black snake out to the center of the throne room. It was by far the most aggressive of all the snakes she had transformed, it even started to come towards her and struck at her. She laughed. It was going to be perfect.

She hit it with her magic and the transformation was again successful. There standing before her stood her perfect assassin. She had not noticed that even the inside of the snake's mouth was also black. She had to admit, Earth realm had some remarkable creatures. She had made her assassin much smarter than even her general as he would be spying and relaying information back to her directly. He also had a map of Silver Moon implanted in his mind so he would know everywhere he would have to travel.

He looked at her with curiosity and looked around her throne room. He spoke, "What have you done to me and what is this place you call Silver Moon?"

She looked at him. "I have given you a life and a purpose other than slithering on your belly. I now need to give you a name, which will be Thresher, and you will understand why I have chosen this name for you in time."

He looked at her and bowed. "Yes my Queen."

"Now go to the barracks and meet your fellow Snakaras

for that is what you truly are now."

She was pleased with how things were progressing and now that she had her commanders and an assassin, she would finish her work with her foot soldiers who were all diamond back rattle snakes. She would have to use a duplication spell to increase their numbers! One thing someone learned being "dead" was patience. Her foot soldiers would be just smart enough to hold a sword and a shield and of course some archers. They would follow her orders or her new general, Midra without question, even if that meant death.

CHAPTER 7
THE ARRIVAL

Traveling through a portal between realms was not a great experience at all. They seemed to be moving at an incredible speed and being thrown this way and that. Sometimes in a straight-line other times side to side and the fun one was the up and down. Logan couldn't see anything; it was impossible to open his eyes as he had tried multiple times. It seemed like they had been in this hell for days. And then a dead stop and a drop, they were now on their knees in some grass, both Logan and Sarah threw up, they looked up at Hawk.

He had a smirk on his face. "The first portal jump is the worst. You get used to them!"

Sarah looked up at him again, she was not amused. "Thanks for the heads-up asshole."

Logan started laughing as this was his exact thought. After their dizziness subsided, Logan and Sarah stood up and started to look around. Logan looked behind him where the large circle made of stone was and he knew that is what they just came through.

The first thing that hit both humans was the air, it was so clean. They both took large breaths of the air and it was very invigorating. No smog or garbage smells, just the smell of fresh flowers and pine trees. Logan felt better than he ever had in his life, the moon was full, he looked up at it.

Hawk and Sarah quickly turned after hearing Logan

scream and drop to his knees. His body was covered with a silver glow. He stood up straight and for a moment his feet left the ground.

Hawk had never seen anything like this he had no idea what was happening. His only thought was he was absorbing the power of the full moon. It finally seemed to calm and then stopped.

Logan was looking at Hawk with a very worried look on his face. "OK. What the fuck was that? I thought I was a goner."

Hawk looked at him and answered Logan with the only thing he could think of. "Logan, now that you are in this realm where your magic originated from you must have absorbed a huge amount of power from the full moon."

Sarah was scared as well. "Is that a normal thing for Elf Mages on a full moon?"

Hawk looked at her. "Well, our magic is at its most powerful on a full moon, but to answer your question, no, I have never seen a person slightly levitate and glow that bright before. I am one of the strongest Mages we have and although some spells will cause my body to glow slightly it looks nothing like what we just saw!" Hawk looked back at Logan. "Are you OK?"

He just nodded his head. "Yes."

Hawk tried to smile. "Welcome to Silver Moon!"

Sarah and Logan looked at each other wondering if they both made a huge mistake. It was night and there were many Elves out and about.

Hawk was trying to figure out how to get the humans up to Dark Owl without them being seen. He finally decided to use a cloaking spell, he just hoped none of the higher Mages would see them as they would see right through the spell.

He cast the spell and brought Logan and Sarah to the Tree of Power. It was huge with a spiralling set of stairs and it had jet black bark on it. Hawk told them both to run to the very top door which is where the elder Dark Owl would be waiting. They both did as instructed and had found the run quite easy due to how clean the air was, they were not even slightly tired.

They reached the door which Hawk had spoken of and as promised the door opened and there stood an old elf. He looked at the humans with scrutinizing eyes and after a few moments he invited them inside.

Hawk had caught up with them and came inside and shut the door behind him. Hawk looked at his elder and spoke. "Dark Owl, this is Sarah and Logan."

He still seemed to be sizing them up and there was an uncomfortable silence. Logan could not believe what he was seeing. Here inside this giant tree was a perfect living area, it was quite remarkable.

Dark Owl finally started to speak. "Welcome to Silver Moon, Logan and Sarah. I have been anxiously waiting your arrival." He then turned his attention to Hawk and asked how his journey was.

Hawk replied. "Quite uneventful. Logan's power was easy to track in the Earth realm."

Dark Owl nodded and walked towards Logan and looked him dead in the eyes. Logan was not sure what their customs were in this new realm, so he reached his hand out and smiled.

"Hello, Dark Owl. It's an honour to meet you. My full name is Logan Coyle."

Dark Owl looked at Logan's hand, grabbed it and held it in his. He closed his eyes and Logan could feel the magic surge through his body but this time without any strange occurrences.

After a few minutes Dark Owl released his hand and turned to Sarah who introduced herself as Sarah Sinclair. He took her hand and repeated the same gesture as Logan had received. After this ritual or whatever it was, Dark Owl headed to a chair carved out of the tree. He slowly sat down and pulled a blanket over his lap.

He looked at Logan first. "So, you are the one Moonrion chose to bestow this power upon which is the strongest magic I have ever felt. Do you understand the gift you have been given, Logan?"

Logan looked at him and answered. "I truly have no idea and I am confused about why she did not choose one of your kind, I am terrified."

Dark Owl smiled. "Well, at least we have ourselves an honest human."

Hawk Looked at his Elder and asked, "Have you told the other Elves of Logan and Sarah coming to this realm?"

"I have told them about one human. The female is a surprise to me." Dark Owl asked Hawk why the female was with them like she was not even there.

Sarah cut Hawk off and responded on her own behalf. "I have come here to make sure Logan isn't used like a puppet, Dark Owl."

Dark Owl smiled. "I apologize for my indiscretion, forgive my rudeness, Sarah."

She looked at him. "Apology accepted."

Dark Owl looked at Logan again. "You must have many questions for me. You may ask anything on your mind, and I will answer them to the best of my ability."

Logan really did not have many questions, but he asked the big one first. "How did this happen to me? Hawk told me there was no more magic in our realm."

Dark Owl looked at him and thought for a moment and finally answered. "Listen, Logan. You have been honest with me and now let me be honest with you, first how you received this power is still a mystery to us. Although our Goddess Moonrion has given you this gift and it is not our place to question the knowledge of our Goddess. This may also surprise you, Logan and Sarah, Earth was once a very Magical place, even more than this realm, due to Earth's size which is much larger than our realm. As your people moved through the centuries you turned your back on magic and started to use what you call technology and science which in its infancy was still a form of magic. As time went on your war and destruction of your planet through pollution also destroyed the magic that was contained in it and every day you do more and more destruction to your mother earth. I am afraid to say it but if your kind does not change its ways you will become extinct. And your realm will heal over time and restart the cycle of life and magic."

It was unfortunate as this was really no shock to either Sarah or Logan. They knew of climate change and of the mass pollution, it was on the news almost every day.

Logan looked at Dark Owl sadly. "Unfortunately, Dark Owl, the people in power in our realm care little about the environment. The only thing they do seem to care about is money and power. And they will kill and destroy to keep it this way. Most humans are not terrible Barbarians as you have called us. Most of us want to be happy and to live peaceful lives, but as time goes on it just seems to get worse and worse."

Dark Owl looked at Logan and nodded. "Yes, after meeting you two perhaps we have misjudged your kind a little harshly."

"No," Logan said, "for the most part you are right, we are a stupid violent race who commit terrible atrocities towards each other, and it breaks my heart. I have always wished we as humans could come together and live peacefully. But unfortunately, I believe we have gone too far, and our time is running short."

Dark Owl looked at him with knowing eyes. "Well, enough talk of the mistakes of your kind. We need to get back to the problems at hand! First things first we need to introduce you to the people of our town of Eclipse."

Hawk had a worried look on his face and Logan caught it right away.

Logan asked the question that was on everyone's mind. "We are not going to receive much of a warm welcome, are we?"

Hawk answered. "To be honest I do not know, I am sure some will be welcoming, and I know that most of the Mages will not be. You are going to have to remember, Logan, that some of our Mages have been working on their magic for centuries and their power comes nowhere near yours. They will also not be happy that one of them was not chosen by Moonrion. I myself have wondered why you are so powerful as I am head Mage besides our Elder.

Dark Owl looked at them and waved his hand in the air. "There is no use in wondering how everyone is going to react, we will just have to wait until the introductions have been made." Hawk nodded in agreement.

"Dark Owl, when will this take place?" asked Logan.

56

"Tomorrow night, as you should all take time to rest. And Hawk you should go and see Lilly she has been quite worried about you. It will do her well to see you back in one piece. Sarah and Logan, you will stay here, you will find two beds in the back with everything you will need."

They headed back to where Dark Owl pointed, as they were both exhausted. Hawk told them he would be back tomorrow night.

Logan looked at Dark Owl confused. "Why are we waiting until tomorrow night?"

"Ah," Dark Owl looked at them. "In our realm we have twenty hours of night and four hours of day, by your time keeping."

Logan shook his head and thought to himself, 'This is not going to be good for my depression or anxiety.'

He kept it to himself and headed with Sarah towards the beds. Both were exhausted, but once they were alone Sarah looked at Logan.

"Can you believe this place, it's beautiful and we haven't even seen it during the daytime hours."

Logan looked worried. "Yeah, it's great."

She looked at him. "That's it? We are in a totally different realm and I get 'Yeah it's great.' What is going on, Logan?" He looked at her and just shook his head. "Just tell me please!"

"I am just worried about my depression and anxiety. They only have four hours of day light."

She kissed him. "I am sure you will be fine, perhaps Hawk can teach you how to use your magic to get rid of it forever."

He smiled. "Perhaps. And I do find it beautiful here. I just don't trust the Elves fully; I am honestly waiting for them to grow fangs and attack. I mean only four hours of sun is weird!"

Sarah looked at him. "Well, there are places like that on earth like Alaska, I mean I do not know how it all works but I know they have something like that." Logan was a big reader, and he knew she was right. Sarah smiled. "And we are both night owls we always have been."

He nodded. "You're right babe, we will get used to it. Let's get some sleep I have a feeling tomorrow is going to be a shit show."

They got in the same bed and snuggled up; it was a tight fit but neither of them cared. They both fell asleep instantly as the Elder had said portal jumping was very tiring.

Hawk ran all the way home; he had missed his wife immensely. He slowed at the door opening it slowly in case she was sleeping. She was sitting at their dining room table with her head laying in her hands sound asleep. He slowly walked over to her and kissed the back of her head she jumped up startled. When she turned around and saw Hawk standing there she jumped up and hugged him so tightly he could barely breathe.

Hawk smiled. "Miss me?" She stood back and smiled and looked at him as if she had not seen him in years.

She answered his silly question. "You know, for such a smart elf, you do ask silly questions sometimes."

She laughed. "Of course, I missed you, I am so glad you're OK, I have been a mess ever since you left. I thought those barbaric humans would be your end."

He looked at her. "Lilly, I may have judged humanity a little harshly we must no longer call them barbarians. The two that I brought back seem like very good beings and they have the capacity to love like we do."

Lilly frowned. "What do you mean two? I thought you

were just bringing one back with you?"

"Well, that was the plan, but he would not leave without his female love. And even you can respect that regardless of what you think of them!"

Lilly blushed. "You're right, I have not even met them, and I am judging them."

Hawk kissed her forehead. "It's OK my love, I have made the same mistake."

"Can they understand us?"

"The human male Logan who has our magic can understand us, we speak elvish, but he hears English. As for the female I cast a small spell on her so she would have the same ability."

Lilly looked at him. "Does she know?"

"No, she does not I know, I should have asked her permission, but it is a harmless spell."

"Just be careful, you do not know how our magic will affect her."

"I was careful," Hawk answered, "and you do know I am a surprisingly good Mage."

She smiled again. "Yes, I am aware!"

Hawk was exhausted and he knew tomorrow was going to be a difficult day. He and Lilly headed to bed, she kissed his nose and he fell asleep.

Logan was the first to wake, he looked down at Sarah who was still sleeping, she looked like an angel and for a few moments he just laid there and enjoyed the view. He was not looking forward to meeting this town of Elves, and he was sure they felt the same way.

Sarah finally opened her eyes and looked up at Logan. He looked worried and she did not need to ask why. For she was not looking forward to this town meeting either. They both laid in bed for a few more moments enjoying each other's company.

There was a knock on the door and the moment was over. It was Dark Owl, who asked them to meet him in his common area. They both got out of bed and got dressed quickly and walked out into the common area.

Hawk was already there with a female Elf with long silver hair, a perfect complexion and light violet eyes, she was beautiful! Logan wondered if there were any ugly Elves.

Hawk stood up. "Good evening, Logan and Sarah. I would like you to meet my wife Lilly." Lily rose from her chair and bowed.

Sarah looked at her and thought she was stunning. Lilly looked at the humans and was shocked, they looked so different from the books she had seen. The human male was tall with salt and pepper hair with dark blue eyes, he was broad and barrel chested like a dwarf but much more handsome. Lilly then turned her attention to the female, she had the most beautiful fire red hair and stunning green eyes, she was much shorter than her male counterpart, she also had a slim figure.

Sarah and Logan had both bowed. "My full name is Logan Coyle, and this beauty is Sarah Sinclair."

They all sat down.

Lilly looked at Sarah. "I love your hair; it reminds me of the dwarves but much more beautiful."

Sarah smiled. Looking at Lilly, she replied. "And you, I've never seen silver hair like yours, you are beautiful."

"Well, now that we have the introductions out of the way, we must speak of how tonight will be approached," said Dark Owl.

Hawk Looked at Sarah and Logan. "We have informed all of the town Elves of tonight's gathering. Dark Owl will speak first, then myself, then you Logan!"

Logan looked at Hawk. "What in the hell am I going to say? I know nothing of your culture or what I would say."

"Just introduce yourself and Sarah," said hawk.

"Oh, yeah! Hi, I am Logan the human freak from Earth realm and this is Sarah Sinclair my better half."

Hawk smirked. "You are not a freak, Logan, we just do not understand what has happened. But I promise we will figure it out together."

Logan looked at him with doubtful eyes. "And you can speak for your people that they will feel the same way?"

"No, I cannot, but perhaps once they get to know you, things can change!"

Logan felt the uneasiness of Hawk and knew that he only half believed what he had said. Logan then looked at what everyone else was wearing, Hawk had a black suit with a silver vest over it, and Lilly had a beautiful long silver dress on, and Dark Owl was wearing a purple cloak that made him look like a true Mage. Logan and Sarah were wearing jeans and t-shirts, not to mention Logan's shirt had the Punisher skull on it! He figured it might not be the best first impression!

Logan asked Hawk, "And what are we going to wear? You are all dressed up we look like a couple of slobs."

Lilly laughed. "Sarah will come with me and I will help her with a dress. And we will get a suit that fits you Logan."

"How, I am twice as broad as you!"

"First lesson Logan. Never underestimate magic."

The women went to the bedroom and Logan and Hawk stayed in the common room.

Once Lilly and Sarah were together Lilly looked at Sarah for a moment and snapped her fingers.

"I've got it." She smiled. "Take off your clothes."

Sarah started to undress until she got down to her bra and underwear and stopped.

"Oh." Lilly smiled. Turning her head, she asked, "Are you naked?"

"Yes," Sarah replied.

"OK, now this is going to feel a little weird but don't worry."

Lilly closed her eyes and began to speak with a strange tempo, and Sarah knew she was casting a spell, a beautiful colour of green began to swirl around Sarah and within seconds she was standing in a beautiful green dress that was perfect for her eyes and hair colour. She could not believe how beautiful she looked.

She turned to Lilly and smiled. "Thank you so much, you have quite an eye for fashion!"

Lilly smiled. "All Elves can use magic. I am nowhere near as strong as Hawk, but I do have my talents."

They both laughed and Sarah hugged her, and Lilly returned the hug.

Logan was in the common room when Hawk came out with a suit that looked like it was ten times too small. He held it up to Logan and began a spell and within seconds the suit changed size.

"Put this on," said Hawk.

"What right here?" Logan did not like changing in front of another male Elf or human.

"Do not worry, I am not going to look!"

Logan did as he was instructed, and he had to admit the

suit fit perfectly. It was black with green lapels; he was not sure if he had ever looked this good. He heard the bedroom door open behind him. And when Sarah walked out his jaw dropped. She was in a green dress that was perfect for her.

Sarah walked out of the bedroom and when she saw Logan's reaction she smiled. And he looked so handsome, his suit lapels matched her dress perfectly. Logan walked towards her and took her hand, she smiled again.

All he managed to get out was, "Wow!"

Sarah laughed. "You always had a way with words! But 'wow' works."

Logan felt like an idiot, but Sarah knew what he meant by looking into his eyes.

Dark Owl stood up. "Well, now that we have all of that sorted, it is time to head to the centre of town."

Logan sighed. "Let's get this over with."

They all headed down the spiral stairs, once they got to the bottom Lilly and Hawk hooked arms, so Sarah and Logan followed suite. And they headed to the centre of town.

CHAPTER 8
PROGRESS

Rubia sat in her throne tapping her nails on the arm. She was happy with the progression of her army which now numbered five-hundred-foot soldiers. Midra had already set up patrols and the rest guarded the front of her lair. She was going to be increasing the number of soldiers very soon, but for now she was resting as she had been busy. Besides, even with the five hundred soldiers the Moon Elves would not survive a direct attack. Or so she thought, until she felt this unknown human with exceptional power enter the realm.

She had never felt such raw power and although their Goddess Moonrion never directly interfered with Silver Moon, it would seem she had given the Moon Elves a powerful ally. The Moon Elves had become weak and although she was technically one of them, she hated and despised them and soon they would bow to her as their Queen or die.

They did not even have a functional army anymore, for they have had peace for over a century. And they thought her to be dead, so the fools felt there would be no need for their swords and their shields anymore. And this would be their undoing, now they had powerful Mages for protection from the dangers of Silver Moon which right now was non-existent, and even with the Mages they would have little chance of surviving a full attack. As all Mage's tire, this was true even for her.

Although she had all this knowledge, the human was troubling her. She had no idea what he was capable of. And she knew that Dark Owl and some of the more powerful Mages would have felt her using her magic, which they deemed evil where she thought of it as progress. This was why she was banished long ago and the cause of the war.

She was still unsure of what she would do with the human, perhaps she would send a small number of foot soldiers to see what he could do as they were expendable. Her other plan was sending in Thresher, her assassin, to do some observing without the Elves even knowing he was there. She would cast a spell on her creation to make him invisible to magic. Some of the Elf Mages may see through the spell, but with Thresher being jet black and intelligent, she believed he would not be detected. This seemed to be the better of the two plans as she needed as much knowledge on this human as she could possibly get.

She summoned Thresher; it was not long before he was standing before her.

He bowed deeply. "How may I serve you, my Queen?"

She smiled. She had taken the annoying hissing accent from their speech. Although, the constantly flickering tongue was slightly annoying, but she knew this helped increase their sense of smell.

Rubia looked at him for a moment before she spoke. "I need you to go to the town of Eclipse, the home of our enemies."

Thresher looked at her. "And who shall I kill for you?"

Rubia smiled. "No one this time, I want you to find out as much as you can about this human the Elves have brought into our realm." Thresher bowed. Rubia continued her instructions.

"If you are captured or directly seen you will kill yourself for your failure."

Thresher bowed. "Yes, my Queen!"

She smiled. "And now I shall give you your new sword!"

She focused her magic and out of a black mist stood a deadly serrated blade with a large, pointed tip. It was a black blade so it would not reflect any light, the guard was a double headed snake, and the handle and Pommel were of a basic design. Thresher stepped forward and took the sword in his clawed hand. He gave it a couple of strong swings.

"It is perfect. I shall look forward to using it." Rubia smiled, she knew her creation would not fail. Thresher looked at his Queen. "When shall I leave?"

"Immediately," Rubia replied, "the sooner we know what we are facing, the sooner we can plan out attack."

Thresher bowed and turned and headed towards the opening of the lair. The foot soldiers all saluted him for they knew he was the Queens personal assassin. Now that her assassin was on his way, she knew it would take him a couple of days to reach the town of Eclipse. She called for Midra, her general.

He appeared from the front of the throne room. He bowed. "Yes my Queen."

She looked at the large Snakara. "It's time for our foot soldiers to be armed with weapons and armour."

He looked at her. "And where are we to find these items?"

"I have an armoury set up next to the barracks, but the mountain has shifted, and we will need to dig to open it again!"

Midra bowed again. "I will have the soldiers begin the digging right away." He turned towards the foot soldiers and began to round them up and giving orders.

Rubia smiled, this evening had been very productive.

***

Thresher made his way through the darkness swiftly, for his reptilian senses made night travel as easy as day travel. He knew where to avoid for his Queen had imprinted a map of the whole realm of Silver Moon into his mind! He knew exactly his path to the town of Eclipse. He continued to move quickly with his new sword in a sheath on his back. He was disappointed he would not get to use it on this trip, but he had his orders. He knew his blade would spill blood soon enough. He only moved during the night and hid during the day which in this realm was only a few hours making his progress that much quicker. He knew he was getting close to the border of the Elves town. It was well lit which was going to make this a little trickier than he previously anticipated. He knew he would think of something by the time he was closer.

He made his way up a steep embarkment on all fours and stayed as close to the ground as possible. Even crawling in different areas. This was the only time he cursed his arms and legs. For in his previous form, he could easily slither in. It was a small price to pay for his current abilities. He slowly crawled to the town tree line. He had reached his current destination and was now planning the best way to achieve his task as he knew failure was death. He laid thinking and noticed that he had not seen any Elves walking around on the streets, he found this odd.

He had made his decision. He would use the trees as they would offer the best camouflage in this instance. He scaled up a tree quickly and quietly, his clawed hands and feet made the climb easy, he started jumping from tree to tree. Stopping on each new tree to make sure no one was looking towards him. He moved like a shadow until he came to a tree where he could now see why the streets had been so empty. All the Elves had gathered in the center of town waiting for something. He held his position for his curiosity was now peaked, for he knew there must be some reason for the gathering. He waited patiently and was soon rewarded. He noticed an older Elf with a dark purple robe and a cane with some sort of stone in it. He then observed two younger Elves walking slowly behind what Thresher guessed was their elder.

Finally, he saw what he had come for, the human. He observed the male. He was taller than the Elves and much broader, he was dressed in some sort of Elven suit. Thresher did not see what all the fuss was about, he just looked like a normal male human. Although, his Queen said he was immensely powerful, and he wasn't sure if he would want to meet him in an open battlefield. The human male had his arm wrapped around a human female with fire red hair in a green dress. He was quite excited by the female for his Queen did not know about her. He knew she would be pleased with this new information, for if they could capture the female, they would get a reaction from the male. This was true for most animals. They might now be able to get leverage on this male, perhaps even an ally.

The Elder Elf was the first to climb the stairs on the raised platform followed by the rest. The Elves were talking loudly and did not sound happy. He figured it was due to the human who had been blessed with all these powers, instead of one of their own. He knew that the Elves did not like outsiders and the humans were not only outsiders, but they were also from an entirely different realm, as was Thresher himself.

The Elder raised his hands and in a powerful voice simply

said, "Silence."

Thresher was surprised that such a powerful voice could come from such an older elf, instantly all the talking Elves stopped and turned their attention to the elder. He began to speak to the towns Elves, followed by an Elf they called Hawk, and finally the male human they called Logan spoke. Some of the Elves yelled different obscenities during the males speech, to which their Elder would rise and dismiss the troublemakers.

One thing was for sure, they did not want this human here and were not happy that he had been blessed with so much power. Little did the Elves know that the only thing keeping them alive was this powerful human, for his Queen would have already attacked if it were not for him. He had heard enough; he left his tree and began his trip back to his Queen.

CHAPTER 9
THE TOWN MEETING

They had reached the centre of town where a small stage had been set up. Logan could hear the whispers and feel the anger, even hatred, from some of the Elves. Hawk turned and smiled at him to help put him at ease, it did not work. Dark Owl went up the stairs of the stage first and Logan and Sarah climbed them last. Which led to a lot more whispering and anger. Their Elder walked to the front of the stage and with a booming voice called for silence. The Moon Elves obeyed and were quiet almost instantly. Although this did nothing for the feeling of anger the Elves felt towards him.

Dark Owl began to speak. "My fellow Elves, thank you for gathering on this special evening! As you can see, we have gathered to discuss our new guests, I know you all must have many questions and as of right now we have little answers. But we are working on understanding the events of the last few days. As some of you already know, a human has been granted an immensely powerful gift of our magic! Currently, we do not know how or why. If you're questioning this, then you are questioning Moonrion herself. And who are any of us to do so? You all know the answer to this question. None! You will treat our guests with the same respect you treat me with. If I hear of this rule being broken there will be consequences. Next, I will call upon our Professor and Mage, Moon Hawk, for he was the one who made the journey to Earth realm to bring Logan here."

Hawk stood up and began speaking. "Good evening my fellow Elves, you all know Lilly and myself as we are both teachers of your children. I know many of you are angry with what has happened. But I will say Moonrion, who we all owe our magic to, does not make mistakes! If she has chosen this human to wield this power then she has her reasons, and who are we to understand the choices of our Goddess, as Dark Owl has already stated. I have travelled to Earth Realm and yes, it's a sad place with much hatred and violence. But I have gotten to know these two humans particularly well in the short time we have had together, and they are both good people. With the capacity for love, empathy and kindness. The same as our species, so I will also ask that you give them a chance, we are Elves, let us act like it. Now I will call upon one of our guests to speak so you can get to know him a little."

Logan's anxiety was through the roof, he closed his eyes and called upon a small amount of magic to settle his nerves. Sarah gave his hand a small squeeze which was better than the magic. Logan stood up, he felt like a giant for he had not realised that Hawk was tall for an elf, and with his six foot two and broad frame the wood on the stage creaked as he walked. He looked out at all the Elves faces and could still feel the hatred, he was not sure how to start.

"Umm, hello, everyone. My name is Logan. I am from the realm of Earth and for some reason I am now here in front of you, just as confused as you are! The woman with me is Sarah Sinclair. I was given this power in my realm and until a few days ago I did not even know other realms existed. This is a beautiful place and I hope I can help all of you."

A female Elf stepped out of the crowd, she looked at him

with such fury that it felt like Logan had been slapped. She spoke, "What can you teach us, primate? How to kill, or perhaps, how to pollute our realm so badly that in a few years it will be uninhabitable? Or destroy everything you touch! You are not a species; you are a virus."

Dark Owl stood up. "Raven, go to my chambers, now!"

She looked at Logan again and did as instructed. He did not really have much of an argument for he himself had felt the same way for years.

He thought for a few moments. "What was just said is not far from the truth, we humans are constantly at war, we have pretty much destroyed our entire planet, we kill for no reason and are full of hatred! But Since I have stepped on this stage, I have felt your hatred towards me. And I know you've had war and killing here as well, yes you have had peace for over a century or however long, which is something that humans will never experience but I came here of my own free will to a place I knew nothing about, and I brought the one thing I love more than anything with me to help you! So, I will not return that hatred towards you as I would like to get to know your kind before I make any decisions. I hope one day you will give me the same chance. Thank you for listening to me." Logan walked slowly back to his chair.

Even though the Elven woman was accurate, he was pissed he came here to help these assholes, left his home and everything he knew and all he gets is a bunch of Elves who are pissed off. He needed a drink. He hoped they had alcohol here or this was going to be a rough go for him.

Dark Owl dismissed the Elves and they all started to head back to their homes. Dark Owl and his entourage headed back to the Tree of Power. Making their way up the stairs Logan remembered the one Elf they called Raven was sent to the Elders chambers.

He thought to himself, 'This should be interesting.' Oh well, not the first female he had pissed off and it would not be the last.

They reached the top of the stairs and Hawk looked at Logan. "No matter what she says, keep your cool, remember you have much to learn in control."

Logan smiled and nodded. He was worried about what might happen as well if he were to lose his temper. Dark Owl was the first one through the door and Logan was the last. Logan was surprised when he walked through the door for he could feel the fury radiating from Raven. For the first few moments there was an uncomfortable silence. Dark Owl removed his robe and was about to say something but before he could get a word out the young female Elf named Raven shot straight up.

"How dare you embarrass me in front of the entire village. I said nothing that was not true about these humans. And yet you defend them over your own granddaughter!"

Hawk stepped forward and looked at Raven with anger and annoyance. "Raven, have you forgotten you are speaking to an Elder, regardless of him being your grandfather. You are way out of line, now be quiet and listen to what Dark Owl tells you."

Raven looked at Hawk, still truly angry. "Shut your mouth, Hawk. I was not speaking to you, was I?"

Now it was Lilly who had to hold Hawk back. Dark Owl finally had enough and in that powerful voice he simply said, "Silence!" He looked at his young granddaughter and sighed, he looked like he had aged ten years in the last few days. He stroked his beard and looked at Raven. "Sit down, Raven and listen very carefully, you speak of being embarrassed and how do you think I feel, you are a Dark and the last of my bloodline. We must be held to the highest standard for our people and yet you have caused the most trouble! I was young once, too, believe it or not, and I also remember my temper and sometimes speaking before thinking. None of this however excuses what you have done tonight we will hold another town gathering and you will apologize to Logan and Sarah for your little outburst."

Raven stood up and looked at everyone defiantly! "There will be no apology, plan what you want, I will not be there. Good luck with your human freak, hopefully he doesn't end our kind." She pushed through everyone, stopping at Logan and eyeing him up and down. Her eyes started to release a small amount of purple mist; Logan's eyes responded instantly with a quick flash of silver. Raven smiled at him. "Like I said, freak!" She went through the door, slamming it with such force part of the door cracked.

Hawk looked at Dark Owl. "Do you want me to bring her back?"

Dark Owl shook his head. "No, Hawk. Let her go and calm down a little, she will come around soon enough."

"And if she doesn't?" Hawk asked.

"Then she will learn to live with it," replied Dark Owl. Dark Owl looked exhausted, and Lilly offered to take him to his bed, he shook his head. "No, I can manage on my own."

Logan and Sarah were also exhausted after all the excitement if one could call it that. Sarah looked at Lilly and told her she would change and return the dress.

Lilly smiled. "My dear, that was a gift for you keep it and

tomorrow we will get you more casual female clothes. And this goes for you as well, Logan."

He thanked Lilly for her kindness and started towards the bed with Sarah following closely. Dark Owl had requested that Hawk stay for a few more moments and that Lilly should head home, she bowed and hoped Hawk would not be too late.

Once Dark Owl and Hawk were alone, he began to tell Hawk what had happened while he was in Earth realm.

"I have cancelled all classes and I have asked our people to stay indoors."

Hawk could not believe what he was hearing, first the human and now being told that Rubia had returned. Hawk shook his head. "I thought Moon Shatter had driven his blade through her chest and that they had destroyed her and her minions."

Dark Owl responded. "Yes this is the story, but one part was kept out of the story."

"And what was that?" asked Hawk.

Dark Owl sighed. "We never found her body after the battle, and we searched for months."

Hawk could not believe what he was hearing! "So, the burning of her body was a lie?"

Dark Owl frowned. "Yes. When the blade went through her body, she disappeared. She must have foreseen her loss and figured out a way to store her body somewhere where she could slowly regain her power once more."

Hawk said nothing for a while then he asked, "Have you told the other Elves yet?"

"No," replied Dark Owl. "I thought the introduction of the human was enough for one evening."

Hawk was very worried; the Elves no longer had an army

as they thought this peace would last forever now that Rubia was destroyed. How could they have been so stupid and blind, perhaps it was arrogance, he did not know.

"Well, this helps us a little with why Logan is so powerful. This must be why he was given these powers by Moonrion! To level the playing field."

Dark Owl nodded. "These were my thoughts as well. But I am still not sure the human will be enough; I have felt a lot of evil in the realm. I believe she is rebuilding her army of Snakaras."

Hawk went pale. "You mean she has brought snakes from Earth realm again to change them into snake men?"

"Yes," answered Dark Owl, "and if this is true, we will not have the warriors to fight back, she could destroy us all."

"Warriors! we have nothing even close to warriors," answered Hawk. "The Armoury has not been touched since the war. And besides our bow hunters and some Mages we have no defence."

"Be calm, Hawk, have faith in Moonrion, perhaps this Logan is our only hope. Take him out tomorrow night, let's see what he can do."

Hawk looked at Dark Owl. "He has no idea how to control his power, he could destroy our whole town, or perhaps something even worse."

"Then you will teach him control quickly, for our people and the whole realm," replied Dark Owl.

CHAPTER 10
THE RETURN OF THRESHER

Thresher moved through the trees after listening to all the speeches. He was surprised by the female Elf who spoke out against her Elder and verbally attacked the humans. She was sent away, Thresher wondered if he spoke to his Queen like this, what his punishment would be? He shuddered at the thought. He finally cleared the trees and was on his way back to the Onyx mountains. He knew his news would please his Queen.

He was coming around a bend when he heard something coming his way, he hid underneath a fallen tree that was close. He then saw what it was he heard and smelt a large red-tailed buck ran along the area he was just standing in. After a few seconds he could see why the animal was running, for a large pack of wolves were on the hunt and moments later he could smell and hear that they had been successful. He kept moving quickly as he still had a lot of land to cover.

Rubia was getting restless for the return of her assassin. She was looking forward to the news he would bring her. She knew he had not been detected by any of the Elves, which was of little surprise as they believed they were all safe and sound. The only army she knew of that was still active were the Dwarves in the Brimard mountains and that was just for show as they did not like outsiders and did not have the magic abilities that the Elves had. So, they lived by the sword, shield and battle-axes. And the Merpeople cared little about things that happened on dry land. They stayed to the Lakes of eight. And the Plains People who were formidable also did not like outsiders. The only ones she was worried about were the Forest Elves for they were master archers who could use magic and were almost impossible to locate in their territory. Her Snakaras would have a difficult time navigating the woods. And their Elder, Jaded Arrow, was an exceptionally powerful Mage. Rubia knew, however, they would stay out of the battle if she left them be.

Midra, Malay and Sucuri stood in front of her snapping her out of her daydream. Midra spoke. "We have reached the door to the armoury."

She smiled. "Excellent work, general. Now begin arming our men as they have much to learn." The three Snakaras' bowed and went back to work. She had cut out the 'yes, my Queen.' Every time they bowed it was getting on her nerves. And they had won nothing yet and she would not be reckless, as she had been in the last war.

She still had a large scar between her breasts which not even her powerful magic could get rid of. Although, it was a reminder to never underestimate your opponents. A lesson she had learned the hard way. She soon saw one of her foot soldiers from the wall running full tilt, he stopped and bowed before her.

"I have seen Thresher; he will be here soon!"

She smiled. "Excellent, return to the wall, and I will prepare for his arrival, there will be extra food for all soldiers on the wall tonight."

The diamond back foot solider bowed and started back to the wall. She knew keeping up her soldiers' morale was important, and after this feeding she would not have to worry about it for a while as Snakaras did not need to eat like warm blooded creatures.

She returned to her throne and soon after Thresher arrived in the throne room. She smiled. "I am pleased to see you back!" She poured something red into a goblet and handed it to her assassin, he looked at her. She smiled. "Drink it."

He obeyed and drank the whole goblet quickly as he was thirsty from the long journey. He had never tasted anything so good. He looked at his Queen and asked what it was.

She had a wicked look on her face. "It's Elf blood!" He was elated, if this is what Elven blood tasted like he could not wait for the war. Rubia looked at her creation. "So, Thresher, what have you learned about the Elves and this human?"

"Well, I have much to tell you my Queen!" As soon as the words left his mouth a chair appeared behind him, he sat down. "I have learned the name of the Human to be Logan and there are two humans, one was female, he called her Sarah."

Rubia stopped him for a moment. "So, there is a female human as well." She smiled. "This could come in handy!"

Thresher responded. "I was thinking if she could be captured, she would be great leverage."

Rubia smiled. "Perhaps I made you a little too smart, Thresher."

Rubia wondered how she did not feel the female entering the realm, she did not dwell on it long, it must have been due to her lack of magic.

She looked back at Thresher. "Please continue."

He told her all he had seen including the hatred the Elves had for the humans and told her of the one named Raven who spoke out and was sent away. Rubia listened to every word the assassin said, she was not surprised of the Elves hatred. She herself had felt the same hatred when she wanted to expand her horizons and used what the Elves had called dark magic. In their ignorance she became more powerful than all the other Mages and their Elder. Thresher finished up everything he had learned.

Rubia asked out of curiosity. "What did the one they called Logan look like?"

Thresher thought for a moment. "He is much taller than the Elves with broad shoulders and salt and pepper hair."

"Hmmm," she said aloud. "So, the Elves have treated their greatest gift poorly? Perhaps if we show him some kindness and treat him as an equal, he will join me."

Thresher nodded his head. "Yes he would be a powerful ally."

"Indeed," said Rubia, more to herself than to her assassin.

Thresher looked at her and asked. "How would we get him here; from what the Elves have said he is powerful."

Rubia nodded. "They are not wrong, I have never felt so much raw power in any being, if I could somehow show him how the Elves are using him, where we would not." Rubia looked to Thresher. "You have given me much to consider, go to the barracks and get some rest."

He bowed and left the throne room. Rubia was going through her options and she knew one thing she wanted, this human. She knew she would come up with something she headed towards her bed to rest so she would have a clear head. She fell asleep quickly.

CHAPTER 11
TRUTH

Logan could not sleep, so he decided to take a walk around his temporary home. It was daytime so most of the Elves were still asleep. Eclipse was truly beautiful with its black tree bark maples with red and purple leaves and how the Elves homes where carved into the trees themselves. It was truly remarkable how in tune with nature they were. He walked more into the woods for the first time since they had arrived. He noticed some large black Pine trees with purple needles and black pinecones, he also noticed some white Birch trees, so there were some similarities in their realms. He guessed with the realms being close together that there would be some of the same fauna. He also saw some deer that were jet black with red tails. Besides the colour they were the same deer they had in the Earth realm.

Logan looked at the sky, the sun was already setting, which he was still not used to. Only four hours of daylight, which was most likely going to play havoc with his depression and anxiety eventually. He decided to head back to his bed to try and sleep and he did not want Sarah to worry if she woke and he was not there. He climbed the stairs and made it to the bed where Sarah was still sound asleep, he wrapped his body around hers. She turned towards him and snuggled up to him. he quickly fell asleep.

They were both awoken by a light knock on the room's

door. "Just a minute," said Logan. "We will be out in a moment!" He opened the door and there was Hawk waiting for him with a more casual looking black suit.

"Put this on!" It seemed more of a command then a request.

Logan nodded his head and put the suit on, he looked like a priest and he noticed Hawk was wearing the same suit.

He looked at Logan. "This is what male Mages of our land wear, Logan." Hawk seemed much more serious than usual. He looked at Logan. "We have much to discuss today, and you must know I just learned of this myself from Dark Owl last night."

Logan looked at Hawk and he knew this was not going to be a good conversation!

Sarah came out of the room still looking groggy, she looked at Logan. "What the fuck are you wearing?"

He looked at her. "it's a Mage's suit."

"Um, yeah, you look great." She smiled. "Sorry, Father!"

He smiled back. "Thanks, dear, but you know I am far from being a Priest!"

Hawk looked at both of them. "We will be going to my laboratory and where I hold my classes today. As I have already stated, we have much to discuss. Sarah, you are also welcome as this affects all of us. Lilly is already waiting for us."

They all started down the stairs. Sarah was now wearing a green shirt and pants that Lilly had provided her. They were halfway down the stairs when they came upon a door. Hawk opened the door and they all entered; he closed the door behind them. The room looked just as Hawk had described it, part lab and part classroom.

Lilly was sitting in one of the many wooden seats the students must use during class. Again, they were carved into the tree perfectly. Lilly smiled and they all picked a seat which were a little small for Logan, but he said nothing. Hawk went to the front of the room, he sighed and started to tell them what he himself had just learned last night.

"Please let me tell you everything I know, no interruptions." Hawk began. "Dark Owl has informed me that when I was in Earth realm a great evil had returned, her name is Rubia." Lilly gasped. Hawk continued. "She was the reason for the war over a century ago and it would seem she has returned, even though we all thought her to be dead. She has already started to rebuild her army somewhere in the White Onyx mountains. She gets stronger every day and we are not sure why she has not attacked us yet. Our only thought being she has felt Logan's power and she is not sure what he is capable of. Which is something we do not know yet either. So, Logan, we are going to start your training right away and the four of us are the only ones who know this, besides Dark Owl. He has not told our people yet as he does not want to start panic until we know more. And this is all we know right now."

Sarah slammed her hand down on the table which made Lilly Jump. "I fucking knew it! I knew there was something you weren't telling us, goddammit! Hawk, this is bullshit, your Elves hate Logan and now you need him to fight some ancient bitch for you."

Hawk lowered his head. "I am sorry. I truly had no idea, Sarah." Hawk continued. "And they are not my Elves, they are my people and we don't all hate you; everyone is scared as this has never happened before."

Sarah was pacing back and forth. Logan had never seen

her this mad, not even at him, which was a little scary. She looked at Hawk, her face scarlet red. "No, you don't all hate us, just everyone outside of this room and Dark Owl!" She looked at Logan who had said nothing. "And what do you think, Logan?"

"So let me get this straight, I have been brought to a realm on the brink of a war?" Logan looked at Hawk. "This is fucked up. I will say this, if you've been lying and you knew in our realm, you will see just how much of a barbaric human I can be."

Lilly had tears in her eyes. She looked at Logan. "I was the last one to see him before he left, Logan, he truly had no idea. I am just hearing this now as well."

Logan looked at Lilly and he knew she was telling the truth. Logan looked at Hawk again. "So, what would be the plan, how big is your army?"

Hawk looked down again. "We have no army, not since the last war, we have not needed one."

"What?" said Logan, and Sarah at the same time. Logan shook his head. "You know, there is a saying in my realm, '*Si vis pacem, para bellum*'."

Lilly Looked at Hawk for a translation. "It's Latin, a dead language in the Earth realm. It means, 'If you want peace prepare for war'."

Logan continued. "Why would you not have a functioning army you thought this was going to be forever, let me tell you something us stupid humans know nothing lasts forever."

Hawk looked at him. "I never thought you to be stupid, Logan, and I see now that we Elves could perhaps learn quite a lot from your people."

"So," Logan asked, "what are we going to do now, fight

them with just the two of us?"

Sarah looked at them. "Look, it's been nice meeting you all, but Logan never signed up for a war, so I am sorry we are going to be heading back to our realm."

Logan looked at Hawk. "Would you ladies excuse us; I need to speak to Hawk in private."

Sarah looked at Logan like he was crazy. "We are leaving, Logan!"

Logan looked at Sarah. "Please," he said. "I will speak to you more later."

Lilly took Sarah by the hand and they both headed back to the top of the tree. As soon as they left, Logan looked at Hawk and he slammed his hand down hard on the seat beside him. It caused the chair to explode into pieces splinters of wood were everywhere. Hawk jumped when the chair exploded.

Logan looked at him. "Now that I have your attention! I will start. Listen, Hawk, do you know what I was in Earth Realm?"

Hawk nodded. "I believe I do. You were a tavern keeper."

"That's right, or what we call a Bartender, I am also a drunk and a loser I couldn't even keep Sarah happy. I also suffer from anxiety and depression which can be crippling, so I drink to keep it in check. I was happy with drinking myself to death. Now that you have heard all of this I will get to the point. I am no leader, I have never been a solider, I don't know why your Moonrion gave me this power, but I don't want it, I have no clue on training people for this and if you use swords and shields, we are really fucked. I have never even held a sword. It's not that I do not want to help you, but I am afraid your Goddess has fucked up big time!"

Hawk looked at Logan for a moment before he said anything. "Listen, Logan. I have no idea what you're going through right now. You are in a strange land with a power you do not understand surrounded by hostility. I can, however, give you some answers into your anxiety and depression."

Logan laughed. "I doubt that, I have been seen by every doctor, tested by every machine and none of them could help me except to drug the fuck out of me. I chose alcohol instead."

Hawk nodded. "Your doctors were right, they could never help you, for you see as Dark Owl has already mentioned, long ago Earth was a very magical place even more so than Silver Moon! Many of your ancestors used magic all the time through the ages. Unfortunately, as time passed between your wars and using nuclear weapons and the industrial age. You were slowly killing mother nature and your realm in the state it's in now, there is no more magic." Hawk continued. "You have probably felt like something was missing from your life since you were young. And as you got older it probably felt even worse for you.

See, Logan, you were a born magic user. But unfortunately, with there being no magic on Earth, it causes you to have what you call anxiety and depression. And I will bet since you have been here and with this power you have felt much better!"

Logan felt like he had been slapped in the face! Everything Hawk was saying was making so much sense. He had noticed that his anxiety and depression had been much better ever since he was given this power, it was almost non-existent! He had not even had a drink since he had arrived, and he was not having any withdrawal.

"OK, Hawk, perhaps you're right about all of that, it's

great, and I do feel better but that still doesn't make me a warrior or a leader."

"Well, Logan, you were chosen for a reason and in time we will find out why we must trust our Goddess!"

Logan looked at Hawk. "Seriously, don't ever call me chosen or chosen one or any of that shit, it's so cliché it makes me want to be sick."

"Well, what am I supposed to say about all of this?"

"How about you just call me Logan, please!"

Hawk nodded. "Simple enough, do you have any other questions for me?"

"I do," Logan replied. "You mentioned that she was assembling an army? Where is she getting the soldiers from?"

Hawk tried to think of how he was going to explain this one. He looked at Logan. "Well, she calls them Snakaras, which are basically snake men."

Logan laughed. "You're fucking with me, right?"

"No, Logan. I am not fucking with you, as you put it. She can bring different species from your realm and she uses magic on them to make the transformation."

Logan sat forward. "So, you're saying she has snakes with arms and legs!"

"Yes, Logan, that is what I am telling you and they stand straight up just as you and I do."

"OK, say I believe all this craziness, how is she going to make an army with snakes? She would need almost every single one we have on earth and some are harmless," replied Logan.

"Unfortunately for us she uses duplication spells so she would only need one of each species, and she only takes the deadliest species your planet has to offer!"

Logan started rubbing his head. "Well, this is great, snake men who can hold weapons! And most will have a venomous bite. And what do we have besides a bunch of scared Elves. How many of your Elves can fight?"

Hawk thought about it. "Well, we have some excellent archers that hunt for us but none of them have been in battle."

Logan sighed. "Well, that is something but hunting an animal and shooting at a charging enemy is something entirely different."

"I agree!" said Hawk. "We have some Mages who can cast attack and protection spells, again, none have seen battle except for Dark Owl."

Logan asked a question that he had been wondering for a while. "How powerful is Dark Owl really?"

Hawk looked surprised by the question, but he answered it. "When he was younger he was matched by no one in magic but now he is older. And to be honest, I've never seen him at full power but even you must feel the strength of his power."

Logan nodded. "I have, but what concerns me is sometimes I feel almost nothing from him." Hawk was hoping Logan had not picked up on that, for he too had felt this. "And you're going to be the next Elder correct?"

Hawk looked at him. "If they follow the bloodline, Raven is next in line to be Elder!"

"But aren't you more powerful than her?"

"Not in raw power," answered Hawk. "My advantage over Raven is my control over my abilities."

"Well, that is just wonderful, the one who hates me the most is next in line to be your leader." Logan was seeing more cons than pros so far. "So, if Dark Owl died or was killed, she would automatically become the Elder right now?"

Hawk looked at him. "No, she is too young and has not passed all her control tests."

"So, who would it be if that were to happen during this war?"

Hawk smiled. "You're looking at him! Until she becomes of age and proves her abilities, I am the one who would hold the role."

"I am only asking as he will be a major target for our enemies." Hawk once again agreed with Logan.

"How was Rubia defeated in the first war?" asked Logan.

"Well," Hawk answered, "back then we had a large army and our General Moon Shatter drove her men back and drove a sword through her chest and when she died the magic keeping her soldiers form returned them to regular serpents which were all burned by our Mages."

"Moon Shatter, huh? Where did his name come from?" asked Logan.

"They say he had the power to shatter the moon itself," replied Hawk, "which we know is impossible, but he was given powerful weapons blessed by Moonrion herself."

"Where are those weapons now?" asked Logan.

"In our armoury," answered Hawk. "Even Moon Shatter's, although it was said only he could hold the sword and shield. Other Elves have tried, and they could not even lift them off the wall!"

"Well, that is some good news at least. We have weapons to train a new army," said Logan.

Hawk shook his head. "It's not going to be that easy! We Elves have had peace for so long we have become decadent, a shadow of our former selves, we will not have many rushing to join the cause."

"So, you're telling me that your men will not fight to protect their wives and children! You're right, Hawk, our people are vastly different. I would fight her whole army by myself to keep Sarah safe."

"And so would I for Lilly!" yelled Hawk. "But I do not think we will have the men or the time to train them."

Logan stood up. "Fine! Just roll over and fucking die. I am not willing to help those who won't help themselves."

He stood up and walked out the door. He was done hearing about these cowardly Elves. He did not go upstairs to where Sarah and Lilly where waiting. He needed to take another walk to clear his head and try to absorb all this terrible information.

CHAPTER 12
THE PEOPLE OF THE PLAINS

Shadow woke as he felt the warmth of the sun and his mate Aura. It was going to be a beautiful day. Shadow loved the day; it was when his people got to wash in the rivers and the children played games. The older children would practise their hunting skills and play fight. Which was particularly important, for life in the Plains was not always safe or easy. He stood up and stretched, yawned and headed out of their den where all his people slept together. He smiled, some of the young ones were already awake chasing each other and he could see some stalking some butterflies. He wished he still had their youthful energy. The children saw him come out of the den; they doubled their efforts when they noticed their Alpha. He heard a sound behind him and felt a weight on his back as his mate Aura had jumped on him and kissed him on the neck. He laughed and smiled, he picked her up in his muscular arms and kissed her back.

She smiled. "Behave in front of the children."

He laughed again. "You started it!"

"I did and I shall finish it later!"

Shadow moved to the front of the den to look across the Plains, this was something he did every day. It was a short walk and with only four hours of daylight he found it necessary. He looked across the Plains, he saw little except for a few red tail deer which was their main source of food. He took a deep breath to let his nose take in all the scents and that is when it hit him. He smelt something vaguely familiar, and he could also smell large fires burning towards the east. He was curious, the east was where the Merpeople and the lakes of Eight were, so the smell of fire from that direction was strange. The only other thing he could think of were the White Onyx mountains.

The hair on the back of his neck was starting to stand up. Something was not right and as the leader of his people it was his job to be very vigilant. He needed to talk with Sabre, his second in command. He walked to their den and outdoor camp where Aura was playing with their children who were laughing and jumping all over her. They loved playing with their mother. He wished he had more time for the children, but his job was their safety, and it was something he took deadly serious. He made a loud whistling sound and Aura stopped playing with the children and returned to her mates' side and within a few minutes Sabre and Swift were also standing before him.

"Good morning, Shadow!" Sabre and Swift were wondering what was going on as Shadow very rarely whistled to summon them.

"Good Morning to you as well. Sabre and Swift I need you all to follow me."

They walked back to the exact place where he was standing just minutes before. They all looked across the Plains and they saw nothing out of the ordinary. Aura was the first to smell the fire, she was also perplexed, and Sabre and Swift picked it up almost at the same time as Aura.

"Is that fire to the east?" asked Sabre.

"Yes," answered Shadow, "and for us to pick it up here it must either be an exceptionally large fire or remarkably close."

Swift smelt the air again. "What is that other smell? I have never smelt anything like it before."

The rest of them agreed. The smell was bothering Shadow the most, as he had not picked up a scent like this since the time of the war and where he had received a large scar across his face.

Sabre looked at Shadow. "What do you think we should do?"

Shadow thought for a moment. "How is our food situation as of now?"

Swift looked at Shadow. "Praise Moonrion, for we are having a great season with our venison and fish, we are well ahead of what we will need for the winter."

"Excellent!" smiled Shadow. "There will be no hunt tonight. I want to head east to see if we can figure out what is going on. The four of us will head out as soon as night falls," which was only an hour away. "Sabre find Spike I wish to speak to him."

Sabre headed out to find Spike who was their third largest male. It was not hard to find him, he was with the younger females showing his strength to impress them. As soon as Sabre came around the corner the females dispersed, and Spike turned around to see him smiling.

"That's quite the show you have going, Spike."

"Ah, Sabre, good to see you my friend! Although you did interrupt the best part of the show," he smiled.

Sabre smirked. "Do not worry young one, you will find a mate soon enough. Now to business. Shadow has requested to see you so let's get a move on."

Spike was excited his father wanted to see him which meant something interesting was happening. Spike walked until he was standing in front of Shadow and Aura, they looked at Spike and smiled, he returned the smile.

"You summoned me?"

"Yes," replied Shadow. "I need you to do something for me. There will be no hunt tonight. I am taking a small group of us to check something out. I need you to guard our people while we are gone."

Spike frowned. "Can't I come with you? You might need my strength."

"I do need your strength, Spike. I need it right here to guard the den," replied Shadow. "This is the most important job, and I am giving it to you."

Spike smiled. "I will do you proud!"

"I know you will, son." And he gave him a strong pat on his shoulder. "While we are gone no one is to leave the den and if anything seems out of place or you see or smell anything strange you howl like you've never howled before. No heroics, understood?"

"Yes, Father, I understand."

"Good, now go and round up everyone and get them into the den." Spike left immediately.

It was now night-time, and Shadow and the others began to take on their true forms, their transformations took seconds. Where Shadow had once stood, now stood a large black and silver wolf. Aura was beside him; she was a light brown with a red stripe down her back. Sabre was a light silver with small patches of brown throughout his fur. And Swift was almost completely white except for her black ears. Once the transformation was completed, they were all telepathically linked to their Alpha.

"Let us head out, Swift and Aura, do not get too far

ahead."

When they were in wolf form the females were much faster than their male counterparts. Where the males were much stronger. They set out east to see just what was happening there. It could be nothing, but that smell was lingering in Shadow's mind and the others could now feel it. They moved swiftly with the males trying to keep pace. They passed one of the lakes of eight and stopped to drink some water and were back on the scent again.

They were making good progress, they moved as a perfect unit with their telepathic link with Shadow giving small instructions while on the move. They could start to see the White Onyx mountains on the horizon, the scents were coming from somewhere near the mountains as Shadow had suspected.

They travelled another few miles when Shadow ordered them to stop. All four stopped and grouped together wondering what Shadow had picked up. They looked towards the mountains and after taking a hard look they could see some light reflecting off the mountain.

Aura put her nose to the air and smelt something she had never smelt before; it was a pungent terrible smell. Her thought went through the four of them. They looked at Shadow. Aura thought, 'What is that smell?'

They could feel Shadow's uneasiness. "It couldn't be they were destroyed." Now the three of them were worried as Shadow never felt uneasy and they did not understand his thought, they did not know what was destroyed.

Sabre asked, "What was destroyed? What's bothering you so much?"

Shadow looked at them. "Nothing," he answered. "Just old ghosts, we will get closer, and I pray to Moonrion this is not what I believe it to be."

Now they were all uneasy, but they kept on the move. They ran up a large hill and when they reached the bottom, Shadow froze, his ears flattened and he let out a small growl, the other three followed suit, they were all on their bellies now and observing the land in front of them. None of them could believe what they were seeing.

There was a huge hole blown out of the side of the mountain and someone had built large walls of Onyx in front of it. And after closer inspection there seemed to be some sort of creatures patrolling the wall. Sabre slowly crawled forward on his belly which was not an easy task for a wolf. Shadow told him to move no closer, he quickly obeyed.

The pack could feel Shadow's anger and hatred which scared them as they had never felt anything this strong come from Shadow. Shadow knew exactly what he was looking at and smelling, for he was in the first war and it was how he had received the scar across his face. Two names flashed through his mind, Rubia and Snakaras, the other pack members had no idea what the two names meant but they knew it was not a good thing.

Sabre wanted to get a closer look, he went to move again, and Shadow let out a low growl. "Stay still, Sabre. We don't need to get any closer as she may feel our presence."

"Who will?" they all asked at the same time!

Shadow repeated the name. "Rubia."

Aura looked at him. "Who or what is a Rubia," she asked.

Shadow replied. "Rubia, is an Elven Mage. She is the one responsible for the war."

Swift asked, "Who are those creatures guarding the wall?"

Shadow growled. "Those are her warriors, she calls them

Snakaras. They are snake men who are fierce warriors, and most have venomous bites. She brought them from Earth realm. All my darkest fears have now been confirmed. We must return to the den quickly as we will have many things to do in the coming days. And it's time we visited the Moon Elves. I need to speak to their Elder."

CHAPTER 13
MOONRION'S INTERVENTION

Logan walked through the town which was quiet and the Elves he did see avoided him. Which in his current mood only solidified his wanting to go back to his realm. He had walked to the centre of town, which was not his original plan, he wanted to go into the forest. He was looking down thinking and when he looked up again, he noticed a large statue of a fierce warrior. He was holding a sword and shield and he was in full armour. Logan moved closer to the statue to take a better look; he noticed a silver plaque on the front of the statue. It read, 'Our Most blessed General a true son of Moonrion, Moon Shatter' and when he looked down, he noticed thousands of names carved into stone. This must be a war monument from the first war like they had in his realm. All these lives lost just so this bitch could come back. He shook his head sadly. He walked away from the war memorial in a fouler mood than before which he did not think was possible.

He headed out of the town into the forest, which was beautiful at night. He made his way to a small stream, it almost seemed to glow in the moon light, and he noticed small lights flying here and there. They were all different colours from blue to red and every other colour in between. He headed towards the stream he cupped his hands together and splashed some water on his face and then took a drink from it. He could not believe how clean and refreshing the water felt as he drank it, he was starting to feel much better. It still did not solve any of the problems he was facing, he had no idea what to do. He did not know this land and was still trying to decide if he wanted to help the Elves or not. They seemed to hate Sarah and him, yet Hawk wanted him to fight what seemed to be an impossible war to win. The only thing even keeping him thinking about it was the women and children. He could not fathom the thought of women and children being slaughtered by snake men or this Rubia.

He was in deep thought when he noticed an extremely bright light, at first he thought it was Hawk and the rest of them looking for him. As the light came closer, he felt something he had never felt before, his magic was coursing through his veins with such intensity, he was worried his heart was going to explode. Eventually the light dimmed and went out and standing before him was the most beautiful Silver Pegasus.

***

Hawk was not incredibly happy with the discussion he and Logan just had. Mostly because the human was right. He knew Earth realm was a place filled with hate and pollution and constant war. Although he now knew they were not all bad, in fact most were trying to live peaceful lives! It was their political and religious dogma that would be their undoing. Elves had no churches of worship as they knew Moonrion was in all things. So, a building was not necessary and as far as politics, they had Dark Owl as their Elder and after he was gone the Elves always put the strongest and wisest Mage in the Elder position. And that was the way they had done things since the beginning of their existence.

Hawk looked at where Logan had been sitting and the destroyed desk beside it. So much power and potential and they may lose him, as Hawk had already decided that if he and Sarah wanted to go home, he would take them. They were right, it truly wasn't their problem, and he had no idea how he would feel if the roles were reversed. He prayed to Moonrion that Logan would help them. He still could not believe how stupid they had been letting their guard down and how they had not kept a functioning army. He decided to go and speak to Sarah and Lilly, which he was not looking forward to as Sarah scared him a little. He made his way up to Dark Owl's and opened the door to see Sarah and Lilly on their feet looking directly at him.

Lilly looked worried. "What was that huge smashing sound?"

Hawk looked at them. "Logan is upset with the situation and at this point I don't blame him."

"Oh, really, you think?" Sarah said, obviously still upset. "Wait where in the hell is Logan?"

Hawk sighed. "He said he needed to go for a walk to clear his head."

"And you just let him go, what if he gets attacked or hurt?"

"In Logan's current condition and mood, I would feel deeply sorry for anyone who tried to hurt him." Hawk looked at Sarah. "I have decided that if Logan and you wish to leave when he returns, I will take you."

Sarah seemed to calm a little, but she looked Hawk square in the eye's. "We are leaving?"

"Logan has not made any decisions and I doubt you speak for the both of you."

Sarah looked at him, her face red again. "Be careful, Elf!"

***

The Pegasus stretched its wings all the way out and then tucked them back to their side. Logan still could not believe his eyes but for some reason he knew exactly what he was looking at, it was Moonrion herself.

He had no idea what he was supposed to do, his voice was a little shaky when he finally spoke. "Do I bow or kneel or something?" He could hear the Pegasus laugh in his mind. It was a very calming and beautiful laugh.

'Oh, Logan you have quite the sense of humour.' The fact that not a word had been spoken and everything he was hearing was in his mind was something he would need to get used to; it was a little weird. Moonrion spoke again. *'I am sorry that we have to speak through telepathy. I know you humans are not used to such things. I speak the language of the Gods and you would not be able to understand me not even the Elves can.*

Logan thought in his mind, *'OK. I understand.'*

Moonrion looked at him. *'I've chosen well by the looks of things.'*

Logan answered her. *'No, you have made a terrible mistake I am not the one who should have these powers. I am a drunk and a mess and I have zero military background.'*

She continued to look at him before she said anything. *'I have made no mistake with you Logan. I chose you for what I see you becoming, not for what you where on Earth.'*

Logan was still unconvinced. *'Why didn't you pass this power on to one of your Elves? Like you did with Moon Shatter?'*

'Listen, Logan. I know the Elves would have you believe that they are far more advanced than your race.'

'Yeah, I kind of got that feeling ever since we arrived here.'

'You know, Logan, the Elves can be just as bloodthirsty and violent as your people, they are far from perfect and as of now I do not trust them to wield such power for I am worried we would just have another Rubia on our hands. Moon Shatter was a rare Elf who did not want power either. Logan, not even Gods are perfect and Rubia is immensely powerful. I created this realm but like your Gods I have given this realm free will so I cannot directly intervene although I can help, and therefore you are here.'

Logan still had a lot of questions. 'How can I fight with these Elves? I myself have never even held a sword!'

Moonrion laughed. 'You don't think I hadn't thought of this? Go to the Elves armoury and take Moon Shatter's weapons off the wall and you will have all the knowledge of the sword and shield, but you must still practice as much as possible!'

'OK, and how do I convince the Elves to follow me into a battle when none of them have fought for a century or more?' It seems she was waiting for this question.

'Trust in yourself and your power and trust Hawk, the two of you will figure this out! It's time the Elves had some tough love. You have an exceptionally good soul and great strength or the light in the alley would have killed you. I must leave now. You must give your word not to speak of this meeting. I know what that means to you, Logan.'

Logan looked at the beautiful Pegasus and nodded. 'I give you my word, and I will help the Elves.'

She looked at him and he could feel her smile in his mind and as fast as she appeared, she was gone.

Logan could not believe he had met a God, especially seeing how he had never been a religious person. In his own realm he did not believe in any God and to be honest he still didn't with all the things he had seen humans do to each other. Silver Moon was different though, it was beautiful and peaceful, but now he knew it was going to get a lot less peaceful. He decided he was going to head back to town and get started on what he still thought was going to be a slaughter.

CHAPTER 14
RUBIA'S TEST

Rubia sat in her throne deciding what her next move was going to be. She did not want to send in her whole army just yet. She wanted to savour her victory, a true battle, and she knew the Elves would not be even close to being ready. She was also still interested in this human Logan; Thresher was right, if he would join her, they could rule this realm. Even for an evil and terrible female Elf she still had needs.

Her bed had been vacant for so long she could not remember what the flesh of another felt like anymore. And she had never been with a human male before, especially one with such power. She was no fool though she felt much goodness in this man. She had toyed with the idea of sending Thresher back to Eclipse to abduct the human female, but she knew Logan loved this woman very much. She was not afraid of him, but she knew how ruthless humans could be protecting the ones they loved. He would come looking for her and she knew he would destroy anything in his path to get her back. And she was not sure if her strength would be able to stop him if he were in a rage.

Moonrion had given the Elves a powerful weapon. She thought to herself that it was time to see just how ready the Elves and this human were! She called upon her general, he appeared almost instantly, he bowed and looked up at her.

She smiled. "I have a job for you." His forked tongue

started flickering faster in his excitement. "I want you to take a hundred of our men in full battle attire and head to the Moon Elves home of Eclipse. Once there I want you to set up camp just outside their border and wait."

Midra looked confused. "You don't want us to attack?"

"No, just do as instructed. Now if any Elves stroll outside that border, you can kill them. I also want you to light large fires and keep them going. I want them to know you are there. It's time to let the Elves see what they are fighting and to know true fear."

"When shall I leave?" asked Midra.

"Right away, general. We shall hide no more."

Midra bowed and turned to round up his viper army. Rubia was very curious to see how this was going to turn out! Even if the Elves somehow managed to kill all her men it was just a drop in the bucket.

***

Midra started to get the men ready for their task, all one hundred of them were putting on armour and retrieving swords and shields, as was their general. They moved quickly as they had been training to do. The men were ready within an hour and had assembled at the front of the onyx mountains. Rubia was standing there waiting for them.

She looked at them and smiled. "Midra, my general, I am impressed with your haste of getting the men ready, and now, my warriors, you move to the borders of our enemies." The vipers rattled in perfect timing and let out a loud war cry. They were a formidable sight to behold. Rubia raised her hand for silence. "And now, my warriors, begin your journey and know

105

I will be with you in heart and soul, go!"

They rattled again and began their march. Rubia got chills watching them marching in perfect formation.

'Now we shall see what this human can do,' she thought.

Midra led his men quickly as he wanted to get to his destination as soon as possible to drive fear into their hearts and with a little luck kill a few Elves. They took two full nights to reach their destination and as soon as they arrived, they started the large fires, as they had been instructed by their Queen, it was the Elves move now!

CHAPTER 15
LOGAN'S DECISION

After Logan's meeting with the Goddess Moonrion, which he still could not believe. He had decided that he would stay and help the Elves. He knew Sarah would be pissed, but he felt in his heart that it was the right thing to do.

He walked back to the town and headed for the Tree of Power and started up the stairs. He took his time as he knew this was not going to be an easy conversation. He had given his word to Moonrion he would not speak of their meeting and he always kept his word no matter how bad things got. He had finally made it to Dark Owl's door when it flew open and there stood Sarah who slapped him hard this time, it struck home. His magic did not stop the blow at all, perhaps it was because he was getting some control over it, or more likely he figured he deserved it for taking off without saying anything. It stung like hell but after the slap she threw her arms around him and started crying.

"Why would you take off like that? What if something happened to you."

He looked down at her and held her tight. "I am sorry, babe. I just needed some time to clear my head and absorb all this information." Logan's magic had already stopped the pain in his face and the redness was gone.

The tension in the room could be cut with a knife, Hawk and Lilly looked like they were frozen in their seats. Logan released Sarah from their embrace and looked into her beautiful green eyes.

"Go and sit down," he said calmly. "I have had some time to think, I have even visited your war memorial, Hawk. It's too bad Moon Shatter is no longer with us!"

Hawk nodded in agreement. "He died shortly after the war. Some say from a broken heart from all the death. But no one truly knows why he died."

"I have decided to stay and help you."

Hawk smiled. Lilly jumped up and hugged him and Sarah looked at him like he was crazy and took him to the room they were staying in. She looked back at Lilly and Hawk and slammed the door.

Sarah didn't say anything for a few moments, she looked at him. "Logan, why are you doing this? You owe these Elves nothing let's just go home. We can work on us, we can start a life, whatever you want, please don't do this!"

He looked into her eyes and he almost broke, but he was sticking to his guns on this.

He looked at her and smiled. "You and I both know that won't work. I'll end up going back to the bottle and you'll go back to being a nurse who rarely stays in touch. Hawk told me the reason why my anxiety and depression was so bad back in Earth realm, it's because there used to be more magic there than here, you even heard Dark Owl say the same thing about Earth! But with all the pollution we have caused we have destroyed it all. He told me I was a born magic user. It was just that there was none for me to feel, and my symptoms were a side effect of it. And I believe him, for as soon as this power was given to me, I have felt much better."

Sarah looked at him. "I am not going to be able to change

your mind on this, am I?"

He looked at her with a look she had seen many times and she knew what the answer was, but she wanted to hear him say it.

"No, I am staying, but if you want to go back, I will tell Hawk to make it happen. You are important back in our realm, you help heal people, you're a nurse and I feel like a bum and a loser, and nothing you say is going to change that. I could not live with myself if I abandoned them now with what I know. I just cannot get the thought of screaming women and children out of my head."

Sarah looked at him. "That was a low blow, Logan Coyle, and you know it."

"I only said that because you do not know what this bitch is capable of, she has made an entire army of snake men that she took from our realm, she calls them Snakaras."

Sarah went ghost white and sat down on the bed. "You mean in this realm there are snakes with arms and legs?"

"Yes," said Logan, "and they walk upright just like us and that's why I am staying. I do not expect you to stay, I know how you feel about snakes and the Elves."

Logan was about to leave the room when she took his hand and gave it a strong squeeze. "If you're going to war with a crazy bitch, snake men, and a bunch of pussy Elves you're probably going to need a good nurse!"

He pulled her close and kissed her with more passion than he had in a long time and it felt good.

After the kiss she looked at him. "I still think you're fucking nuts."

He laughed. "Maybe that will be my edge in all this!"

Hawk and Lilly were both trying to pretend that they

heard nothing, but with giant smiles on their faces. Logan knew they had heard most of the conversation if not all of it.

"We are going to stay but my help does not come without conditions."

Hawk nodded. "What are those going to be?" Logan looked at him.

"All male Elves fight, no one gets to sit this out, women can fight only if they volunteer."

Hawk nodded. "How are we going to accomplish this little miracle?"

"Any male not willing to fight for his land and people will be banished from Eclipse never to return."

Hawk's jaw dropped. "Don't you think that's a little harsh?"

"Not as harsh as watching everyone getting slaughtered. You know what we are facing."

Just as Logan finished his first condition, Dark Owl came out of his room. He looked at Logan.

"Do what he has asked, gather our people and give them the ultimatum. For he is right, if you're not willing to fight for your land and people then you do not get the right to enjoy that land."

Dark Owl then simply turned around and went back to his room.

Hawk looked at Logan. "OK. But this is going to get ugly!"

Logan smiled. "That is why I will tell them and if they do not like it, they can start packing. It's better to die fighting than being curled up in a ball like a coward. And with Rubia those are their choices."

Hawk could not argue with that logic, so he decided to

ring the town bell and have the meeting. He just hoped there would not be a riot.

All the Elves heard the bell and they headed towards the centre of town. As the bell was only used in rare occasions, so many where curious as to what was happening. Lilly, Sarah and Logan headed towards the stage that was in the centre of town. Logan, could hear the whispers when they saw him and could feel the dirty looks. This time he did not give a shit, for all he knew Rubia was moving her Snakaras towards them right now. All three met Hawk on the stage and Hawk could see the look in Logan's eyes.

Hawk looked at him. "Just take it easy, Logan, they don't even know about Rubia."

Logan looked back at Hawk who he now considered his friend. "The time for half measures is over my friend."

Hawk nodded and sat down with Lilly and Sarah. Logan went to the front of the stage he could feel hatred and fear and by the end of this he was certain it was going to be worse, he no longer cared. Logan looked down at them and said nothing for a moment. He then looked at all the Elves piled into the centre of town.

"You may wonder why Hawk rang the bell and called you all here. Well let me tell you. Rubia has returned, and she has already rebuilt her army."

Hawk smacked his forehead. 'Real subtle, Logan!' he thought to himself.

The Elves were all talking amongst themselves and one of the males stepped forward. "This is some trick to scare us into thinking we need this human freak."

Logan looked at all of them. "Be quiet!" His voice sounded like thunder. He was not sure how he did it, but he knew it was his magic. "I speak the truth; you can ask Hawk or your Elder if you wish. We don't have time for this, but I will tell you now the next person that insults me or Sarah will feel my wrath." A glow of silver came out of his eyes just to get his point across. "Listen, everyone, I am here to help you, not hurt you and I am going to fight Rubia and her army, but I need your help. I am not even from this realm and I could have left but I chose to stay. The love of my life who has no magical powers is staying to help you. Now I know you have not fought in over a century, but I am asking all male Elves to join us and rebuild our army! Women may fight as well on a volunteer basis. I will give you twenty-four hours to come forward on your own accord. If you do not then you will be banished for life."

The Elves started yelling questions and calling him all kinds of things most of which he did not understand. Eventually they quieted down, and he heard someone yell something he could understand.

"You cannot do this! You don't have any authority over us. Dark Owl will never agree to this blasphemy."

Hawk stood up and walked to the front of the stage. He spoke with a little anger to his voice. "Logan speaks the truth with full support from Dark Owl. We have agreed if you won't fight for your land and people then you do not deserve to continue to reap its rewards."

Logan looked at all the Elves who looked terrified. "You need to become the Elves you were when Moon Shatter led your people into battle against Rubia and her army. You have a war memorial and every name on that memorial died and bled to give you all the peace you have enjoyed. And now you must fight again so your children can also know peace." He looked at them. "This will be the last thing I will say. I am sorry it had to come to this, but I need warriors and we need to start now. I hope all of you do the right thing.! And when we step on the battlefield know I will lead, and I will not stop fighting until we have won, or I am dead. That is all, your twenty-four hours to choose starts now." Logan walked off the stage hoping they would choose to fight.

Hawk looked at his people. "We will meet in twenty-four hours for your decisions." And he too walked off the stage with Lilly and Sarah.

They returned to Dark Owl's. Once everyone was inside Hawk looked at Logan.

"I thought we agreed to take it easy."

Logan turned to Hawk. "I thought I told you the time for half measures is over. This Rubia is not going to wait forever. I am surprised we haven't been attacked already."

Hawk nodded. He wished Moonrion had picked a human who did not make valid points all the damn time.

"So, do you think they will step up and volunteer or choose to leave?" Logan asked Hawk.

Hawk shook his head. "I do not have high hopes to be honest."

Logan looked at Lilly. "And what do you think?"

She looked scared. "I don't know, Logan. They are terrified and to be honest so am I."

Logan nodded. "So am I but we either fight and die trying, or we die a coward's death! And I would rather pick the first one personally."

Lilly looked at him. "I understand and must admit I agree with you."

Sarah looked at Logan. "You could've been a little gentler

with them."

"Do you think Rubia will be gentle with us?" Logan replied. No one said anything to that.

Sarah looked at Hawk. "I could use a drink. Do you have a pub or something in this town?"

"Of course, we do, it's near the centre of town, but I don't think now would be a good time to go."

"Listen, Hawk, we cannot hide up here forever and if Logan is to lead these men, they need to see him among them and who knows, maybe we will win some of them over."

Logan looked at Sarah. "Hawk is right, now is not the time, we must have clear heads and the Elves will need some time right now."

Lilly spoke up. "I have some Elven wine at our home. I will go and get it and we can have a drink here."

Sarah smiled. "Elven wine, that sounds interesting!"

Lilly smiled. "You will love it. I will be right back."

Logan could only think about tomorrow night and if he would have anyone volunteer.

CHAPTER 16
FIRST ATTACK

Midra and his men were getting antsy. He hoped some of the Elves would cross the border so his new large Broad sword would taste blood. His Queen had made it for him, the blade was long and wide and as sharp as a razor. It was a beautiful and deadly looking weapon with a simple cross guard and a red handle with the head of a cobra for the pommel. Shortly after he was done admiring his blade, he ordered his men to add more wood to the fires. They could smell the Elves in the air and Midra had a hard time keeping them calm. It would not take long for the Elves to know they were there. He did see some tactical disadvantages for them. The large black pine trees with their purple needles made seeing deep into the forest difficult even with his men's heat pits that could see heat from anything warm blooded. He had ordered his men to take some time to rest as they had been on the march for two days. Now came the worse part, which was waiting to see what the Elves would do. He did not think they would attack. More likely they would run away pissing themselves.

***

The three Elves moved through the woods in total silence.

Their bows at the ready, they were on the hunt for red tail deer which was a nightly job for the three of them. They walked in a V formation with Peregrine in the front and Stag on the right and Thorn on the left. They were all masters of the bow with Peregrine being the best but not by much. All Moon Elves are trained on the bow at a young age. Most, however, wanted to become Mages and magic users. Now that is not to say Peregrine could not use magic. He used it to enhance all his senses including the speed in which he moved. These were all novice spells, but they were all he needed. Depending on the Mage, he could drop them with an arrow before they even had a chance to use a spell.

The hunt was going as it usually did, they had just stalked a nice sized Buck. Peregrine nocked his arrow with lightning speed. He drew it back and was just about to shoot when he smelled fire and heard a voice that had a strange accent. He relaxed his bow, and the three Elves ducked down. They were listening to what sounded like a large group moving and clanking around.

Stag looked at the other two. "What should we do?"

Peregrine smelt the air; it was filled with a foul-smelling musk he had never smelt before. He knew something was not right, but his curiosity was getting the better of him.

Peregrine looked at Thorn and Stag. "I say we get as close as we can and look."

They both nodded. Slowly and quietly, they started to crawl towards the fires. They had heard the speech made by the human and the three had already decided to help as they had agreed with him. Better to die with bow in hand than to die a coward, which these three were not. They continued their crawl when they started seeing shadows moving about. They froze and waited before the shadows were gone. They were getting closer to the treeline and they slowed their crawling. Now Stag and Thorn smelt the musk.

Thorn whispered. "What is that terrible smell?"

Peregrine shuddered. "I think it's those Snakaras, Logan was speaking of."

"Then we should get the hell out of here and tell everyone."

Stag was right but Peregrine wanted to get a look at one of these beasts to be sure. They crawled right to the end of the trees and finally saw what a Snakara looked like. Peregrine did not scare easily but these freaks where damn scary to look at, especially the large one who was huge and had a large hood that the others did not. Peregrine figured the large one was the leader; the others were not nearly as big although they were still bigger than the largest elf.

Thorn noticed that it seemed that they had same sort of tail that rattled when they moved it. They also noticed they all had weapons and armour; they even had some archers with them. Peregrine wondered just how good they were.

They had seen enough and were backing up slowly when they saw one of the smaller Snakaras turn and look right at them. The beast started to rattle his tail at a rapid pace. Peregrine could not believe it; how did it see them? They were all dressed in black and the forest at night was almost impossible to see into.

As soon as the others heard the rattle, they moved to its location. That is when they heard a loud hiss and one word, "Elves."

The large one shouted, "Kill them!" They were past the border, and he figured that if they stayed away from the town his Queen wouldn't mind.

The Snakaras where coming directly towards them. Peregrine nocked an arrow, he aimed for the throat of the first one that would reach them his arrow hit home and the beast dropped. They had to choose their shots carefully to avoid hitting their armour. Stag and Thorn each released an arrow dropping two more of the snake men. Peregrine knew now was the time to run and finish this fight another day, he only had three arrows left.

"Run!" yelled Peregrine.

The other two Elves needed little motivation, all three turned and started to run faster than they had ever ran in their lives. This is where the Elves had a huge advantage, they knew this forest like the back of their hands and the Snakaras were wearing armour and were clumsy through the trees.

Peregrine heard many of them fall, hissing when they hit the ground. He kept moving at full speed, he looked beside him and saw Thorn, but Stag was nowhere to be seen. Peregrine's stomach fell but they had to keep moving, they were almost there.

Stag was well ahead of the Snakaras when out of nowhere a huge arm stuck itself out from behind a tree, it flipped him, and he hit the ground hard and when he looked up he saw the large Snakara with the hood.

The Snakara picked the Elf up with one arm as if he were a feather, the beast let out a hiss so loud it was painful to the ears. He hooked Stag under his arm, that is when he passed out.

Peregrine and Thorn cleared the forest and were at the edge of town, for some reason the Snakaras had stopped pursuing them and seemed to be heading back to the border.

They both looked at each other not knowing what had happened to their friend, Stag. They hoped he was hiding and would show up later. Neither one of them said anything about it as they knew this was highly unlikely.

Peregrine looked at Thorn. "We need to get to Dark Owl and report this now." Thorn nodded and they both took off towards the Tree of Power.

CHAPTER 17
THE POWER OF KNOWLEDGE

It had almost been twenty-four hours and Logan had started to worry that the Elves would not come together and fight. He could not remember the last time he slept. Sarah was resting, there was no sense for them both to be a mess. Hawk was pacing and Lilly was passed out in the chair she was sitting in. All of them were in such deep thought or asleep that when someone pounded on the door, all of them jumped. Hawk opened the door and two Elves dressed in black with bows and quivers walked in. Both were extremely out of breath and needed a few moments before either of them could speak.

While they waited, Hawk introduced them both. "Logan, this is Peregrine and Thorn."

Logan smiled. "You Elves really like your Raptors don't you."

Hawk smiled. "They are majestic and powerful creatures so yes, we do."

Peregrine finally began to speak. "At our border, Snakaras, we came across them while we were hunting."

Logan and Hawk looked at each other, they both thought the same thing. 'We are not ready for this.'

Hawk looked at them. "Why did they not invade the town?"

Thorn answered. "They stopped chasing us as soon as we cleared the trees into town."

"And where is Stag, you always hunt together?"

Peregrine shook his head. "We hope he is hiding somewhere but I doubt it. I still don't know how they saw us; we were so careful."

Logan looked at both. "What can you tell me about the Snakaras themselves?"

"The leader was huge and had a large hood. The main soldiers seemed to have rattles on the end of their tails."

Logan nodded. "That is how they saw you; some snake species have heat pits."

Hawk looked at Logan. "What do these heat pits do?"

"They can see the heat that comes off our bodies, even in pitch black. And the leader sounds like a cobra, most likely a King Cobra as they are the largest venomous snake back in the Earth realm."

"How do you know all this?" asked Hawk.

"I was always fascinated with snakes when I was a boy, and I watched a lot of nature shows."

"Nature shows?" Hawk looked confused.

"It's not important right now, just trust me on this," replied Logan. "What else did you see?"

Peregrine answered. "They have set large fires on the border and we each dropped one before we started running."

Logan smiled. "You each killed one, I am impressed!"

"Don't be, there is still a lot of them," replied Thorn.

Hawk told Logan that even if these three Elves were blind they would still outshoot Earth's fabled Robin Hood.

"I am going to the edge of town; I want to see if I can make anything out."

Hawk looked at him. "Do you think that's a good idea?"

"I think right now we will be OK. I think she just wants

to scare us, or they would have continued their pursuit of these two."

Hawk thought about it. "I am going with you."

"And so are we," replied Peregrine and Thorn.

Lilly was awake and so was Sarah, they had heard everything.

Lilly looked at Hawk. "Are you crazy?"

Sarah looked at Logan. "Yeah, what she said."

"I am just going to the edge of town, we will be OK and besides, I have two of the best archers in town backing me up," Logan said smiling.

They walked down the stairs and hurried towards the edge of town. That's when they heard a strange voice. "We have one of your Elves, we will trade his life for the humans, you have two hours."

Logan was tired of this shit and focusing his magic and he replied with a thundering voice. "Then we shall meet in two hours."

Hawk grabbed him. "What did you just do?"

"If I let them kill Stag, we will never have our army."

"You have no idea how to use your powers, you could get killed or kill us all."

"I am not letting anyone die on my behalf," replied Logan. "I need you to open the armoury and show me Moon Shatter's weapons."

Hawk sighed. "I already told you, Logan, no one can remove them from the wall."

"I know, so what is the harm in me trying."

"None, I guess," replied Hawk.

"So, let's get a move on, Stag only has two hours. Peregrine and Thorn go and notify Dark Owl as to what is

122

going on here. We will meet back here in an hour."

The four headed to their destinations with Hawk and Logan heading to the armoury. Hawk and Logan moved quickly to the centre of town where the war monument was. Logan could feel magic under his feet, he looked over at Hawk who was casting a spell. A moment later a large set of stairs heading down underground was visible, they both made their way down.

They moved through cobwebs and so much dust they could hardly breathe. Logan could not believe what he was looking at, the armoury was huge with everything from bows to swords and shields. And on the very back wall was a beautiful sword and shield.

Logan looked at Hawk. "I would take it that the sword and shield at the back belonged to Moon Shatter?"

"Yes, that is the sword and shield he used." Hawk looked at him. "This may be dangerous, if you can get the weapons off the wall, I have no idea what will happen."

Logan began to move towards the sword and shield and the closer he got he heard a male voice. *'It's time for these weapons to be used again, may they protect you and bring you victory.'*

He shook his head and continued towards the weapons. The sword was beautiful with Pegasus wings as a guard and a moon on the pommel with a black leather grip. It looked like they were brand new, there was no dust on either of them. The blade had a small curvature near the tip. It was a very intimidating looking weapon. Logan reached towards the grip and tried to move the sword off the wall as soon as he contacted the grip. Logan dropped to his knees with what looked like ghosts surrounding his whole body, some even going through him at a rapid pace. This lasted for seconds but it felt like hours.

Logan was now completely covered in a silver and black dome. Hawk was worried, he reached out towards the dome and was thrown back. After a few moments he could see Logan stand up. Hawk gasped for Logan was in complete armour that was silver with black accents with the Pegasus and two swords emblem on the left side of his chest piece that was identical to the symbol on the black shield still on the wall. His helmet left only his mouth exposed, it had two black horns on either side of the helmet that curved like the moon in the waning crescent phase.

Hawk stood up. "What in the name of Moonrion is going on?"

Logan was looking down at himself and examining the armour. "Um, OK, that was crazy, it was like thousands of voices were going through my head and now I know military tactics, sword rhythm, timing and distance. And other terminology I've never even heard of."

Hawk looked at him. "Remarkable, it would seem you have absorbed the knowledge of other warriors from the past. You had spirits passing through your body."

"What!" said Logan. "I really don't remember anything. I just have the knowledge." He swung the sword from side to side then spun the handle behind his back catching it with his other hand with ease. It was as if he had been using a sword his entire life and then some.

Logan looked at the armour. "This will eventually come off, right?"

Hawk looked at him. "I have no idea."

"Well, we will figure that out later we have an Elf to save."

They left the armoury. Logan could not believe how easy it was to move in the armour, and it did not seem to slow him down in fact he felt like he was moving faster. He felt confidence with the new sword and shield and the remarkable armour. They met Peregrine and Thorn back at the town line near the forest. When they saw Logan in his armour with the sword and shield, they were in awe and a little scared.

They looked at him. "Where did you get all this?"

Hawk looked at them. "It's a story for later as Stag needs our help."

They nodded. "Dark Owl cast a spell of protection on the forest, but we must move quickly as he cannot hold it forever."

They all started into the woods moving as quietly as possible. That is when they heard the Snakaras voice again.

"Thirty minutes left before the Elf dies."

"How long to the border?" asked Logan.

Peregrine answered. "If we make haste, twenty minutes."

"It is going to be close, but I will not let your friend die."

They were both unsure if the human could keep this from happening. Perhaps now with his armour and weapons they had a chance. They moved as quickly and quietly as possible with Logan's armour making little to no noise. They were close to the tree line of the border. Peregrine and Thorn scaled two trees bows at the ready.

Logan looked up at them. "Remember, only start shooting if a fight starts."

Hawk looked at Logan. "I will stay back and help you with some magic attacks from the trees."

Logan nodded. "If things go south, you three get back to town."

Hawk smiled. "Sorry, my friend, we will be staying until

the end with you."

Logan smiled as this was the first time Hawk called him his friend. "Well, let's hope it doesn't go south then."

Logan walked through the trees and crossed the border where he came face to face with the Snakaras for the first time. At first sight he was revolted but he was slightly impressed by them as well. He was right, the foot soldiers were Vipers, most looked like Diamond back rattlesnakes. He did not see the leader at first. He did notice that the foot soldiers were moving out of the way and he finally got to see their leader. And again, he was right, he was a large King Cobra. He had his hood closed and in dramatic fashion he opened it quickly and let out a loud hiss. If it was supposed to intimidate Logan, he was not impressed, in fact it only strengthened his resolve.

Logan spoke first. "I am here as promised, where is the Elf?"

The large cobra laughed. "You're a fool, human. I am Midra, the general of this army and I take no prisoners."

Something flew and struck Logan's foot. It was the head of the Elf they had called Stag. Logan's body filled with rage, mostly at his own stupidity. Why had he trusted this snake man to keep his word? Before Logan could say anything, two arrows struck this so called general in the right arm.

He hissed in pain and ripped both arrows out of his arm. "You'll pay for that, human."

Logan looked at him. "And you will pay for your treachery, freak."

Logan said no more. He let out a war cry which felt like it shook the very ground. He smashed into the front soldiers with his shield sending most of them flying back, he continued his assault, he swung his sword with deadly accuracy, heads flying in some directions along with various other body parts. He hacked and slashed through the foot soldiers, he parried and blocked and continued to make his way through the battalion of Snakaras as if they weren't even there. He had a Snakara jump onto his back only to be filled with arrows seconds later.

Hawk was supposed to be casting attack spells, but he could not believe what he was seeing. He could not take his eyes off Logan, watching him was like watching a deadly dance! Body after body dropped all around him. The foot soldiers were backing up, trying to avoid the slaughter taking place all around them.

Midra pushed his soldiers out of the way and drew his large broad sword from its scabbard, he swung it with ease. It struck Logan's shield, knocking him back a few feet. Logan quickly rolled to the left and swung his blade right into the hood of the large cobra. The general let out a loud roar and dropped to his knees.

The foot soldiers were all standing behind him but none of them moved towards Logan. Logan kicked the cobra in the face and now stood over him. He grabbed him by the front of his chest plate and pulled him up, so they were face to face. Logan was still filled with rage at the death of the Elf.

He looked the general directly in the eyes. "You're a piece of shit and I should kill you right here and now, but I am not going to. I want you to go to your Rubia or Queen, whatever she is to you, and tell her we will not be intimidated and if she keeps sending your kind, I will continue to kill them and then I will come for her."

He dropped the general and headed back towards the Elves border and entered the trees taking the elf's body with him. The remaining Snakaras picked up their general and turned around towards the White Onyx mountains.

CHAPTER 18
UNEXPECTED VISITOR'S

Logan's silver armour was completely covered in blood. He set Stag's body on the ground, Peregrine and Thorn dropped from the trees, both had tears in their eyes as did Hawk. Logan was still too angry for mourning, he looked at the Elves.

"Did he have a family?" asked Logan.

Thorn nodded. "Yes, a wife and a daughter."

Logan dropped to his knees grief stricken, he had promised to save their friend's life. Instead, they looked down at a headless body. Logan stood up and punched a large pine tree, wood flew everywhere, and the tree went down.

He looked at the Elves. "I am sorry. I know how you respect nature; I did not know I could do that."

Hawk looked at Logan, he put his hand on Logan's shoulder and said gently. "Don't worry, I can fix the tree, we should get back to town."

Logan nodded; his heart broken for Stag's family. They did not even know he was missing, now they must tell his wife and daughter that he was dead. Logan insisted on carrying the body back to town, he set it down by the Tree of Power.

The town was deserted, all the Elves staying in their homes.

"What do you do in this realm for the dead?" asked Logan.

"We have a pyre set up to burn his body and send him home," replied Hawk. "We have not used it in a long time."

Logan looked at him with sadness in his eyes. "Well, that may change soon unfortunately."

Hawk smiled sadly. "I know, now we must get you cleaned up, you reek and are covered in dried blood."

Logan sat the sword and shield down, there was a bright sliver of light and black flash, and there stood Logan in his black shirt and pants.

"Remarkable," said Hawk. "I guess that makes things easier."

Logan looked at Hawk. "So does the armour only work with the sword and shield?"

"I do not know," replied Hawk. "Pick them up and see what happens."

Logan picked up the sword and shield and nothing. Logan looked worried. "I hope that was not a one-time event."

Hawk thought about it for a minute. "I think it may only work when you truly feel threatened."

"That makes sense, let us not test it right now, I am tired, and I want to see Sarah."

Hawk agreed. "Let's go."

They got to Dark Owl's and Sarah grabbed Logan, she hugged and kissed him until he laughed and stopped her. Lilly's reaction was similar when she saw Hawk. After the love fest, Sarah and Lilly asked what had happened. Hawk retold the story of Logan and his magical armour and how he killed at least fifty men on his own and dropped their leader to his knees. Then he informed them that Stag had been killed as the general had lied to them.

Lilly shook her head. "Poor Star, she is going to be crushed." Logan wanted to tell her but Peregrine and Thorn went ahead instead. Lilly looked at Logan. "It's not your fault,

Rubia and her Snakaras are evil and have no honour. You saved us and the town, you should be proud."

Logan looked at her. "I do not feel pride, I feel pain for his widow and pain for his little girl. Now if you will excuse me, I am tired."

He went into the room and sat on the bed still furious. He had tears running down his face. Sarah came into the room, she saw his tears, she took him in her arms.

"You won't be able to save them all, Logan. You tried while they all hid in their warm homes with only three that had the courage to help you."

Logan snuggled in closer to her. "I promised Peregrine and Thorn, I was so sure I could save him. I thought these Snakaras had some sort of honour. I will not make the mistake again; I feel like going to this Rubia now and killing the bitch."

Sarah hugged him tighter. "We will figure it out, my love."

She rolled over and kissed him, he returned the kiss and soon they were taking each other's clothes off. As Logan became more and more excited, his magic started to make his body glow a light silver. He suddenly stopped. Sarah looked at him as her eye's had been closed and then she stopped as she was not sure what was happening.

Logan smiled. "I think maybe we will make this a cuddle night until I can ask Hawk about this."

"I don't want Hawk hearing about this," replied Sarah.

Logan shrugged. "Well, I just don't want to hurt you."

"Well, you are kind of glowing," she answered.

"I will make it up to you tomorrow night, I promise."

"I am holding you to that, mister!"

He smiled and they both held each other close and fell asleep.

Logan woke up and noticed Sarah was gone, she must have just let him sleep in. He got dressed and walked into the common area.

Hawk was there, he looked at Logan. "That was quite the sleep."

Logan looked at him. "How long have I been out?"

"Long enough, but we have a meeting with Dark Owl in his room right now so let's go," replied Hawk.

Hawk knocked on the door and Dark Owl told them to enter. Dark Owl was lying in his bed, he was not looking particularly good. Dark Owl told the two of them to sit down.

After they were seated Dark Owl looked at Hawk. "I am dying, my friend, and I am afraid I can no longer perform my duties as our people's Elder."

Hawk looked sad but not surprised. He looked at Dark Owl and asked, "What would you like me to do?"

"Well, I am not going to drop tomorrow, my friend, but we will let our people know you will take my place until Raven has passed her tests and is old enough to hold the position." He then turned his attention to Logan. "You've had a couple of rough days here, and you'll never understand my gratitude for protecting us even when we have not been so kind to you. Moonrion saw the warrior and felt the goodness in your soul, you must not let Rubia blacken your heart with hate and rage. You must work together and trust in Moonrion. Now we have more pressing matters, we must arrange Stag's funeral."

Hawk agreed and they left Dark Owl to rest. Once they left the room, they both looked at each other but neither of them said anything. They headed down the stairs where Peregrine and Thorn were waiting for them.

Hawk looked at both. "How did Star handle the news?"

he asked. He knew it was a stupid question, but he had to know.

Peregrine looked at him. "She is crushed, angry, sad, but mostly angry right now."

"Whom is she angry with?" asked Logan.

"With all the other Elves who wouldn't help us."

"Wow!" said Logan. "I figured it was going to be me for sure."

"No, we told her you tried to save him," answered Thorn, "but she will need time to grieve."

On that they all agreed.

"Is the pyre ready?" asked Hawk.

"Yes," they both answered. "And we have set the body inside as well."

"OK," Hawk nodded. "The funeral will be held tomorrow night."

They were just about to head to Hawk's Laboratory when they heard a loud howl and then seconds later another one.

"OK, what is going on?" Logan asked, his body starting to swirl with magic.

Hawk took him by the shoulder. "You are not in any danger. You are about to meet the People of the Plains. The howls are just them asking permission to come on our land."

"What, are they werewolves?"

Hawk cringed. "Whatever you do, please do not call them werewolves."

"Why?" Logan asked.

"It would be like you calling a black person the N word in your realm."

"Ah, OK, gotcha!"

Hawk looked at him. "I will explain later." Hawk put his hands over his mouth and let out a howl as a response. "Just follow my lead, you might find this strange."

Moments later four large wolves walked through the trees. The one in the lead was a large black wolf with some silver, Logan assumed that was the Alpha. The one on his left was smaller with a red stripe down it's back, the third one on the right was all white with black ears and the large wolf in the back was silver with brown patches. They were a little bigger than the Timber wolves they had in the Earth realm, but not by much.

Hawk stepped forward greeting Shadow. "It's good to see you again."

There were multiple flashes and where the wolves had stood were two males and two females. They looked human in this form, but Logan did not want to assume anything. The large Alpha male was very tall in this form, he was at least six foot seven with arms like tree trunks. Even the females were tall, both standing around six foot, just a little shorter than Logan himself.

The one who Hawk had called Shadow looked at both of them, he did not look happy. He started speaking. "Hello, Hawk, where is Dark Owl? I wish to speak to him, not to you."

Hawk answered. "He is ill now, and I am handling all of· our peoples affairs. So how may I help you?"

Shadow growled lightly. "I want to know why Rubia is back with another army of Snakaras."

Hawk figured that this was the reason for the unexpected visit. Hawk sighed. "To be honest we don't know how she has returned."

Shadow and the rest of the pack did not seem happy with Hawk's answer. Shadow paced back and forth, he looked at Hawk and he pointed to his face.

"You see this scar across my face, my people fought with you Elves and were almost wiped out completely, only now do our numbers recover."

Hawk nodded. "I have read of your heroics in the first war."

"Yes, you've read all about war, but know nothing of it. Who is this human? And what is his kind doing here?" Asked Shadow.

Logan stepped forward. "My name is Logan Coyle, and I was brought here by Hawk to help."

Shadow laughed. "And how will you do that? Humans are weak and have no magic."

Logan did not like being insulted, he looked at their Alpha. "Careful, wolf. I am being polite."

Shadow laughed and then looked Logan directly in the eyes. "Or what?"

Logan locked eyes with the Alpha and his eyes turned completely silver, they were almost glowing. All the wolves jumped back a little growling. Logan relaxed and his eyes went back to blue.

Shadow looked at Hawk. "What the hell was that? How can this human use your magic?"

Hawk smiled. "He was blessed by Moonrion herself."

"And why would she do that?"

"The only answer I can give is Logan has proved to be a good soul with a good heart."

Just as Hawk had given his answer, Lilly and Sarah had returned from their day in town.

Shadow looked at Sarah. "He brought his bitch as well."

Sarah just looked at the large man who basically had no clothes on. "Did you just call me a bitch?" She started walking towards the man who was easily three times her size.

Lilly grabbed Sarah by the arm. "Sarah, this is just a misunderstanding. These are the Plains People; he did not mean it the way you think." Sarah looked at Lilly confused. "Can one of you just show her, please?" asked Lilly.

The large male looked to the female to his left. "Aura, show them."

There was a quick red flash and where the woman had stood was now a large wolf with a red stripe down her back.

Sarah jumped back a little bit. "Holy shit, so they're werewolves."

Logan and Hawk both slapped their foreheads with their hands.

"What did you just call us?" asked the Large male. They were all looking at her like they wanted to kill her. "What did she just say?"

Lilly whispered something in Sarah's ear, and she blushed. She looked at the large male again. "Oh my god, I am so sorry, I didn't know, we are still learning the customs."

"You should train your humans better, Hawk."

Logan looked at him again. "Keep pushing, asshole."

"I agree," replied Hawk, "but they are still very new to this realm and there is much to learn."

"I have come here to tell your people you are on your own if a second war starts. Rubia is your mess you can clean it up yourselves."

Logan stepped forward. "That's fine, but if they attack you know you can come here, regardless of how you feel about me."

Shadow looked at the human. "We need no help from a human."

Logan locked eyes with the Alpha again. "We shall see, won't we?"

Shadow and the rest of the wolves transformed back to their wolf form and left quickly through the trees.

Hawk looked at Logan. "Let's all go to my classroom."

CHAPTER 19
FAILURE

The Snakaras were moving slowly back to their lair in the White Onyx mountains. Some of it was due to injury for the fortunate ones who avoided the human's sword, and for others it was the fear of their Queen, who was not going to be happy with this failure. Midra was the most miserable, he had his hood tucked back to alleviate some of the pain from the human's strike. He was terrified as to what his punishment was going to be as he was the general and would take the brunt of her anger.

They continued moving as they had more than just Moon Elves as enemies and now with being a much smaller squad, they were much more vulnerable. They could see the mountains on the horizon and decided to make camp to buy them another day. None of them slept as tomorrow they would be home.

They made the rest of their journey during the day as most creatures of Silver Moon were nocturnal. They finally reached the mouth of the mountain. The Snakaras, keeping watch on the wall, said nothing after seeing the shape of their brothers.

Midra sent his men to the barracks as he would face Queen Rubia by himself. He limped in pain to the throne room where Rubia was just leaving her bed, still naked she walked over to her robe and put it on she stretched and yawned. She slowly walked to her throne and sat down, Sucuri and Malay stood on either side of her. He hated the female constrictors, with their size they acted superior to all Rubia's creations, when Midra knew one bite from his venomous fangs would kill them quickly.

Rubia looked at her general. She noticed the cut on hood which went all the way through, it looked painful. She closed her eyes and Midra gasped as he could feel his wound closing and the pain slowly going away until finally it was gone. He had a nasty scar, but he was just grateful it no longer brought him agony.

He looked at his Queen confused. "Why did you heal my wound, we failed you."

She smiled at him. "How did you fail me, general?"

"We lost the fight; we are all bloodied and beaten and those are just the ones who made it back."

"Midra, did you kill any Elves?"

"Yes, one my Queen."

"And did you contact the human?"

"Yes," he answered. "I used the Elf to draw him out, I gave him two hours to show himself. Even though I had already killed the Elf." Rubia took a sip of something dark red. "Continue, general."

"He showed up on time like he said he would, but he was not what I expected, he was much bigger than the Elves. He had some sort of armour and a deadly looking sword and shield with a winged horse and two swords crossing on the shield and left side of the armour. He asked me to return the Elf, I instead tossed the Elves head at his feet."

Rubia laughed at this. "What was his reaction to that?"

"Not a good one, my Queen, he let out a war cry that sounded like an earthquake and thunder. He attacked with no fear, it was like trying to fight a ghost. He moved so quickly you could barely see the blade of his sword and the shield blasted us and sent men flying. He gave me a message for me to give to you."

"Oh, he did, and what was the message?"

"He told me to tell you that they would not be intimidated. And every time you send more of us, he would kill them and then come for you."

She smiled. "Ah yes, the Elves must have retrieved Moon Shatter's weapons, although the armour is news to me. So, you said his rage peaked when you threw the Elves head at him?"

"Yes, my Queen."

Rubia smiled again. "Well, we may have found the chink in his armour, he has honour and a heart and cares for others. This could be used to our advantage. For I care little for any of those things, I can play with his mind and hurt others and he will come running."

Midra looked at his Queen. "I would be cautious for when he is enraged, he is a deadly advisory."

She looked to her general. "Yes, I can see this Do you fear him, Midra?"

"No, my Queen. I just have respect for his battle prowess, you did not witness him in action, it is a sight to behold, I will say that."

"Ah, so I have a worthy adversary, if I could only get him to join me," she said, pacing.

"I do not think that will happen, my Queen, after seeing what happened when we killed just one Elf."

She turned her head quickly. "What would you know of my power? Say something like that again and you will be back on your belly! Now get out of my sight, send the wounded men to me so I may heal them."

She returned to her throne with a new plan for this human, she would open a telepathic link with him and show him images from the first war and perhaps some seductive suggestions. Maybe he would come to her. Now she had to pick another target for her men to attack, which she had to consider carefully. She knew the Forest Elves would be difficult for they were nearly invisible in their territory and would have many traps set. She smiled and decided that the People of the Plains would be an excellent target.

CHAPTER 20
A BRIEF HISTORY LESSON AND A FUNERAL

The four of them went into Hawk's classroom and everyone sat down except where Logan had smashed one of the desks, he felt kind of bad about it now.

Hawk looked at them. "OK, so I should have done this a while ago but after the misunderstanding with the Plains People, we need to get this out of the way. So, I will start with the whole bitch fiasco! When Shadow called you a bitch, Sarah, he meant female."

"Well, I know that now," responded Sarah. "How was I supposed to know that they were also wolves?"

"You could not have, that is why we are having this discussion. Also, the reason they hate being called werewolves is because long ago a small group of young wolves went to the Earth realm to see what the wolves were like there. Once they were there they met humans, some fell in love with them and when they mated it created a hybrid of man and wolf, except these beasts were nothing like the Plains People we have here they were uncontrollable mindless beasts. Luckily, your people killed them all and they no longer exist. One time your love of killing was a good thing."

"So, why do the Plains People look human when they are not in wolf form?" Logan asked.

Hawk looked at him. "They are actually an Elven species,

the largest in fact, why they look so much like humans I truly don't know."

"So that's where all the lore came from, remarkable," replied Logan.

"What about vampires, were they real?" Sarah asked.

"No, you are looking at what your people thought were vampires and as time went on the stories became more and more elaborate. I guess it was our pale skin, strange ears and the fact they only saw us at night. Now there were Necromancers in your realm which could make the dead rise, so that could also be where your vampire and zombie Lore came from."

Hawk smiled. "No more monster questions, now our neighbours are the Forest Elves, they look like us except they have tan skin and are all masters of the bow. They are very territorial, and, in their woods, they are virtually invisible, even with the help of magic. Their Elder's name is Jaded Arrow and not many have ever seen her."

Logan looked at Hawk with hope. "So maybe these Elves will help us with Rubia."

Hawk shook his head. "I doubt it, for that is one place Rubia will not attack."

"Well, we could try," replied Logan.

"We could discuss that later. Now, one of the last species you might see is the Merpeople. They inhabit two of the lakes of Eight so you can never go into these waters."

"Why?" asked Logan.

"Well, Logan, once you hit their lake they would attack and tear you apart, they are like your Piranhas on earth. Except they are the size of an elf."

"Ah," said Logan, "that is a damn good reason."

"Fun fact, Moon Shatter used to push Snakaras into their lakes on purpose, only to be torn apart, they say there is thousands of swords and armour in the bottom of the lakes. You will probably never see one, they can only be on land for about ten minutes. There are other species in our Realm, but we will discuss them at another time as most will stay hidden while Rubia is alive."

"OK, any other things we should know?"

"Our wildlife is similar, we have deer, bears and moose, some will be different colours, but we have them and lots of birds and raptors where many of us get our names. As you pointed out already, Logan, most will go into hiding as they are all magic sensitive. One thing you do not have is Thyrions, which is like a Clydesdale crossed with a ram. We have some here in the stables, I will show you later as we use them for farming and travel. OK, so that pretty much wraps it."

Logan had a final question. "What about the Dwarves in the Brimard mountains?"

"Oh, yes, them They still have an exceptionally large army led by King Ember and Queen Azurite, they are great warriors and the best weapon makers in the land. In fact, the weapons you now have, Logan, were made by a Dwarven smith who was blessed by Moonrion while he worked."

"So, they absolutely will not help us?" Logan asked again.

"I highly doubt it, they lost many during the first war like the Plains People. And they will feel like them, as this is our mess to clean up." Logan said nothing more on the matter. "Now unfortunately we all must get ready for Stag's funeral. You will find clothes upstairs for the gathering." They all stood up, Lilly and Sarah left first, Hawk was about to follow them when Logan grabbed him lightly by the arm. "Yes, Logan?"

"Listen, I need to ask you something and it's not easy to ask but I need to know."

"OK, what is going on?" Hawk asked.

"OK, last night Sarah and I were being intimate and when I became excited, I started to glow a little."

Hawk laughed out loud. "Our little magic user Logan is growing up!"

"Hey, this was not easy to ask, dick. I just want to make sure I do not hurt her or anything."

Hawk patted Logan on the shoulder. "No, you will not hurt her, we Elves glow as well. And anytime your magic comes from love it's always a special thing."

"OK, good, thank you, do not say anything to Lilly, please."

Hawk smiled. "I will not say anything. Is that everything for right now?"

"Yes," Logan blushed.

"How are you feeling about the funeral?" Hawk asked.

Logan looked at him. "You know, for such a smart Elf, sometimes you ask dumb questions. I feel horrible, I do not think I can look at his widow and child."

"You tried, Logan. That's more than anyone else can say."

"Yeah, that is what I keep telling myself." Hawk handed Logan a small flask, Logan took a sip of it. "what is that?"

"Dwarven Mead, just take it easy, it's strong!"

Logan nodded he really was not that interested in drinking at all since he was blessed with this magic or cursed, he still had not decided. They both headed upstairs when they opened the door Lilly and Sarah where almost ready. Both were told to hurry up. Logan was provided with a genuinely nice black suit. He cleaned himself up and put the suit on, it fit like a glove which he was not surprised about anymore.

They all met in the common area. "Well, we should get this over with," frowned Logan.

They all knew how he felt about the situation. They headed towards the town's pyre, Logan had never seen so many Elves, not even when they had their town meetings. Everyone was in a sombre mood as they headed towards the pyre.

The four of them finally made it to the pyre, they took their positions and there lay Stag covered in a silver sheet of some kind. Logan had never seen a pyre except in history books. This one was round with the body in the centre like the moon above them. Logan could see no wood or anything to start a fire with. He looked and Dark Owl was standing in the middle at an alter and next to the widow and her small child.

Logan whispered. "What's the daughter's name?"

"Moon Petal," replied Hawk.

Logan sighed. "This is going to be a long night."

Dark Owl began the proceedings, he spoke very highly of Stag and his ability as a hunter and archer. Peregrine and Thorn both had their bows with them. Logan wondered why but figured it was like a twenty-one-gun salute. They all sang a song praising Moonrion and after the song both Peregrine and Thorn lit two arrows and fired them into the air. The arrows came down and hit the silver cover that had been laid on Stag's body.

As soon as the fire hit the silver cloth there was a large flash and where Stag's body once laid there was nothing. His wife was crying on Peregrine's shoulder and Thorn had picked Petal up who had tears running down her little face.

Logan's heart broke, he had not felt like this since the loss of his parents in a terrible car crash when he was seven years old. He looked up at Peregrine who was pointing directly at Logan. He knew this was going to be a disaster, he was ready for a slap across the face. He stood still as he saw Star and her daughter start towards him; the little Elf had a purple rose in her hand. Logan held his head down; they were both right in front of him now.

He felt a finger under his chin as Star brought his head up, she looked him in the eyes which now had tears in them. She spoke, her voice was a little shaky. "Peregrine and Thorn told me what you did to try and save my husband, I thank you for your bravery, you should not hold your head down today for you tried to save a life of an Elf you did not even know." She kissed his forehead. "And now my daughter has something to give you."

Logan crouched down and the little Elven girl gave him a purple rose and hugged him. And then returned to her mothers' side. Sarah and Lilly were both crying, even Hawk had a few tears in his eyes. Logan stood up; he had not expected that reaction at all.

Dark Owl raised his hands. "This concludes the funeral for our brother Stag who now sits by our Goddess Moonrion. There is one more thing that needs to be said tonight, however. My fellow Elves, I have become ill, and I fear my time to join Moonrion will be soon. Hawk, our High Mage, will be taking my place as your elder until my granddaughter has passed her control tests and comes of age. I am sorry for this timing and bad manners to do this right after our brother's funeral, but I do not think I have much time left. That is all, it has been an honour being your Elder."

The Elves were starting to leave, and most were heading

to the one pub in town.

Hawk looked at Logan. "That went as well as it could have."

Logan looked at Hawk. "What does the purple rose represent?"

Hawk patted his shoulder. "It is given to warriors for bravery. You should feel honoured."

"I do, but I wish it went another way."

Hawk looked at him. "You've got to let this pass my friend, you did everything you could, now you must move on. You know this is not going to be the last one of these."

Logan nodded. He knew his friend was right, but he truly wished that there were no need for this one or any more of them.

Hawk looked at him. "Now we are going the pub, you look like you need a drink."

"Hawk, you know my history in the Earth realm."

"I do, but with your magic you will not go down that path again, trust me."

"All right if you're sure about this. I have not had anything since I arrived, except from your flask." He looked at Sarah who gave him the 'it's OK' look and she smiled at him.

They arrived at the pub called The Silver Pegasus which made him smile thinking of the meeting he had with Moonrion herself. Hawk had tucked the purple rose into his left lapel and they walked into the pub. Almost immediately everyone went silent, all of them looking at Logan and Sarah. Hawk led them to a booth in the centre of the pub. Soon the Elves continued to talk amongst themselves, there was music and dancing, Elves were laughing and drinking, slamming their mugs together. The only two Elves who looked sombre were

Peregrine and Thorn who had lost a friend. Logan was confused as to what everyone was so happy about.

Hawk looked at him and said, "we celebrate life not the death, like your Irish in the Earth Realm."

Logan nodded but Sarah was worried, she had seen that look in Logan's eyes before and they were full of disgust not sadness.

Soon a pretty Elf came up to the booth and asked what they would like. The ladies ordered the Elven wine and Logan and Hawk ordered Dwarven mead.

The waitress looked at Logan. "All drinks are on the house for the hero."

Hawk and Sarah looked at each other, very worried as the Elves did not understand he had considered his actions as a failure. He smiled and thanked her. They both relaxed, they were not sure how that was going to go.

The night went on with the laughing, dancing and drinking. Logan was starting to get a little tipsy and the more he drank the angrier he became, as these Elves had done nothing but hide while he had fought to save one of their own. The only people who had thanked him were Star and her little girl Petal and Peregrine and Thorn.

He had finally hit his limit; he pushed his way out of the booth almost knocking Hawk on his ass. He stood in the middle of the room with his mug, he shouted so loud that everything stopped in the bar and all eyes were on him.

"I want to give a toast!" The Elves cheered. Logan looked furious. "Shut your fucking mouths!" Everyone gasped, Logan guessed they knew the word. "So, my toast, here's to Stag, one of your own brothers who had his head chopped off by the very evil I asked you to help me fight, while all of you hid in your warm homes. And due to your cowardice, Star is a widow and Petal will grow up without a father, the only three Elves who helped me were Peregrine, Thorn and Hawk. Maybe if all of you had helped me none of this would have happened so fuck you and your celebration of life! On your way home every one of you should stop and beg forgiveness from Star and her little girl. You all disgust me."

Logan walked out of the bar and headed back to the Tree of Power, Sarah chased after him and helped him walk.

The Elves looked at each other, Peregrine stood up and looked at his fellow Elves. "The human is right, you know." And he and Thorn left as well.

Logan stumbled up the stairs and with Sarah's help they finally made it to the bed they had been staying in. She helped him get undressed and set the purple rose on the table beside the bed. She kissed him gently at first and he helped her with her clothes as she pushed him back into the bed, he kissed her neck and pulled her close, he had that silver shine to him again but neither of them cared.

They made love most of the night with Logan's magic making Sarah feel things in places she didn't even know could be made to feel that way. They eventually ended up in each other's arms and neither of them said anything, they just fell asleep.

They were both startled out of sleep by a loud knock on their door. It was Lilly's voice they heard. "You need to come downstairs; something has happened."

Logan and Sarah got up. Logan looked at Sarah. "I wonder what it's about now. I am getting tired of these fucking Elves, maybe we should go back to the Earth realm."

Sarah kissed his shoulder. "Just go and see babe, and if

you decide you have had enough, we will go. I love you, Logan."

He looked at her. "I know I love you too, angel. I will be back after I see what they want." He got dressed and headed towards the door.

CHAPTER 21
LINES CROSSED

The Plains people were still asleep in their den not knowing the evil that was descending upon them. Thresher moved quickly and quietly, the only thing that was on his mind was the mission. He had the potion that would draw out the one they called Aura. He would be there soon, and the sun was still up. The Plains were much closer to the Mountains than the Elves town. He reached a good vantage point and studied the land, he noticed a guard in the front of the lair, he would not see Thresher. Thresher pulled out the potion he was given by his Queen. He poured a small line down the hill until he had a good ambush point.

***

Aura woke suddenly and began to sniff the air, she smelt something and was not sure what it was, but she had to go and look, all her pups were accounted for last night. She walked to the front of their lair, she smiled at Spike.

"Anything to report?"

"Nothing, Aura. It has been a long quiet night."

She looked at him. "Do you smell that?"

Spike sniffed the air. "I don't smell anything out of the ordinary."

She was worried, how could Spike not smell that? She

decided that she would follow the scent.

Spike looked at her. "Where are you going?"

She looked at him. "I just want to check something out; I will not be long."

"Do you want me to go with you?"

She thought for a moment. "No, stay put, it's probably nothing."

Spike nodded, and she was off. She followed the scent path which headed down the hill and seemed to stop beside a black bush which she thought was strange but against her better judgement she went to the end of the scent trail, once she reached it a strange feeling came over her, she tried to shift but instead she passed out completely. Thresher was delighted, his Queen had told him she would not be able to resist the scent and she was right. He picked her up and headed back to the mountains.

***

Shadow stretched out to reach for his mate and found she was already awake. She enjoyed the sun, so this did not surprise him. He walked to the front of their den and patted Spike on the shoulder.

"How was the night?"

"All quiet, Shadow."

"Have you seen Aura this morning?"

Spike nodded his head. "Actually, I have, she went to follow some scent, it was strange," Spike said. "I couldn't smell anything."

Shadow looked worried. "Which way did she go?"

"Just over the hill," pointed Spike.

Shadow ran up the hill and followed Aura's scent, it led down the hill and then it just stopped. He was very worried now. And that is when it hit him, the scent of a Snakara. He let out a loud howl and within moments Spike was beside him.

"What's wrong, Shadow?" Spike looked scared.

"Rubia has taken her!"

His rage built inside him, the animal in him wanted to follow the trail right away. The Elf in him, which was still full of rage, knew now was not the time. He ran up the hill, Spike closely behind him. Most of the pack were now awake upon hearing Shadow's howl, Sabre and Swift were at his side almost immediately.

"What's wrong?" asked Sabre.

"I think Rubia has taken Aura," replied Shadow.

Sabre and Swift both growled! Sabre looked at Shadow. "What are we waiting for, let's go after her trail."

"We will not be able to, who ever took her used magic and is probably already back at their mountain sanctuary."

"OK, so what do we do?"

Shadow looked at them. "Looks like the human was right, we are going to need help."

They left Spike in charge as per usual and told him to close the den and not to leave it until they returned. They all changed quickly and ran as fast as they could towards Eclipse.

CHAPTER 22
FACE TO FACE

Logan made his way down the stairs and when he reached the bottom, Lilly ran up to him and hugged him. All around the Tree of Power were male Elves, along with some females.

Logan looked at Hawk. "Looks like your toast last night worked." It still took Logan a minute to figure out what he meant as he was still half asleep. Hawk looked at him. "All of these Elves want to join your cause against Rubia."

Logan was elated. 'Finally,' he thought to himself.

Sarah came up to Lilly. "What's going on?"

"These Elves are here to fight with Logan."

Sarah could not believe it, after all this time they wanted to fight and protect their lands and families.

"This is great," Logan replied. "So now what?"

"Well, let's get them organized into three groups, Archers, Foot soldiers, and Mages," answered Hawk.

"That sounds like an excellent place to start."

Just as Logan finished his sentence, they heard a loud howl. 'The Plains People, what would they be doing here so soon after our last meeting,' thought Hawk.

Logan howled back.

"Hey, that is my job," replied Hawk.

"Sorry," said Logan.

The three wolves came through the trees, they transformed immediately. Hawk looked worried and Logan knew why there was only three of them.

Shadow looked at Logan and Hawk, he was out of breath. "We need your help please. I know our last meeting was a little rough. But Rubia has taken Aura."

Hawk looked at Logan. "You mean she is in her mountain fortress, or whatever it is?" asked Logan.

"Yes," said Shadow, "and every second we waste I fear she will not survive. It's probably payback for the first war, she is my whole world, please help me."

Hawk and Logan looked at each other. "Shadow, Logan is not ready to face Rubia on his own," replied Hawk. "He still has little control over his powers."

Logan looked at Hawk. "We knew this day was coming and I have Moonrion on my side."

Hawk sighed. "Logan, this is a stupid idea."

Logan looked at Shadow. "Will you help us fight Rubia if I help you?"

"If you get her out of there, I will do anything you want, she has crossed a line of no return with me."

Logan smiled. "I shall go and get my sword and shield," he headed up the stairs.

Sarah ran up to him. "Logan, please don't do this now, you heard Hawk!"

"I am sorry, Sarah. I understand Shadow's position, if she had you, I would stop at nothing to get you back. This bitch needs to learn some manners."

Hawk sighed when he saw Logan with his sword and shield. "I am coming with you."

"No, I need you to stay here and get the Elves organized, like we talked about. I will be OK, I have Shadow with me, and he is a veteran of the first war."

Hawk shook his head. "Good luck, my friend, but this is still an unbelievably bad idea, but if you will not listen, fine. May Moonrion protect you and the pack."

Logan looked back at Shadow. "Shall we get going?"

He nodded. "Listen, Logan, about before, I am sorry, I was so rude to you."

Logan looked at Shadow. "I understand, but now is not the time, we need to move."

The pack changed back to their wolf forms. They were running at an incredible pace and somehow Logan was keeping up with the wolves. Well, the males anyways, Swift lived up to her name. They had been running for about an hour when they heard Shadow tell them to stop for a five-minute rest through the pack's telepathy.

'Sounds good!' said Logan using the packs telepathic link.

'How can you hear us? Only other wolves can hear this link, not even the other Elves can hear us in this form?'

Shadow answered this. *'There was once one who could and that was Moon Shatter from the first war. OK let's get moving, we still have a lot of ground to cover.'*

'I must admit, this telepathy thing is quite handy' thought Logan.

'It helps us work as a unit when we hunt now let's stay focused Logan,' replied Shadow.

They were getting close to the mountains, Logan could see the White Onyx, it was beautiful! It was a shame such evil lurked inside of it. The mountain was huge, and they were getting closer and closer by the second. Shadow and the pack stopped and lowered themselves to the ground.

'What's wrong?' asked Logan.

'You probably can't smell it,' answered Shadow.

Logan closed his eyes and tried to concentrate on his senses. That's when the smell hit him, Snakaras, and lots of them. Shadow was thinking of a plan to get in and out without being detected. That's when Logan heard a female voice in his head.

'Welcome, Logan. I look forward to meeting you!'

By the packs reaction they did not hear the voice. Logan broke his telepathic link to the pack.

"We are not going to be able to make any plans, she knows I am here."

The pack returned to its elven form. Shadow looked at Logan. "Are you sure?"

"Yes, unfortunately she must have felt my power as we got closer."

"So, what now?" asked Sabre.

Logan looked at them all. "I am going through the front of the mountain." They all looked at him like he was crazy. "It's the only way now, none of you have to come with me, I will get Aura back."

"How?" asked Swift.

Logan looked at them. "Listen, I am not going to lie, I am making this up as I go, this is uncharted territory for me."

Shadow looked at Sabre and Swift. "Wait here, I will go with Logan."

"I cannot allow that," growled Sabre.

Shadow looked at him. "Are you challenging me for the Alpha position? We do not have time for this right now, stay here."

"This is suicide, Shadow."

Shadow looked at him with sad eyes. "I am going with Logan, stay here." Logan and Shadow started towards the front of the mountain.

"This is tactically stupid, Logan, you know that, right?" asked Shadow.

"Of course, I do. But she knows I am here, so stupid is our only choice."

They reached the entrance of the mountain only to be welcomed by a battalion of Snakaras. Logan drew his weapons, and he had the same silver and black power swirl around his body and moments later he was in full armour. Shadow looked over impressed.

"All right, Shadow, ready to get stupid," Shadow smiled and nodded his head.

He looked at the battalion. "I am here for the one called Aura."

The battalion did not move. Logan focused his power to his shield and released a large blast which sent most of the battalion flying back. The rest of the Snakaras backed off and cleared a path for Logan and Shadow, they were still staring at Logan and his armour and weapons. It was impressive and it did give him some hope that they may get out of this alive. They walked down a long hall until they came to a large room with a black floor and red walls. Sitting in a throne with two exceptionally large Snakaras on either side of her was Rubia.

Rubia looked at him and smiled. "You definitely know how to make an entrance, I will give you that, Logan."

Logan looked at her for a moment. "And you're the bitch who fucked with my life."

Rubia laughed. "From what I know, it wasn't much of a life, trying to kill yourself with a bottle."

"Fuck you, it was my life and my choice on how I wanted to live it."

Rubia looked at him. "Oh, I am sorry, did I hit a nerve?"

Logan looked at Shadow. "Look, this isn't about you and me right now. I am here for Aura and you know that."

Rubia stood up, her dress pretty much left nothing to the imagination. "Well, Logan. I am afraid I can't do that. You see, Shadow and I have some history and I like seeing him in pain."

Logan was trying to remain calm. "Wasn't almost destroying his entire species and killing his first Alpha female not enough pain?"

Rubia looked at Shadow. "Your wound healed nicely, too bad about the scar."

He growled. "Yes, too bad, how's yours these days?"

Rubia did not like that, a flash of what looked like lightning flew across the room heading towards Shadow. Logan reacted quickly and stood in front of Shadow and blocked the bolt with his shield.

Rubia looked at Logan. "Why are you helping this mutt?"

Logan looked at her. "That's my business, not yours, now what will it take for you to release Aura."

Rubia looked at him. "Oh, Logan, even you humans know in order to negotiate you must have something the other person wants."

Logan looked at her, the thought of trying to kill her then and there crossed his mind. He also knew he had no idea what she was capable of and underestimating your opponent could land you in a world of hurt. He could only think of one thing to do to get Aura back.

Logan looked at her. "How about a life for a life, would that be enough for you?"

Shadow grabbed his arm and whispered. "I cannot allow that."

"It's the only way," Logan whispered back.

Rubia looked at Logan and laughed. "So, let me get this straight, you're offering your life for Aura's? Wow," she smiled, "you are as heroic as they say, and stupid." Rubia looked at Logan directly. "What if I just take both of you right now?"

Logan was losing the fight with his anger. "You can try, bitch." Logan began drawing on his power ready for a fight!

Rubia laughed again. "Oh, Logan, all that power, it's orgasmic, fine I will trade your life for Aura's." She looked at two Snakaras and they headed into a chamber. Rubia looked at Logan. "Will you be giving me your weapons and armour?"

Logan shook his head. "It won't help you. I am the only one who can use the sword and shield and the armour is a part of me that magically covers my body when I feel threatened."

"Just the sword and shield, then," Rubia smiled.

"Fine," answered Logan. "I will set them down."

A few moments later the guards brought Aura out, she looked unhurt, just a little dirty.

"Release her." They did as they were told.

Aura ran to Shadow, he hugged her tightly. "Did they hurt you?" asked Shadow.

Aura shook her head. "No," she said. "I am just so glad to see you. And is this the Human we met?"

"Yes," said Shadow.

Rubia looked at the two of them. "Leave now before I change my mind."

Shadow looked at Logan. "I cannot repay you for this, we are now brothers."

Logan smiled. "If I don't come back just keep Sarah safe for me."

"I give you my word." Shadow and Aura took their wolf forms and ran out of the throne room.

"Well, aren't you just the hero," Rubia laughed. "Now, what shall I do with you? I know, perhaps a conversation."

Next to Logan a chair appeared, he sat down in it. "So, you're the one with all this power. I have been wanting to meet you for some time now," smiled Rubia.

Logan was really beginning to hate that smile. "Well, now we have met, and I am no hero. I just detest cowardly beings with no honour like you."

Rubia looked at him and laughed. "Why do you care so much for these Elves and why trade your life for a Plains woman you don't even know?" She continued, "how have the Elves treated you since you have been in this realm? Let me guess, with hatred and contempt. I know that feeling, Logan, more than you know."

Logan looked at her. "And why do you hate them so much, why make these abominations, why must you start another war? You cheated death once, and now you have all of this, why not just be happy with that?"

Rubia answered. "Well, I would've thought, as a human, you would understand that I want more than this and I also want my revenge on the Elves, and I shall have it."

Logan looked at her. "Yes, as a human I understand vengeance and war and I will tell you it's almost completely destroyed our realm." Logan asked one more time. "So, you will not agree to peace?"

Rubia looked at him. "No, I will not agree to peace. Do you think I was born evil, Logan? I used to live amongst the Moon Elves. I was one of their most powerful Mages at a noticeably young age. They all feared me and my power and when I started to dabble in Magic they did not approve of, I was banished from my home, and my daughter, and for that I will never forgive them. Especially Dark Owl, my own brother who did nothing to help me." Logan felt dizzy with all the knowledge that was just dropped on him. Rubia looked at him. "Oh. Did they not let you know any of this information, I wonder why?" Logan was furious with Rubia and the Elves. "Think, Logan." Rubia looked at him. "You are just a weapon to them, a human they need. But even if you win the war, what then? You live here happily ever after?"

Logan knew she was trying to get into his head, and even though the Elves left out a few bits of information he still knew they were the lesser of the two evils. He would deal with them when he got out of this throne room.

"Do you find me attractive, Logan?" Rubia asked with a big smile as her dress seemed to hide nothing now.

Logan looked at her. "Physically, you are beautiful, but I can see the demon underneath."

"Does this look not please you?" Rubia asked. "How about this one?" And in a flash Sarah stood right in front of him.

He got closer for a look and he could still see Rubia's eyes they were not Sarah's beautiful green eyes. "Rubia, you will never be Sarah, no matter what you look like!" Logan sneered. "And if you think you can seduce me into being at your side, then you're crazier than they said."

"In time I think you will see things differently, Logan."

"Well, we have nothing further to discuss, do we?" Logan stood up to leave when he was hit with what felt like a sledgehammer, he was pinned to the wall.

Rubia had her hand raised holding him there. "Did you

162

think I would just let you leave?"

Logan's eyes turned completely silver, his whole body was glowing with power, he focused and pushed Rubia's magic back at her and the two large Snakaras, all three went flying. He dropped to his feet, picked up his weapons and ran straight towards the front of the mountain, some Snakaras tried to stop him and were cut down so fast that most never even got their swords out of their scabbards before they died.

Rubia was now somehow in front of him she fired two bolts from her hands, he blocked them with his shield, they didn't even slow him down. He went to hit her with his shield, she moved out of the way just in time. He felt her scratch him under his lower lip. It was the only part that the armour did not cover. He kept running, he could not figure out why no one was following him.

Midra looked at his Queen. "Why are you letting him just leave? You saw his power."

Rubia looked at him. "Yes, I have seen his power, and I am not sure we had a choice. Do not worry, general. He's dead, he just doesn't know it yet."

CHAPTER 23
THE FALL OF LOGAN

Logan was making good time back to Eclipse, if he kept his current pace he would be there by nightfall. He was worried, getting out of Rubia's mountain fortress seemed way too easy. The scratch she had given him under his lip was becoming painful. He tried to use his magic to subside the pain. It was not working, and he had a feeling that is why his escape was so easy, the scratch was doing something to him. He kept going towards town, he was almost there. That is when the pain started to become excruciating, he became dizzy. He knew he had to make it to town, or he would be in serious trouble. He kept moving towards town much slower now, he made it to the border and pushed through the trees. He dropped to his knees now, crawling forward and after a few minutes he stopped moving.

***

Hawk was pacing back and forth, when Aura and Shadow came back without Logan he was extremely worried. Shadow had told them Logan traded his life for Aura's. Sarah did not know who she was angrier with, the Wolves or Logan. Lilly put her arm around Sarah, who was too mad to cry.

Hawk shook his head, "Dammit, Logan, why do you think you have to save everyone."

Shadow looked at Sarah. "I am sorry. I never asked him to do this. He insisted and I am now your guardian and protector until he returns."

"I don't know why he keeps taking these risks, Hawk was clearly worried for him." Sarah looked at Hawk. "Logan's no saint and he has done and said some terrible things and I think he is trying to right these wrongs."

Peregrine was leading a small group of Elves through the woods to watch for Rubia's men and hunt. That's when they saw the body. Peregrine and Thorn ran quickly to Logan's side. Thorn checked for a pulse he looked at Peregrine.

"He has a pulse but it's weak, we need to move fast."

The Elves picked Logan up, he no longer had his armour on. They moved as quickly as possible as the human was heavy. They finally reached the edge of town. Thorn headed to the Tree of Power, when he reached the top of the stairs he pushed through the door.

He looked at Hawk. "We need you, now!"

Hawk had no chance to say anything, he just ran after Thorn. They reached the bottom of the stairs and Hawk's worst fear was laying directly in front of him.

Hawk looked at the Elves. "Get him upstairs, now!" They did as they were instructed. "Get him on the bed and be careful."

Sarah was not sure what was happening until all the Elves were out of the way. Peregrine and Thorn stayed behind. She walked into the room and what she saw was Logan laying on the bed his face was so swollen he looked unrecognizable, and he had a scratch that was leaking a white foam.

Thorn looked at Hawk. "He had a pulse when we checked in the woods."

Sarah took two fingers and felt for a pulse and there was one, but it was still very weak. Being a nurse in the Earth realm she had seen some terrible things, but this was by far the worst. Hawk moved to Logan's side and started to use some sort of magic on him. Logan gurgled but that was all. Hawk continued his efforts, but nothing seemed to be working.

Dark Owl made his way into the room and Hawk let him take over. He looked at Logan and closed his eyes, he touched Logan's forehead and started to use his magic. Logan began to glow a light purple, his body spasmed and shook, he then calmed, and the purple glow subsided.

Dark Owl stood up and almost fell, Hawk caught him. Dark Owl looked at everyone in the room. "I have bought him some time. I do not know for how long, but he will survive the night."

Sarah looked at Dark Owl and thanked him. Hawk took Dark Owl back to his bed. Dark Owl looked at Hawk. "I won't be able to do that again, so you must call upon all of our Elves who have healing abilities, no matter how little."

Hawk nodded. He asked Dark Owl if he knew what was causing the symptoms.

Dark Owl looked grim. "I do, I felt it. Rubia has managed to mix all of the different venoms of the serpents of Earth into one immensely powerful poison. I do not think he will survive this, Hawk." Hawk nodded and pulled a blanket over his Elder and left the room.

Hawk looked at Lilly and she had seen that look before, but she managed to hold it together for Sarah's sake. Sarah was still in the room with Logan, she said nothing, her anger was building, for Logan was all she had now.

She came out of the room and looked at Hawk, she looked

evil and scary. "I am going to the armoury and I am going to kill this fucking cunt."

Hawk looked shocked as even humans very rarely used those words. He was still afraid to say anything. Sarah let out a scream of frustration and fell to her knees, Lilly was by her side instantly with her arms around her shoulders. Shadow and Aura left as Shadow felt guilty for his role in all this, Aura had tears in her eyes.

Sarah was shaking and crying. "I want Rubia's head!"

Lilly rocked her gently. "Sarah, let's go to the guest house and you can rest."

She shook her head. "I am not leaving Logan's side until he wakes up."

Hawk looked at Lilly and she knew not to push any more right now. Sarah went back to Logan's side and shut the door.

Lilly looked at Hawk. "What do we do now?"

He thought for a moment. "I need you to get Raven and Orchid, they are my top students."

Lilly looked at Hawk. "Raven hates Logan, she won't help!"

Hawk looked angry. "She will help or feel my wrath! Now I need you to move, quickly, love." Lilly nodded. "And tell Peregrine and Thorn I need to see them, oh, and Shadow."

"OK, I will tell them on the way." She left right away.

Peregrine and Thorn were waiting at the bottom of the Stairs. Lilly looked at them. "Hawk wants to see you two and Shadow right away."

They nodded. "We will get Shadow and be right back."

Lilly took off without saying anything else. Hawk did not have to wait long for the trio to appear.

Hawk looked at them with a serious look in his eyes.

"Thorn and Peregrine, I want all Elves that can now use a bow at our borders night and day, set up a rotation." He then turned his attention to Shadow. "I want all of your wolves here; you can decide what to do with your young ones, I will need any who can fight."

Shadow looked at Hawk. "I have already sent Aura to bring our people here, we figured you would need us."

Hawk shook his head. "Thank you."

Shadow looked at him. "After what Logan did for my people, your Elves never need to thank us for anything anymore."

Hawk nodded and his thoughts went to Logan, he went into the room where Sarah was still by his side. He could feel her anger, he put his hand on her shoulder.

"I am so sorry, Sarah, we will do everything we can to heal him."

She looked at Hawk. "And if you can't, who gives a fuck, right? He's just a human, not like you sophisticated Elves." She was right in his face now. "Let me ask you something, Hawk, did you ever actually care about him or was it the power he had?"

Hawk put his head down. "Honestly, in the beginning it was the power but now that I know him, I look at him as a friend and brother."

He turned and left the room. Hawk did not know what to do, which was something he was not used to. He was deep in thought when Lilly came through the door with Raven and Orchid.

He looked at his students. "I don't have a lot of time to explain everything, I need your help in trying to heal Logan, have you been practising your healing spells?"

"Yes, sir." answered Orchid. Raven just looked at Hawk which he took as a yes.

"We will take shifts, one healing while the other two rest." Orchid nodded.

Raven looked at Hawk. "Why bother, he's going to die."

Raven had no idea Sarah was right in the other room and before anyone had a chance to say anything Sarah flew through the door and punched Raven directly in the nose, blood flooded out of her nose and onto the floor.

She was on the ground. "That was very stupid, human." She was healing her nose quite quickly.

Sarah raised her fist again but found her arm would not move.

Hawk yelled. "Enough! We have enough problems. Sarah, back away now."

Sarah moved back and let Raven stand up. Her nose was completely healed, she looked at Sarah. "This isn't over."

Sarah walked back to the room and before closing the door she looked back. "I look forward to it, bitch."

Hawk very rarely lost his temper, but he was tired of Raven's attitude. He looked at her, she stared him down and walked out. Hawk was losing valuable time.

Lilly looked at him. "What about the Forest Elves, Elder Jaded Arrow, she might have the power to save Logan?"

Hawk thought about it. "They will blame us for the return of Rubia and will most likely not want to get involved. And we need all our men here."

Sarah came out of the room, she looked at Hawk. "I will go."

Hawk looked at her. "I can't allow that, Sarah, if anything happens to you and Logan wakes up, I'll be a very dead Elf."

Sarah looked at him. "And if Logan dies, I will be dead inside, so it doesn't matter."

Hawk sighed. "You will have to go alone."

Sarah looked at him. "That's fine, when can I leave?"

"I will have to put a few spells on you, one with directions and the other is so you will be able to understand them, as they use a different dialect of Elvish then we do."

Lilly looked at Sarah. "If you really want to do this, I will pack you a travel bag."

"I am going, that's the end of the discussion, so let's get these spells going."

Hawk nodded. "OK, we will get started right away."

Lilly left to pack Sarah a travel bag.

CHAPTER 24
NIGHTMARE

Logan was in Rubia's Throne room again sitting beside his Queen in his throne. He was now the King of Silver Moon and with his new Queen he had taken to the role quite well. The Moon Elves were easily defeated with his army and his own power. Some of the Elves were kept as workers and others for food for his Snakaras. The Plains People were completely wiped out except their two Alphas. Logan's next campaign was to destroy the Forest Elves which would be a difficult battle, but he was looking forward to the challenge.

He leaned over and kissed his Queen and smiled. "What would make you happy today, my love?"

She smiled. "I am thirsty for some Elven blood."

Logan smiled at her. "Sucuri, bring us an Elf!"

The large constrictor returned shortly with a female Elf.

Logan looked at Sucuri. "Could you fill our goblets for us?"

Sucuri brought the goblets and placed them next to the Elf and in an instant she bit the Elf on the jugular, blood sprayed everywhere. Sucuri picked the Elf up and tipped her like a bottle and poured blood into the goblets. She moved towards her King and Queen and presented them with the goblets. Logan and Rubia both took a large gulp of the blood and smiled at each other. They kissed each other sharing the blood that was in their mouths.

Rubia looked at Sucuri. "Bring the remaining blood and Elf to the side of my bed, I want to fuck my King in it."

They headed to the bed. They were tearing each other's clothes off. They covered each other in the Elves remaining blood. They licked the blood off each other slowly and poured more over themselves as they continued to fuck. Neither of them were capable of true love as this was just a companionship of power. They continued their activities for most of the night. They had finally been satisfied with their sick desires. Logan held Rubia close. Rubia looked up at him and asked when he was going to execute the female human that had come with him from the Earth realm.

He looked down at her. "I was having so much fun with you, love, that I forgot about her."

Rubia smiled. "She still loves you."

Logan laughed. "Love is for fools, only power lasts."

Rubia looked at him. "Yes but we must be careful of power for it can be a tricky ally as well."

Logan looked at her. "Always so wise, my beauty."

He kissed her and got out of bed. He instructed Thresher to bring the human female to the throne room. Rubia got out of bed as well, they both stood there naked still covered in blood. Thresher brought the red headed female to the throne.

He looked at Thresher. "Bring the chopping block and my sword."

The human female looked at him with tears in her eyes. "I love you, Logan, this isn't you, please don't do this."

He smiled wickedly. "This is exactly who I am."

Thresher held her head down. Logan raised his sword. Everything flashed and the image shattered like glass. He was now falling in darkness, when he landed, he stood up and was in a wooded area. He looked around, there seemed to be nothing here except for trees, he could not even hear birds or anything for that matter. He caught a flash of silver out of the corner of his eye. He tensed and a moment later Moonrion stood in front of him in the form of the beautiful silver Pegasus.

He looked at her. "Where am I?" he asked.

Moonrion looked at him. *'This is purgatory, Logan, a place for souls who get lost not knowing which way to go.'*

Logan looked at her. "So, I am dead?"

She thought for a moment so she could put it in a way he could understand. *'Right now, you are neither dead nor alive, you must decide which way your soul will go.'*

"So, until I figure it out, I am trapped here?"

She looked at him. *'Logan, don't think of it as a trap, it's just a place for your soul to decide if it wants to move on or stay in your body, this is all of the information I can give you, the rest is up to you.'*

Logan looked at her. "Please don't leave me alone."

Moonrion looked at him. *'You're never alone, Logan.'*

With that she was gone. Logan had no idea what to do so he sat on a fallen tree and thought about what Moonrion had said.

CHAPTER 25
THE FOREST ELVES

Hawk had placed the spells on Sarah, and Lilly had brought her a travel bag with food, water and a blanket. Hawk had also given Sarah enhanced night vision as he only wanted her moving at night.

Hawk looked at Sarah. "Are you ready for this?"

Sarah nodded her head and smiled. Sarah hugged Hawk and Lilly and headed towards the door. She turned. "Please, Hawk, keep him alive until I return."

Hawk nodded. "I will." With that she turned and walked out the door.

Lilly looked at Hawk. "Do you think the Forest Elves will help?"

Hawk shrugged. "Who knows, I feel like our world has gone insane. I really wish I had more knowledge as an Elder right now."

Lilly kissed his forehead. "You're doing fine, my love, this is an event that has surprised us all."

Hawk looked at his wife. "I love you, now I need your council."

She looked at him. "What is bugging you?"

"I don't know what to do with Raven and her behaviour, her hatred has blinded her, and who does that remind you of?"

Lilly nodded. "You don't think she would seek out Rubia do you?"

Hawk looked at her. "I don't know, she is young, powerful and full of rage, and Sarah did break her nose."

Lilly thought for a moment. "I see your logic, but not even Raven is that reckless, and she deserved the punch in the nose if you ask me."

Hawk smiled at his wife. "I thought you hated violence."

She smiled. "I do, but I understand Sarah's reaction and Raven should've known better than to say that, so in this case she got what she deserved."

"I agree," answered Hawk. "Do me a favour, find someone to keep an eye on her."

Lilly nodded. "I shall find someone right away."

"Thank you," replied Hawk.

***

It took Sarah a while to get used to the night vision spell. It felt unnatural to be able to see so well in the dark and she could not see any colour. Sarah was just leaving the forest around Eclipse and heading to the border. She kept moving, always checking her surroundings as she had no weapons, and she did not think her martial arts training would help her much if she ran into a bear. She knew exactly how to get to the Forest Elves border, she just hoped she would not be killed by an arrow. She moved as fast as she could, she was dressed all in black to make her harder to see. Even her hair was tucked under a black hood. She did not take many rests for she knew every second she rested was time Logan may not have. She was getting closer to her destination, her hope growing with every step. She would be there sometime tomorrow night and she would find out her fate with the Forest Elves then.

She was resting when she heard voices, she ducked down into the tall grass. Two Snakaras were coming right towards her. She froze, she was terrified, they were getting close. The first one was so close now if he took one more step, he would surely see her. She saw the foot in the air, she knew this was the end when at the final second both Snakaras ran to the right quickly. She heard some sort of animal scream as it died. She still did not move; she listened carefully and heard the Snakaras voices getting further away from her. She looked up slightly and saw them tearing apart a rabbit. She felt sorry for the poor thing. It had, in its own way, saved her life. She had lost more time hiding, she crawled for a little way and then she stood up and sprinted for a small distance looking back and stopped when she thought it was safe.

She could see a battalion of Snakaras heading to Eclipse. She thought of going back to warn them. She looked at the size of the battalion and with the number of new archers and the Plains People that were now there, she was sure they could handle a battalion of this size. She kept her focus on her mission and continued, according to the map in her head she was almost there. She looked up and gasped, there in front of her looked to be a rainforest, which seemed strange between the pines and maples. She started towards the forest very slowly, she was waiting for an arrow to pierce her chest. And just as the thought left her mind three arrows landed in a perfect triangle around her foot.

She stopped with her hands up. She heard a voice. "That is close enough, this is our land! Turn back, this is your only warning."

Sarah did not move but she did call back. "I need your Elders help! I need to speak with Jaded Arrow please." She did not move as she waited for them to answer.

"What do you want with her? And what are you, we have not seen one like you?"

"I already told you, I need her help. And I am a human, my name is Sarah. Please, this is a matter of life and death."

"Human Sarah, we will ask if she wants to meet you. Do not move, I will be back shortly."

Sarah stood there for what seemed like forever. She thought she was going to fall over. Finally, she heard the voice call again.

"OK, human Sarah. Jaded Arrow will meet with you."

Sarah let out a gasp of air as she was wondering what would have happened if she had said no. She moved slowly towards the strange forest when she reached what seemed to be the entrance. She only saw one elf. He had tan skin and long brown hair that was braided. He was in a tree, he flipped out of the tree and landed in front of her. He had eyes like a cat, yellow with vertical pupils. They were quite beautiful.

He looked at her and ran his hand through her hair. "I have never seen hair of this colour, I like it."

Sarah smiled. "I like your eyes. What is your name?"

He stood up straight. "I am Jaguar, second in command to Jade."

She smiled. "My name is Sarah."

He looked at her. "Hmm, strange name." He looked at her seriously now. "Did you bring any weapons?"

"No," said Sarah. "I have come from Eclipse, they said it was bad manners."

Jaguar looked at her. "Ah. They were right, I am surprised the stupid Moon Elves remembered." Jaguar looked at her. "Enough talking, we will go to see my Elder now, come, human Sarah." She started to walk into the forest with Jaguar telling her, "Don't step there." By the time they reached a small domed house made of roots he probably had to say it over a hundred times. He looked at her. "Wait here and I will let our Elder know you are here."

She nodded. He went inside. Moments later he waved her in, she moved slowly as she had no idea what was in the dome. When she made it to the entrance, she lowered her head and went inside. She looked around, there were different bottles and plants just about everywhere, and on the far side sat the one they called Jaded Arrow. She was beautiful, she had light green hair with large dark green eyes, which were also cat like. Sarah also noticed that the Forest Elves did not have the longer ears like the Moon Elves. Their ears were the traditional looking Elf ears she had seen in some of Logan's books. She noticed their Elder was looking at her as well. She said nothing for a few minutes. She seemed to be using magic to tend to a flower which seemed dead, but within moments it looked like it was just freshly grown.

She looked at Sarah. "Why have you come to my forest?"

"I need your help and I was told you may be the only person who can help me."

The Elder looked at her again. "So, you have made this journey for love."

Sarah looked at her. "How would you know that?" Sarah asked.

Jaded Arrow laughed. "Oh, my dear, I am quite old and the only thing that makes almost all species take such risks is love."

"Where are all the other Elves?" Sarah asked.

Jaded Arrow laughed. "You passed all of them on your way in, when Forest Elves do not wish to be seen they will not be."

Sarah smiled. "So can you help me, Jaded Arrow?"

The Elder looked at her. "First off, just call me Jade, the whole Jaded Arrow is actually not my true name but the name of a powerful weapon which we protect."

Sarah blushed. "I apologize, Jade."

"None needed," said Jade. "It's a common mistake with the Moon Elves as they use a different dialect of Elvish than we do. It's strange," Jade said aloud, "in all my years, I have never seen a human, I must say your red hair is beautiful, it's much like the Dwarves but silkier."

"Thank you," Sarah said.

Jade smiled. "Now, down to business. This human male they call Logan, I have heard of his exploits, we Forest Elves have been watching very carefully. And I can feel your love for him, Sarah. What has happened to him that has brought you to me?"

Sarah looked at her. "He went after a Plains woman when Shadow asked him for his help as it was his Alpha female. They went to Rubia's lair and Logan saved them both. He also escaped, but, on the way out Rubia scratched him with some sort of super venom." Sarah had tears in her eyes. "And now he lays dying. The Moon Elves are doing their best, but they sent me to you for your guidance."

Jade could feel the human's hurt and anguish, but she said nothing about it. Sarah punched the ground, her rage taking over now.

Jade looked at her. "You must not let hatred fill your heart as it will slowly poison you as well, Sarah."

Sarah nodded. "I know, but it seems to be the only thing keeping me sane."

Jade had listened to every word Sarah had said. "So, this Logan went to save a woman he did not even know and stood against Rubia herself in doing so?"

"Yes," responded Sarah. "I know, not the best move."

Jade looked at her. "Risking your life to save another is never a wasted action, Sarah."

She smiled. "Now you sound like him. And I know you're right, I am sorry."

"Don't be, my dear. After hearing of this Logan, I will help you."

Sarah moved up to her and hugged her tightly crying. "Thank you, Jade. I will do anything to repay your kindness!"

Jade smiled. "Don't thank me yet, I have not done anything, and I have two conditions."

"Anything," replied Sarah.

"I would like a lock of your hair, as it's unique! And if this human Logan recovers, I wish to meet him."

"OK," Sarah said. "What do you mean though, by if Logan recovers?" Sarah asked.

Jade looked at her. "I do have something that I think will cure your Logan, but all magic has a price, it could also kill him, it will depend greatly on his body and constitution."

Sarah looked sad, but she knew she had to be strong. "Well, he's going to die if I do nothing, so I'll have to risk it."

Jade nodded. "If this is your choice, I will give you this." She reached up on one of her shelves and passed her a small round bottle with a black cork in it.

"What is it?" Sarah asked.

"What you hold is exceedingly rare, it's dragon saliva, it will burn all of the venom out of Logan's system."

"You have Dragons in this realm?"

Jade smiled. "Yes, my dear. But that is a story for another time. Now take this and make haste, use every drop of the saliva."

Sarah looked at her. "Thank you for your help. I will

forever be in your debt."

Jade pulled out a small knife and cut a large piece of Sarah's hair off, as per the agreement. They both smiled at each other.

Jade looked at her. "It is time to go, Jaguar will lead you out of the woods."

When he arrived, she thanked Jaguar and started back to Eclipse.

CHAPTER 26
THE MOMENT OF TRUTH

Hawk and Orchid were exhausted. Taking healing shifts had them both almost at their breaking point. Hawk heard a knock on the door. He opened the door and there stood Star and her daughter Petal.

Hawk was surprised to see them. "Is everything OK, Star?"

Star looked at Hawk. "I heard that you needed healers, I thought I could help." Petal pushed passed her mother and Hawk and headed to the room where Logan was laying. Star went after her. "Petal, you should not do that, it's rude!"

She looked at her mother sadly. "I am sorry, Mama, but I am here to help Logan get better." She took the purple rose she had given him at the funeral and placed it on his chest.

Star looked down at Petal. "He is extremely sick, honey. He will need all the help he can get." Petal sat down beside the bed with a look that said she was not going anywhere.

Hawk smiled as he and Star had been friends growing up. "I wonder where she gets that stubbornness from?"

Star smiled. "I have no idea, Hawk."

The door opened; it was Lilly. Hawk looked at her. "Did you find someone to watch Raven?"

"Yes," replied Lilly. "Shadow and the pack are going to watch to make sure she stays in Eclipse."

"OK, good, that is one problem solved."

Lilly looked at Hawk again. "We also have a medium sized Snakara battalion heading this way."

Hawk looked frustrated. "What does medium sized mean? Dammit, get Peregrine."

"He has already told me for you not to worry, he said between our archers and the pack we will be able to hold them off."

Hawk nodded his head. "If that's what Peregrine said, I trust his judgement."

Star walked out of Logan's room. Lilly smiled. "I didn't know you were here, it's good to see you, where is Petal?"

"I heard they needed healers and Petal is holding vigil next to Logan." Star looked at Hawk. "I just used my healing powers, he should be OK for a while, he looks terrible."

"We know," Hawk said. "We sent Sarah to the Forest Elves to talk to Jaded Arrow about a cure."

"You did what?" asked Star.

"We had no choice and she wanted to go," replied Lilly.

Star shook her head. "Well, hopefully they don't kill her."

"They're not savages," replied Hawk.

"No," said Star, "but they will blame us for the return of Rubia."

"Well, she is gone, so we will find out one way or the other." Lilly gave Hawk a look. Hawk apologised. "I am sorry, I am just so tired right now!"

The others nodded, knowing Hawk had been trying to hold everything together almost completely alone. They heard Elves whistling in the trees which meant this battalion was getting closer.

Hawk looked at everyone. "I will go down and help with some magic attacks."

Lilly looked at him. "Hawk, you don't have the energy right now, trust in Peregrine, he has been doing wonders with the Elves and Shadow and his pack have been extremely effective and lethal after the kidnapping of Aura."

Hawk nodded. "I know, I just hate not being there to help. I will keep working on Logan as he is my priority right now. How many Mages do we have fighting right now?"

Lilly shook her head. "I do not know, that would be a question for Peregrine."

Hawk nodded. "Well, hopefully our lines hold."

Star looked at Hawk with a darkness in her eyes. "I will go and help, I have not used attack spells in ages."

Hawk looked at her. "I will still need your healing powers here."

She nodded. "I will only cast a few and then return."

Hawk smiled. "Please be careful." And with that she was gone.

Hawk wondered how long Sarah was going to be, he knew that Rubia was sending these small battalions just to hamper any attempts to help Logan. For all he knew she was close to the border but could not move due to the battalion. He was almost certain Logan would not survive this.

***

Sarah was getting close to the border of Eclipse. She could see fire and hear the battle which was frustrating as she was so close but if she got too close, she might be hit with a stray arrow or run into a Snakara. She cursed as she was so close, she crawled as far as she could and decided to wait it out. That is when she felt a warm breath on her neck, and she froze as

184

she thought she was dead. She was not sure if she wanted to know what was going to kill her. She looked to her right and there stood a wolf, she sighed, thank God or Moonrion or whoever. The wolf nuzzled her and ran a bit ahead, it hopped a little forward like a dog on Earth would if it wanted you to follow it. She stayed close to the wolf as they both moved slowly towards the forest. That is when the wolf stopped and growled with its ears against its head. The wolf took Sarah by the hand gently with its mouth and hid her behind a tree.

Three Snakaras came over the ridge. They looked at the single wolf.

The leader laughed. "Looks like we have a stray here, men, kill the mutt."

The wolf wasted no time in his attack. Sarah could not believe the speed of the wolf, the first Snakara went down quickly, both of its Achilles tendons were ripped out. The wolf kept moving, taking all three down the same way. He then stood close to the three of them and let out a howl and ran towards the tree and stood behind it with Sarah.

Seconds later arrows fell from the sky and put the Snakaras out of their misery. Sarah was impressed as this was a brilliant system they had in place. The wolf continued to guide her through the forest trying to avoid any more Snakaras.

They were almost at the tree line to town when five Snakaras broke through and went after Sarah and her wolf companion. They were gaining on Sarah when she saw Star step out from behind a tree.

She looked at Sarah. "Get down."

Sarah dropped and the Elf released what looked like red and silver lightning from the palms of her hands. She looked behind her and there were five very dead Snakaras. Sarah almost threw up at the smell of the burnt flesh but ran to Star.

Sarah looked at her. "I did not know you were a Mage."

She smiled. "I am a Battle Mage. Just a little rusty is all." Star grabbed her arm. "We can talk about this later. Logan needs you now!"

They both headed up the stairs of the Tree of Power at full speed. Sarah broke through the door and looked at Hawk who was too out of it to be startled.

Sarah looked at him. "Hawk, you look like shit."

He looked at her. "So do you," he smiled.

Lilly hugged Sarah. "So, the Forest Elves didn't kill you."

Sarah looked at her like she was crazy. "Um, no, they were actually very friendly to me, and Jade is a sweetheart."

Hawk and Lilly looked at each other, Hawk shrugged.

Hawk looked at her and asked. "So, please tell me she gave you something to help Logan?"

Sarah pulled the bottle out of her pack; it was small and had a black cork.

"What is it?" asked Lilly.

Sarah looked at her. "It's dragon saliva."

Hawk's eyes widened. "Jaded Arrow told you that's dragon saliva? I didn't think there were any left in Silver Moon."

Sarah smiled. "And Dragons!"

Hawk looked at her. "I doubt that one," replied Hawk.

Sarah looked at him. "Who gives a shit right now, I need to give this to Logan ASAP."

Lilly looked at her. "ASAP?"

'Yes," said Sarah. "It means as soon as possible."

She ran towards the room where Logan was laying. She was surprised to see Petal sitting beside Logan's bed.

"Hello, Petal, what are you doing here?"

She looked up. "I am protecting Logan until we can heal him."

Sarah looked at the little girl and kissed her forehead. "Thank you, honey! You did an excellent job."

She smiled. "It's OK, I like him."

"Me too," replied Sarah.

Hawk came into the room. "Sarah, did Jaded Arrow tell you that this could also kill Logan?"

Sarah looked at him. "Yes she did, and she likes being called Jade, not Jaded Arrow."

Sarah looked at Logan and popped the cork on the bottle. She looked back at everyone in the room. "Here goes nothing."

She opened Logan's mouth, emptied the bottle and stepped back. At first nothing happened. Sarah stood there worried as she thought everything would happen right away.

It was Petal who noticed it first. "Look," the little one said pointing to Logan's arm.

There was a golden light traveling through the veins of his arms and it was spreading through his whole body now. His face and arms were fire red now. Hawk grabbed Petal and took her out of the room. Logan's whole body looked like it was on fire from the inside. Sarah was worried it was probably going to kill him and it was all over. Out of nowhere Logan let out a scream so loud it shattered the windows in Dark Owl's home. He looked like he was rising from the bed, there was one large blast wave that came from Logan's body. And finally, there was nothing, just Logan's body lying in the bed, his body was smoking from the magic.

Sarah looked at him and noticed all his swelling was gone, he looked like Logan again. There was still no movement from him. Hawk walked over to him and looked at his face very closely. Logan opened his eyes and Hawk fell back and tripped onto the floor. Sarah looked at him and went to hug him, but he was still too hot to touch.

He looked around confused. He looked at Sarah, his first word was "Water!"

Hawk ran to get him a canteen of water. He passed it to Logan who took it from him, he was still very weak, and Sarah had to help him. After Logan drank about five canteens of water, he took a break. He still looked confused but said nothing as he seemed to still be in a large amount of pain. Hawk used some healing magic on him again. It seemed to have a much better effect on him now and his body temperature was coming down. Everyone had tears in their eyes.

Petal pushed through the adults and looked at Logan. "Wow, you look like you again." She smiled. "Please don't do that again."

Everyone started laughing as Petal was pointing her little finger at him.

Logan even tried to smile, and he slowly moved his arm to touch the little one's face. "OK," was all he managed to get out.

Star had returned and noticed all the glass everywhere and she could tell by everyone's reaction that whatever Logan was given worked.

Star looked at Petal. "Watch your feet, there is glass everywhere."

Hawk walked out of the room looked at her and asked, how is the battle going?"

Star looked at Hawk. "They are retreating again, our army

is getting much more organized, we lost no men or wolves this time."

Star looked at Hawk. "I don't know why she doesn't just send her whole army against us."

Hawk looked at her. "I've been wondering the same thing, and the only two things I can come up with is, she wants to be more careful because the first war she lost and was almost killed. The only other thing I can think of is she wants to make sure Logan is one hundred percent dead."

Star looked at him. "She is going to be furious when she realizes that her plan failed. I fear for the Forest Elves if she finds out they helped us."

Hawk smiled. "Rubia won't attack them as her army would be decimated and Rubia would not want to face Jaded Arrow, or Jade, as she likes being called."

"How do you know she goes only by Jade now?" Star asked.

"Sarah told us when she returned."

"Why are all the windows broken?"

Hawk looked at Star. "We gave Logan Dragon saliva and he let out a scream that broke the windows."

"What?" Star looked stunned. "She had Dragon saliva? I didn't think there was any left in the realm."

"Neither did I," responded Hawk. "But it seemed to work, it burnt all the venom out of his body."

"That was risky! This human continues to fascinate me, I cannot believe he survived that." Star shook her head. "It's crazy."

Hawk looked at her and agreed completely, he was also sure Logan was going to die. Hawk wondered if there were going to be any side effects.

Sarah walked out of the room.

"How is the patient?" Lilly asked.

"He is still very weak and tired, it will take some time before he is up and about, but he is alive." Sarah started crying when she saw Star. "You saved us out there, how can I ever thank you!"

Star looked at Sarah. "You owe me nothing. Logan tried to save my husband. And besides, Petal has taken a liking to him."

Sarah smiled. "I noticed, and the feeling is mutual. As Logan does not have many friends around here."

Star smiled. "I think most of the Elves do not feel the same anymore."

Sarah thought about Raven and hitting her, she felt terrible for her actions. She looked at Hawk. "How is Raven? I am so sorry I did that; I feel terrible, I was just so angry at the time."

Hawk answered her. "She was out of line and I understand your reaction, but we have the wolves watching her."

"Why are you watching her?" Sarah asked.

Lilly looked at her. "We are afraid she will leave Eclipse and do something she will regret later."

"As Logan gains more and more of the Elves support, she becomes angrier by the day." Hawk had a dark look on his face. "I am afraid she will seek out Rubia to teach her more powerful magic."

Star looked at him. "Really! Hawk, she is young and angry no doubt, but she would never do something like that, you're wrong about her."

Hawk still had a dark look on his face. "And what if I am right, does anyone in here want to take that chance?" He looked around the room and no one said a word.

CHAPTER 27
THE WOLF AND THE RAVEN

Shadow and the rest of the pack were resting after the latest attack from Rubia's Snakaras. Shadow was proud of the way his pack was becoming such a deadly unit. He was especially proud of hearing about Spike saving Sarah so she could help Logan. Word was spreading through the town that Logan was alive and recovering. Shadow thanked Moonrion for he had felt responsible for what had happened.

Aura smiled and walked towards him. "Have you heard the news? It seems Logan will survive."

Shadow looked down at his mate. "Yes, I had heard that, love."

Aura looked at him. "This may sound selfish, but I am relieved he will be OK. I may get some sleep tonight."

Shadow understood, Aura had taken it almost as hard as Sarah. She was not his mate of course, but she had felt terrible that she had escaped because of him and he lay dying.

Shadow thought about it. "Don't feel guilty, it's been hard on all of us, and you need rest and to eat something." She had no arguments with that.

Peregrine walked up to Shadow. "Great job and thank you for helping us."

Shadow smiled. "The take down howl and arrow technique has been working well."

Peregrine nodded. "I meant to ask you where you came

up with that, it's brilliant!"

Shadow smiled. "I cannot take credit on the technique. It was your Moon Shatter who came up with it. In the first war."

Peregrine looked at up at Shadow. "I wish I could've met him."

Shadow smiled. "He was a fearless and cunning warrior who gave his life to save us all, I think of him every day."

Peregrine looked at Shadow. "Thank you again. I must go and check on my men."

They shook hands and Peregrine was on his way. Shadow looked at the Elves who all looked happy, patting each other on the back smiling and laughing. Shadow's face darkened, he did not have the heart to tell them that they had not truly seen a full-fledged face to face battle, and he hoped they wouldn't have to, but he knew that was a fools hope.

Shadow went back to his people who were all resting, he walked up to Spike and gave him a light tap on the paw. Shadow quickly took his Elven form, and looked him directly in the eyes, he smiled and put both hands on Spike's shoulders.

"Don't let this go to your head, Son, but your actions tonight were brave and perhaps the most important thing any of us will do during this war, helping Sarah, I couldn't be prouder of you. You are now promoted to part of our main pack."

Spike hugged Shadow. "Thank you, Shadow. I will not let you down." Shadow was surprised by the increase in Spike's strength as his hug was crushing him. "I know you won't, now go get some rest."

With everything going on, Shadow almost forgot about keeping an eye on Raven. He called upon Swift and asked her to see if she was still in the town, she took off like a shot.

Shadow went to lay with Aura, but she was not with the pack.

"She went to see Sarah and Logan." Sabre informed him.

He thought he would go and join her but after having second thoughts he decided perhaps this was something she needed to do on her own.

Aura walked up the stairs to where she knew Logan was recovering. She had no idea what she was going to say as this man had traded his life for hers without even knowing her. She arrived at the door and noticed broken glass everywhere, she could see Hawk standing at a large round table. He looked up at her and smiled, which she took as an invitation to come in.

"Aura, how are you?" Hawk asked.

She looked at him awkwardly. "I wanted to come and see how Logan was doing. There is talk amongst the pack that he is cured of the venom."

Hawk looked at her and nodded. "Yes he is, thanks to one of your people and Star, he is still very weak and tired right now."

Sarah stepped out of the room, she looked at Aura and smiled. "Hello, Aura. Logan is resting right now."

Aura looked at her. "Would I just be able to look at him."

"Sure," Sarah answered.

Aura looked in through the door at Logan, he was asleep, but he looked like she remembered, she was relieved.

She turned and looked at Sarah. "Thank you." She went to leave.

Sarah looked at her. "I just wanted you to know that none of this was your fault. Logan did what he did because that's what he thought was right."

Aura nodded. "You have chosen a good mate, Sarah, he's

brave and puts others before himself."

Sarah nodded. "I know."

Aura made one more request. "Could you please let me know when he is feeling better, I would like to thank him in person."

Sarah nodded. "Of course."

Aura turned and walked out and headed back to the pack.

Shadow was lying down. She joined him; he pulled her close. "How did it go?"

"It went well," replied Aura. "He looks tired but OK."

Swift had returned and reported Raven was still in her home for now. The pack could finally rest for now.

***

Raven was furious, she could not believe that bitch had punched her. She was only stating the obvious. She had started packing a small bag, she had decided she needed to get out of Eclipse. She could not be with a group of Elves who basically worshipped a human. She was not sure, perhaps she would try to visit the Forest Elves if they did not fill her with arrows. And in her rage, she had the thought of going to meet this Rubia as she was immensely powerful and could perhaps teach her more magic.

It was obvious the Moon Elves did not appreciate her power, perhaps Rubia would. She continued to pack all the things she would need on this journey, as she did not plan on coming back until this Logan and Sarah were dead or gone. She was just about ready; she used a spell to make her harder to detect by magic. She slipped out quietly into the night, avoiding anywhere where she thought she may run into any other Elves.

Shadow could not sleep so he was walking in the woods checking on the men who were on watch making sure no one was sleeping. He was just about to go back and lie down when he caught a familiar scent. It was Raven, Shadow went back into the woods, it looked like Hawk had been right. She had used some sort of magic on herself, so it was difficult to see her at first. Her mistake had been that the magic made her hard to see but her scent was easily picked up by Shadow, even in his Elven form.

Raven was making good time, and no one had seen her. She was just about to enter the forest; she was almost home free. She entered the forest to the far right as she knew there was no watch setup here. She quickened her pace; she was looking left when she bumped into something. She looked up and was mistaken, it was a someone she had bumped into.

She looked up at Shadow. "Get out of the way, please."

She had never been this close to him before and she had never really realized just how big he was, it was like talking to a tree.

Shadow looked at her. "You know I cannot let you leave, Raven."

She had underestimated Hawk, she never thought he would use the Plains People to keep watch over her. Clever, but it did nothing to help her rage.

She looked at Shadow. "Please move, why do you even care if I leave?"

He looked at her. "I care because a friend asked me to watch over you and it looks like he was right."

She decided to try a new tactic. "Get out of the way or I will make you. I am a powerful Mage you know."

Shadow nodded. "Hawk has told me you are his top student, and you are to become an Elder when you come of age."

She tried to look as scary as she could against this giant Elf with the large scar across his face.

"Hawk is right, so if you don't back down, I will drop you."

Shadow smiled and he had the scary face thing down to an art as she backed up a little.

"Listen, Raven. I know you hate the humans and you disobeyed Hawk's direct order to help heal Logan who saved my mates life." Now he looked angry. "I am a veteran of the first war and have seen men cut down screaming and some not quite dead wishing for death from their wounds. I have seen the crying widows and orphans." He looked at her. "Have you ever smelt burning flesh?"

She looked at him. "No, I have not."

"It is a terrible smell." Shadow continued. "And if you have even thought of going to Rubia, you are truly mad or stupid for she will not help you, she may use you for a while and when she is done with you, she will kill you and feel nothing after it is done."

She looked at him. "This is your last chance, Shadow."

He growled. "After all I have said you still want to leave? OK, 'Mage', let's see how powerful you really are."

The flash was lightning fast, and the next thing Raven knew she had a large wolf on top of her with its teeth holding her gently by the throat. Raven thought she was dead, she was frozen, the large wolf gave a gentle squeeze and then released her.

Shadow took his Elven form. "You are not even close to

being ready. Now do you see?" She stood up and rubbed her throat. Shadow looked at her. "If you truly want a purpose, Raven, help your people here, they need you. With the way things are now maybe Hawk will start to teach you new spells, and how to cast them quickly."

She sighed and turned around. "This isn't over yet, wolf."

Shadow smiled. "I am looking forward to your next lesson."

CHAPTER 28
RESURRECTION

Logan was getting better every day physically but the dream and being in purgatory had taken a toll on him mentally, he was not sure he would ever tell anyone about any of it. The dream was not real anyways, as terrible as it was. Now, purgatory he was sure was real a place where his soul had been deciding. He figured no one knowing would not hurt anything except maybe him. It was a cross he was strong enough to bare.

The dragon saliva had burnt all the venom out of his body, but it was the most painful thing he ever had to endure, he was certain he was going to die. Although as quickly as it started it had ended. And now, day by day he was getting back to normal, he could even feel his magic coming back to him. He wondered what had happened in the Earth realm seeing as they had been gone for months and Sarah had left her car in the alley. They both no longer had parents and they were both from a single child home. He figured the hospital would call the police to look for Sarah as she never missed a shift.

He was not sure what Colin would do. He probably just figured Logan was dead or took off somewhere as he was always talking about it. He missed them, he wondered if Jessica ever thought of him, not that it mattered much now but thinking about them made him feel a little better. Back when everything was simple, and Logan was just a drunk bartender not the saviour of a race. He sighed, he had always wanted to be special, to be able to help people.

'Be careful what you wish for,' he thought.

The darkness of everything he had been through had left an imprint on his soul, he hoped in time it would heal. Sarah came into the room, she looked more beautiful than ever. Logan had a quick flash of his dream where he was going to kill her. He shook his head, and it was gone for now.

Sarah looked at him and smiled. She kissed his forehead. "How are you feeling today?" she asked.

He sat up and everything in his body hurt. "Like hammered shit." He looked at her. "But I do feel better now that you are here, care to join me?" He patted the pillow beside his.

Sarah smiled. "I don't think you're that strong yet, mister."

He smiled. "No faith, huh!"

"Do you want to know a secret?"

Sarah looked at him. "Of course."

Sarah smiled. "Did you know I have special powers in this realm?"

"When it comes down to it you had special powers in the Earth realm as well!"

"Why do you think I stuck around?" laughed Sarah.

He smiled. "I guess it was not all that money I had."

She laughed again. "How much did you have in your account when we left the Earth realm?"

Logan smiled. "Sixteen dollars and twelve cents. Oh, but I had about seventy dollars in tips, so I was going to look at Ferrari's if all this had not happened." He laughed even though it hurt like hell.

Sarah smiled again. "You're such a dork." She sat next to

him and rubbed his back gently. "Hawk was worried you would not be the same after going through all of this, which makes sense." She smiled. "You can talk to me about anything you know that, right?"

He smiled, he wished that were true, but he would die with that terrible dream in his mind, he would not even tell it on his death bed. Just as the thought left his mind, Hawk walked into the room, he looked terrible.

Sarah got up and stepped out of the room. Logan smiled at Hawk as he entered the room, he looked like he had aged fifty years since the last time he had seen him.

Logan was concerned. "Hawk, are you OK? You look a little rough, my friend."

Hawk nodded. "I will admit, without you, things have been difficult, and I have much to tell you."

Logan looked at Hawk. "I am sorry for what I did, it was stupid and reckless."

Hawk shook his head. "No, Logan, your actions actually got the Elves and The Plains People to start working together." Hawk looked at him. "We have held off multiple small attacks."

"So, we have warriors now?" Logan smiled.

"No, Logan, we have a lot of archers and some Mages, we have no one who knows the sword or the shield! And we will need that to win this war."

Logan looked at Hawk. "OK, so who do we have to teach them the sword and shield?"

Hawk smiled sadly. "Maybe some of that venom gave you some brain damage or the dragons saliva we used to cure you."

Logan looked at Hawk. "Wait, did you say dragon saliva?"

"Yes, Sarah was given some by the Forest Elves."

Logan looked at Hawk. "You let Sarah go to the fucking Forest Elves, are you crazy?"

Hawk looked at him. "I had little choice, you don't know how close you were to death, and you try to stop Sarah when she has her mind set on something."

Logan nodded; he knew when Sarah had her mind set on anything there was nothing that was going to stop her. Logan got back to the dragon saliva thing. "You never told me there are dragons here."

Hawk shrugged his shoulders. "It was news to me as well, I thought they had left long ago."

Logan looked at him. "What do you mean left?"

Hawk threw his hands up in the air. "I have no idea; I've never seen one and the legends say they can travel to different realms like we open doors to a different room."

Logan put his hands up. "OK, sorry. I didn't know, so back to the sword and shield training. How are we going to accomplish that?"

Hawk looked at him. "You will train them; you have the knowledge of all the warriors that came before you and I don't even know how many that is."

Logan felt dumb for not thinking of that, but his mind was still a little hazy. "OK, well as you can see, I can barely move right now so that will have to wait."

Hawk looked him in the eyes. "You feel different somehow, Logan, are you OK?"

He nodded. "I am just coming to terms with being here again. You don't know just how close to death I was, and I had terrible dreams."

Hawk looked at him for a moment. "I guess that would

take its toll on any man's soul. I will let you rest; we still have much to discuss."

Logan laid back in the bed. "Thank you, Hawk"

"Don't thank me yet, you may have woken up in a place worse than you were before."

Logan smiled. "That's not possible, my friend." Hawk nodded and walked out of the room.

Sarah looked at Hawk and asked, "So, what do you think?"

Hawk thought about it before he answered. "Well, he's definitely different, but we have no idea what he was going through or what he saw when he was filled with that venom, we may have snatched his soul from what you humans call hell itself."

Sarah looked at Hawk. "I know Logan was never perfect, but he would not have been in hell."

"OK," replied Hawk. "He will need time to work through everything, but other than that he is the Logan you always loved."

Sarah smiled. "Thank you, Hawk."

He smiled back. "Anytime. Oh, and by the way, he is healing extremely fast, he should be up and about soon."

Their conversation was interrupted by Star and Petal who walked into Dark Owl's home. Hawk had fixed all the glass that had shattered. Petal ran from her mother's side and into where Logan was resting. Logan looked up to see a smiling little Elven girl. She gave him a thorough look over. She seemed to be happy with what she saw.

"Hi, Logan, I am glad that you are getting better!" She pointed at him. "And I am reminding you, do not do that again, you scared us."

Logan smiled. "I promise I won't, little one."

She looked at him, she smiled and nodded. She asked him when he would be able to play.

Logan looked at his new little friend and smiled. "It won't be much longer."

Star came into the room. "Petal, Logan needs his rest right now." She smiled at him. "Sorry, Logan, she has become quite smitten with you."

"It's OK, Star. I am always open to new friends, and here I need as many as I can get."

Star smiled. "Things are changing Logan."

Logan rolled over to rest; he was glad some of the Elves had started to fight while he had been recovering. He tried to get some sleep and hoped it would be nightmare free.

CHAPTER 29
THE CAPTURE OF THRESHER

Rubia was getting tired of waiting for Logan to die, she had to admit he had an inner strength she had underestimated. She thought he would have been dead by now. She was getting tired of playing cat and mouse. She was ready to crush the Elves, although they had started fighting back and with the help of the Plains People, they had killed all the small battalions she had sent with a few managing to escape. She should have just killed Shadow's bitch when she had her. For she knew Shadow was a powerful warrior, he had almost killed her in the first war. Instead, he now carried a scar across his face which had been pure luck for her with a dropped blade catching him in the face.

She had felt small flickers of power which had to be Logan fighting for his life. She wanted him dead, and she was tired of waiting for the poison to work. She called upon Thresher, he walked into the Throne room.

She looked at him. "Thresher, I have been pleased with all of your work. But now I give you your most important job yet. I want this human killed; I care little how it's done."

Thresher looked at her. "What about his power, I will be no match for him."

"He is on his death bed, Thresher. Sneak in and finish the job."

Thresher looked at her again. "What about the Elves and

Wolves now working together, how will I sneak through?"

She thought about this. "I will mask your scent from the wolves and the rest is up to you. I will send Sucuri and Malay with you to cause a distraction."

He bowed. "Thank you. I will begin my journey when they are ready."

Sucuri and Malay were a sight to behold in their armour, both females stood close to ten feet tall with rippling muscles and each of them held a spear twice as long as any elf, with a sword on each hip they were frightening even to Thresher.

They both looked at the assassin, Sucuri spoke. "We are ready when you are."

The three left out of the main entrance and began the journey. Thresher admired the size of Sucuri and Malay, but they were both much slower than he was, which was frustrating to him as he relied on speed as an ally. He knew, though, that they would draw all the attention from him when they reached the border of Eclipse. He was hoping it would be a quick, in and out, and they could finally destroy the Elves, for without the human there was no way they could win.

As before, they only travelled at night, it was much harder hiding the two behemoths he had with him, he wondered if it was a mistake bringing them. They were getting closer to Eclipse. He looked at Sucuri and Malay.

"OK, we are getting closer now, when we get there, I want you to cause as much carnage as possible, so I have time to work."

They both nodded, Thresher hoped that this worked, it seemed like a suicide mission to him.

Rubia was sitting in her throne room drinking some red wine when it hit her, she felt strong magic. It was not as strong as before, but she knew that the Elves had somehow figured out a cure for her venom. She also knew that Logan would only get stronger the more time he had to recover. She just hoped Thresher made it there in time to kill him.

The trio had just made it to the border, Thresher looked at the two of them. "If I do not return by sunrise, no matter what, you both retreat and report to Rubia." They nodded. "Now, give me a few minutes and then attack."

Thresher moved like a ghost across and into the trees, the two constrictors could hardly believe it. They waited as instructed and then they both stood to their full size and began to cross the Moon Elves border. The first arrows struck their armour, they kept moving forward. More arrows flew at them, this time some struck their scales but were little more than a nuisance. They kept advancing, they could hear the scared cries of the Elves as their arrows had no effect on the two giants.

Shadow looked through the trees, he cursed under his breath. He had seen large Snakaras like this in the first war. He knew the Elves and his pack were not ready for this. He had to find Peregrine for he knew that they needed to retreat to the armoury where not even these giants could get into. Aura and Swift were behind him, they saw the two giants and gasped.

Shadow shook Aura and she looked at him. "You and Swift round up the women and children, get them to the armoury." She nodded. They both shifted quickly and took off. He looked at Sabre and Spike. "OK, it's only going to be the three of us, the rest of the pack goes to the armoury!" Shadow looked at Sabre and Spike. "Listen, I know they look huge, and they are. All we are going to do is try and slow them down. No direct attacks and watch their reach, no heroics, you hear me,

Spike." Spike nodded and with that they all shifted.

They ran towards the giants, growling and barking. Shadow was right, they were big but terribly slow, they tried spearing the wolves multiple times, missing their marks by a large margin. A spear smashed the ground near Spike, he grabbed and held it for a moment and at the last second he let it go, it almost struck the large Snakara in the face. Their plan was working but the giant Snakaras were still advancing. They were at the tree line where the wolves knew this tactic would not work anymore. They broke off into the woods howling for the Elves to retreat to the armoury.

Sucuri and Malay were doing a splendid job, Thresher was waiting in a large tree next to what the Elves called the Tree of Power, waiting for the few remaining Elves to retreat or to join the fight. He knew Logan was in there, the only one he was worried about was the one they called Hawk. As he knew him to be a powerful Battle Mage.

Shadow shifted back to his Elven form as he ran into Peregrine. He looked at the Elf. "You need to retreat; I have seen this type of Snakara from the first war. Their scales are too thick for your arrows to penetrate, only swords and magic will bring them down."

Peregrine nodded and let out a loud series of chirps. The two giant Snakaras were still advancing and a dead Elf went flying into a tree right beside Shadow. There were more screams but most of the Elves had begun to head to the armoury.

The giants had almost made it to town. Hawk was trying to figure out what to do, they needed to head to the armoury, but he was not sure how to move Logan. Hawk ran into the room where Sarah was with Logan, who was awake and aware, but he was in no position to fight.

"Sarah, we need to get to the armoury now."

She looked at Hawk. "Why can't you go down there and fight them with your magic?"

Hawk looked at her. "Because I am the only one who can seal the armoury against attack, if those beasts get in there, we are all doomed."

Logan looked at Hawk. "Take Sarah, I will be fine, trust me."

Sarah looked at Logan. "I am not leaving you here by yourself."

Logan looked at Hawk. "Go, now, and I will look after Sarah."

Hawk looked at him. "You can't even get out of bed. I am not leaving you both here."

"Just go now. Have faith, Hawk, go now and protect your people."

Hawk knew by the looks on the faces of Sarah and Logan there was no sense in arguing.

"Fine," he turned and grabbed Lilly and they started down the stairs.

Just as they reached the bottom, the giant Snakaras broke the tree line into town. Hawk couldn't believe how big they were. Lilly screamed, he pulled her towards him and they both ran towards the armoury. He noticed a few dead Elves scattered here and there, one was still on the spear of the large Snakara, she flicked the Elf off like a rag doll. They were almost at the armoury. He looked back; he was worried he would not have time to seal it. He could see most of the Elves were heading into the armoury. When he noticed out of the corner of his eye, one female Elf walking towards the giants.

Hawk shook his head, he could not believe what he was seeing, it was Raven. Hawk got Lilly down the stairs and ran to grab Raven, she was in the middle of a spell, she pointed her hands towards the giants, her fingers released ten ice daggers into the flesh of the giants who both cried out in pain. They both slowed down, not knowing what to do.

Hawk ran towards Raven; he grabbed her hand. "C'mon, we must get out of here!"

She looked at Hawk. "Go and seal the armoury, I will buy you time, I will be fine."

Hawk looked at Raven. "If you wanted to impress me, mission accomplished, but let's go."

She jerked her hand out of his. "Just go!"

Hawk had no more time to argue, he ran to the armoury and went down the stairs, he began the spell to seal the door. He sighed; it was done.

Raven looked at the two large Snakaras, she had one more spell and then she would run. She called upon her magic, a large burst of green lightning flew out of her fingertips, again both giants cried out, and this time were dropped to their knees as the armour they were wearing was a perfect conductor.

She opened her eyes to see them both kneeling. She smiled and started to run to find somewhere to hide. The two constrictors rose to their feet after the spell had travelled through them, it was extremely painful, but it had not killed them. They continued towards the armoury, they smashed their spears and fists against the door. Whatever magic was cast on the door was much too strong even for them to break through.

They headed back to the forest; they had accomplished what they needed to.

Sarah and Logan were still in the room. Logan had sat all

the way up which caused him immense pain. They had heard the screams and then nothing. It was deadly silent. Sarah looked at him and smiled when out of nowhere a jet-black hand grabbed her by the head and pulled her into the next room. She screamed, there was a thud and whatever grabbed her called her a 'stupid bitch,' and then he heard what sounded like a slap across the face and someone hit the floor.

Logan felt a rage build in him that he did not know he possessed. He rose to his feet feeling his magic repairing him at a rapid pace. He stepped out of the room and there in front of him was a jet black Snakara which Logan knew was a Black Mamba from the Earth realm. He looked to the right and saw Sarah laying on the ground unconscious with a small amount of blood coming out of her mouth.

Logan's rage was beyond anything he had ever felt, he grabbed the Snakara by the throat and lifted it easily off the ground. His eyes were completely silver even the whites were gone. The Snakara struggled in his hand, he squeezed harder and pulled the snake man face to face.

"That was a mistake, freak."

He threw the Snakara out the window and he knew it was a long way down but not far enough to kill. He went to Sarah's side.

She looked up at him. "Logan?"

The next thing she knew he jumped out of a broken window. Logan dropped down onto the Snakaras chest, it spit up blood he picked it up and threw it against the tree, he was just warming up.

Sarah did not know what was happening, but she knew Logan was well beyond angry. And she remembered Hawk's warning about his control. She knew after the Snakara hit her it was game over for the creature. She ran down the stairs where Logan had it pinned to the tree. His eyes were completely silver, he looked like some sort of demon. She was scared, she did not know what to do. She called his name, he looked at her, his hands were also glowing silver.

She slowly walked towards him. "Logan, stop. I am OK, you need to calm down, babe, please."

He looked at her, he seemed to be lost in his rage but just when she thought she had lost him, the silver left his eyes and his breathing slowed down. She ran to him and took his hand, he was gentle, and slowly Logan was back in control. That did not mean he was not still pissed, he walked up to the Snakara, still pinned to the tree.

Logan looked at him. "She just saved you from being torn apart. You have some questions to answer." He punched the Snakara, and it went limp.

CHAPTER 30
INTERROGATION

After the attack of the two giant Snakaras and the assassination attempt on Logan's life, many things had changed. Logan was back on his feet, it seemed that all he needed was an attempt on his life for the motivation to fully heal. They had lost thirty Elves in the attack which was a much lower number than they had expected. Identifying the bodies was proving to be difficult as the giants left little to identify at all. They had lost their first battle and many of the Elves were shaken up. Peregrine and Thorn were doing a good job at calming the Elves.

Hawk and Logan were in the Tree of Power where Dark Owl was close to his final days, he did not even have the power to get out of bed anymore. Lilly had been tending to him. Sarah was resting as she was a little tired after Logan had seen to her wound, and she was still a little shaken up. Although Logan was not sure who scared her more, the Snakara assassin or him when he had lost his temper. He would talk to her when she was ready. The Elves were now out of the armoury. Shadow and his people had taken no losses due to his leadership. Hawk and Logan now stood on opposite sides of the table looking at each other. Neither of them knew where to begin as Logan still had a Snakara pinned to a tree downstairs.

Hawk looked at Logan. "What is it with you and breaking glass, I just fixed this place."

Logan nodded. "I am sorry for that, the bastard hit Sarah, I was angry."

Hawk looked at him. "I would say angry is putting it mildly, perhaps border line psychotic! Did you have any control at all?"

Logan looked at Hawk. "I don't know, it all happened so fast. What if it had been Lilly? And besides, I did not kill anyone, and don't call me psychotic, asshole."

Hawk thought on Logan's words. "I understand you were protecting Sarah. But what if she had not been there to stop you? What would you have done if she were not there? Would you have killed it?"

Logan looked at Hawk angrily. "Yes. I would have torn the beast apart and anything else that had stepped in my way."

"Even me?" asked Hawk. "What if I had stepped in your way?"

Now Logan was angry. "I would never hurt you, or any of the other Elves here, you know that."

Hawk shook his head. "I am not so sure, Logan."

Logan put his head down. "Well, I guess we will never know. I am done with hypothetical situations we have enough of a real problem right now, don't we?"

Hawk sighed. "Unfortunately, we do."

Logan looked at Hawk. "Well, what happens from here?"

Hawk sighed. "I don't know to be honest, we just had two Snakaras breach our defences, so we are not even close to fighting an army. What are your thoughts, Logan?"

"Well, we can set traps throughout the woods big enough to take down even the largest Snakara. We will make the forest a death trap, I have some ideas. I will begin to train the Elves in how to make these traps, after what happened here today, I figure we won't have much time before Rubia sends her entire army against us. She has to be getting tired of this, I know I am."

Hawk looked at Logan with a confused look. "You want her to send her whole army against us?"

Logan ran his fingers through his hair. "To be honest, no, but I am getting tired of this cat and mouse game. There is no doubt fighting her on open ground would be suicide, that's where we have to outsmart her."

Hawk thought about what Logan had said, he was right about trying to fight her on open ground, although he was not sure how easily Rubia would be outsmarted, as she may be crazy, but she was not stupid.

Lilly walked out of Dark Owl's room, she looked grim. "He is reaching his final hours I fear."

Hawk hugged his wife tightly. "Are you OK?"

She smiled. "I am doing as well as can be."

Peregrine entered the room looking at Hawk. "We have gathered what parts of the Elves we could, it was grim work, the pyre is ready. I don't think we will have time for the usual ceremonies."

Hawk agreed, they would burn the bodies together and they would be in a better place, all the Elves families would receive a purple rose for bravery. He wished they could be more formal but there was just no time. They were not even sure whose family most of the men belonged to. They would find out mostly from the families themselves when men did not come home. Hawk was acting Elder and would visit those families.

Hawk looked at Peregrine. "Start the pyre, we will deal with the families individually."

Peregrine looked at Hawk and nodded sadly. He left right away to carry out his instructions. Logan wished he had been able to do more when the giants attacked so he could have stopped the death of the Elves. Logan knew the two large Snakaras were just a distraction to get to him while he was weak. Which had been a mistake and had only given him the motivation to heal and be back to his former self. Hawk asked Logan if he would train the Elves in using swords and shields.

Logan's answer surprised him. "No, I will need everyone helping with the traps in the woods."

Hawk looked at him. "What are you not telling me about this plan?"

Logan smiled. "Don't worry, once I have figured everything out, I will tell you everything."

"Fine, but something tells me I won't like it!"

Logan nodded. "We shall see."

"Something else happened during the attack that I have not told you about yet. When the two giants were heading for the armoury, Raven attacked both beasts and bought me time to seal the door. I am worried that something may have happened to her."

Logan looked to Lilly. "Could you ask Shadow to join us? His people could find her faster than we can."

Lilly smiled and headed down the stairs.

Logan was still thinking about what Hawk had told him about Raven and he was not that surprised, she hated him not her people. What he did not know was about the fight that she and Sarah had when he was fighting for his life. He just looked at Hawk and told him the same thing. Hawk never brought up the fight as it was not important now.

Lilly had returned with Shadow, he looked tired. He spoke

before anyone else said anything. "I am sorry for the Elves you lost, Hawk, may they rest with Moonrion."

Hawk thanked him and they asked if Shadow knew where Raven was. He was not sure if he should tell them about the lesson he had given Raven. He decided not to.

"I have not seen her since the battle, and we have had no time to keep an eye on her."

Hawk nodded and thanked Shadow for his wolves bravery in trying to slow down the two large Snakaras. Shadow was only glad they had not taken any casualties but felt slightly guilty, so he did not speak of it.

Shadow asked Hawk. "Would you like us to look around to see if we can find her?"

Hawk smiled at Shadow. "You read my mind friend and please ask her to come here, I would like to speak to her."

Shadow went to leave when he turned around. "You might want to figure out what you're doing with that Snakara stuck to the tree, it's not looking so good."

Hawk and Logan looked at each other. "Time to get some answers."

Hawk looked at Lilly. "Stay here and watch over Dark Owl and Sarah."

Logan and Hawk went down to their prisoner only to find Elves throwing rocks and whatever they could find at it, someone had even put an arrow in its shoulder. Hawk looked at his people and yelled at them to stop and the crowd scattered with a few last rocks being thrown.

Logan released the creature from the tree it fell to the ground; it looked like it was pretty much dead. Hawk could not believe he was going to have to heal the snake man if they wanted any answers. Logan looked at Hawk and set a hand on the snake man, it woke up instantly and hissed in Hawk's face who fell back.

"Thanks for the heads-up, dipshit." Hawk wiped his pants off and stood up.

Logan laughed. "Dip-shit? You really have been hanging out with Sarah too much."

Hawk smiled. "Yes she does have a way with words."

The snake man looked to the left and to the right. Logan had brought his sword and shield and promised the snake man that if he tried to run, he would be down a leg.

The thing looked at them and hissed. "I am not a snake man, I am Snakara. I am an honourable member of Queen Rubia's army. One who will soon destroy all of you."

"Well, I am so sorry. I did not know we were dealing with a Royal assassin, should I bow?"

The Snakara looked at Logan. "You're fucked, human."

Logan smirked. "I would look around and think about who's fucked right now."

Hawk gave Logan a 'what now?' look.

Logan looked at the Snakara. "Has your Queen given you a name?"

The Snakara looked at him. "Yes, I am called Thresher."

Logan looked at Thresher. "Kind of a stupid name for a snake, but that's none of my business, so here's how this is going to work, I am going to ask you some questions and you will answer them. If you are truthful I will heal you a little more, if you lie to me I will break something, do we have an understanding?"

The Snakara looked at Logan. "Fuck you, human."

Logan shook his head. "I guess not."

There was a large cracking sound and the Snakaras leg

217

was at an angle it should not have been.

Thresher screamed in pain. "OK, fine!"

Logan looked at him and within seconds the leg was healed. The Snakara looked at Hawk and Logan with hatred but Logan knew he understood how this was going to go now.

Logan went first. "I am assuming that the reason you attacked me was because you knew I was in a weakened state?"

Thresher nodded. "Yes, that is what my Queen's instructions were."

Hawk looked at Thresher. "Was Logan your only target?"

Thresher looked at Hawk. "Yes."

Logan healed the Snakara a little more.

Hawk asked another question. "Why hasn't Rubia sent her whole army against us?"

Thresher laughed. "She likes the game and the fear she is causing your people, also she is hesitant as she does not know what the human is capable of, but after this she will not care."

Logan looked at Hawk. "Do you have any other questions for our guest?" Hawk shook his head. Logan healed the Snakara. "I want you go back to your so-called Queen and tell her that her plan failed, and I will be coming soon."

Thresher nodded. The Snakara stood up. Logan looked at him. "Oh, one more thing, which hand did you strike Sarah with?"

Thresher looked at Logan. "The right."

With a flash of Logan's blade, the right hand of the Snakara flew off. Logan's hand was glowing silver and when he touched the stump it cauterized the wound. Thresher screamed.

Logan looked at him. "Now leave. And if I see you again,

I will kill you!"

Hawk watched the Snakara running out of town holding his right hand.

Logan looked at Hawk. "Now we need to talk about a few things Rubia told me."

Hawk looked at Logan with a strange look on his face. "OK, let's head back upstairs."

They walked back to the table. They had not been spending so much time on their next move and Hawk could not fathom what Logan wanted to talk about.

Logan looked at him. "So, when I was with Rubia in her lair or whatever, she told me a few things. I want to know if they are true."

Hawk nodded. "OK, what exactly did she tell you?"

"So, I know it's probably all lies but she said Raven is her daughter and Dark Owl was her brother and when she started using magic Dark Owl didn't approve of, he banished her and took Raven away from her."

Hawk looked at Logan and shook his head. "Is that what she told you?" Hawk looked at Logan. "Listen, that is almost all a lie."

Logan nodded. "OK, so what parts are the truth?"

Hawk frowned. "OK, Logan, yes Dark Owl is her brother, and he did banish her for using the dark arts. However, she is not Raven's mother, in fact when she started using dark magic, she became sterile. She had taken a liking to Raven when she was young and one night, she killed both her mother and father as they slept and tried to take Raven and leave Eclipse. Dark Owl confronted her and at the time he just thought she had stolen the child; he knew nothing of the murders. During this time, Rubia knew she was no match for her brother. So, she set

219

the babe down and left Eclipse forever. She knew if Dark Owl had discovered the murders before she was gone, he would have put her to death. That is Elven law, if you take life for no reason then your life is forfeited."

Hawk looked over Logan's shoulder and turned white. Logan turned around to see Shadow and Raven standing there. By the look on Raven's face, she knew none of this until now. This was going to be bad.

CHAPTER 31
ULTIMATUM

Sucuri and Malay had returned from their attack on the Elves. Midra was standing next to Rubia who sat on her throne. She looked at the two giants, she was not happy.

"Where is Thresher?"

Neither of them knew as they had left as Thresher had told them to. They explained what had taken place and the deaths of the Elves. This seemed to put Rubia in a better mood which was not saying much.

She looked at both. "Take your armour off and return to me."

They left as instructed. She already knew Thresher had failed in his mission as she could feel Logan's strong power return. She was livid as she was certain the magical venom she had concocted would kill him. That had been the only reason she had allowed him to escape. And now it would seem he had fully recovered. She could now see Thresher holding his right hand entering the throne room.

She looked at him with disgust and rage. "You have failed in your mission, why have you returned, you know the punishment for failure."

He looked at his Queen. "I didn't know where else to go and I have a message from the human."

She shattered the glass she was holding. "A message you say. What threat does he have for me now?"

Thresher looked at her not wanting to say anything for he knew once the message was delivered, he would most likely be dead. He continued anyways. "He told me to tell you that your plan had failed, and he would be coming for you soon."

She nodded. "He is like a broken record. What happened to your hand?"

Thresher looked at her. "The human took it for striking his female."

She looked at him. "Well, thank you for the message, but the cost of failure has not been changed."

She looked at Thresher and seconds later he was screaming in pain as his body burned from the inside out until there was nothing left but ash which blew away in the wind.

Midra shivered, he had never seen anything like that or did he care too again.

Rubia was tired with this human, she decided it was time to find out just how powerful he was. She was going to pay Eclipse a visit, she was tired of failure and threats. She put on one of her finest and most revealing dresses and called upon her bow staff. She looked at herself in the mirror and was happy with her appearance, even though she was evil she had always been one of the most beautiful Elves. She hoped her brother had not died yet; she had felt his power slowly draining away. She would like to see him one last time not for sentimental reasons, just to see how he had become so old, and she was still young. If he had listened to her and had started using the dark arts, he would still be young. She had even escaped death itself.

She looked at Midra. "We are going to Eclipse."

She hoped she would get a clean shot at Sarah so that she could shatter Logan's heart and finally he would witness her power. She did not need to walk; she would use her magic to put herself right in the centre of town. She made her final preparations and told Sucuri and Malay to watch the lair. Rubia and Midra vanished and appeared in the centre of Eclipse, she smiled, this was going to be fun.

***

Raven had heard what Hawk and Logan had been discussing. She had no idea what to say or where to start. Her whole life had been a lie, she was told her parents were killed in a hunting accident and that is why Dark Owl had raised her but now, she was not sure if he was even her grandfather. She pushed past everyone and went into Dark Owl's room; he was awake for he too must have heard Hawk and Logan talking.

He looked so tired and sick. He looked at her. "I am sorry I never told you, Raven. Rubia murdered my only son and his wife, she tried to take you. As she practised her black magic, she could have no children of her own. I love you more than anything. Do not let this news blacken your heart as you have a good one. You are the last of my blood line and you are strong but do not try to rush. Your magic will be beyond your wildest dreams when it's time and you will become the Elder of Eclipse. Hawk will hold the seat for now, he is wise and a good Elf, he will know when it's time, please trust him as I will not be here for much longer child. Rubia was my sister but that woman died long ago. Now she is nothing but evil in an Elven shell. Please forgive me for all of this, I should have told you long ago, but I never had the heart to."

Raven had tears flowing down her cheeks. She took Dark Owl's hand. "So, Rubia's blood runs through my veins as well."

Dark Owl looked at her. "No, Raven, like I said, she is no longer that Rubia."

Raven was speechless, she was experiencing every emotion she knew of all at once. She sat there and looked down at the man who had raised her so lovingly, who had taught her so many things, even her first spell as a child.

She squeezed his hand gently. "I love you, Grandfather, and none of this is your fault. I blame Rubia and I will avenge my parents' death and for what she has put you through."

He looked at her. "Be careful, child, vengeance is a dangerous road and many who walk it rarely return. Remember there is power in the light and do not dwell too long in the darkness. This was Rubia's mistake. I would save you that pain! Become powerful fall in love, live life, have children, be happy. For this is how you truly battle evil."

Raven thought about her grandfather's words and felt his hand go limp. She looked up to see his eyes close, she knew he was gone. She hugged him and cried out loud. Hawk opened the door and saw Raven laying on Dark Owl, crying to the point that her whole body shook. Lilly went into the room to comfort her, she was crying as well, even Hawk could not hide his tears. He turned and looked at Logan and shook his head.

Logan left the room, he needed to see Sarah. Sarah woke to see Logan with tears in his eyes. "What's wrong, babe?"

"Dark Owl has passed."

Sarah bowed her head and pulled Logan closer, they both had tears in their eyes as he had been so kind to them. Logan still had so many questions to ask him, he felt like he had lost a family member again. They held each other for some time when out of nowhere Logan felt it right in his heart, Rubia was in Eclipse, he was furious, only such an evil bitch like Rubia would show up in a time like this. Sarah felt Logan tense and she knew something was very wrong.

Hawk ran into the room. "Logan, we have a problem."

He nodded. "I felt it, too."

Sarah looked at both. "Felt what?"

Logan looked at her. "Rubia is here."

Sarah looked scared and pissed at the same time. "I am getting tired of this bitch."

Logan looked at her. "We all are."

Logan got up and they went into the common room. Raven and Lilly were there, as was Shadow.

Hawk looked at Shadow. "Go and take your people and hide them somewhere, this is not a fight you can help with."

Shadow understood, his people could shape shift but when it came to a direct magic battle, they were out of their depth.

Hawk looked at Raven. "You need to sit this out, she is going to play with your head, and you have been through enough this evening."

Raven looked at Hawk and she was scary calm. "No, I would like to help if you would have me."

Logan looked at both. "Listen, she is here now, we need to get to the centre of town, if she wishes to join us, let her."

Hawk looked at him. "You still don't get it."

"You're right, I don't, maybe we need to lose some control to fend her off or kill her."

Hawk looked at both. "Fine. Lilly and Sarah will stay here, let's go."

Sarah came out of the room. "I am going with you."

Logan looked at her. "Dammit, Sarah, we do not have time for this, stay here."

Lilly took her hand. "We will go and help round up the children and try to find Star. She will kill you, just to hurt Logan."

Sarah looked at Logan. "OK, but please be careful, I love you."

"I love you, too." Logan responded.

Hawk hugged Lilly and they headed down the stairs. It was just the three of them now.

Logan picked up his sword and shield. "Let's go."

Hawk looked at him. "What's the plan?"

Logan shrugged. "Don't die!"

Hawk nodded. As the three headed down the stairs, Hawk was seriously worried, he was in between two hot heads with great power. He hoped the town survived this. They headed towards the centre of town. Elves were running into the woods and anywhere else they could hide.

Peregrine and Thorn ran to Hawk. "We will fight with you."

Hawk looked at them. "Thank you both, but you need to help protect the Elves in the woods, try and find Shadow."

Peregrine nodded and they both took off.

They kept heading to the centre of town. Hawk was just thankful she had not started to attack anything yet. They were just about to their destination when they saw Star walking towards them, she said nothing, she just joined them. They finally entered the centre of town. Rubia was sitting on the war memorial.

Hawk looked at her. "Get off that, you were banished and now you shall leave." Hawk, cast some sort of spell. It had no effect.

Rubia laughed. "Sorry, Elf, that spell will not work anymore with the death of Dark Owl. It was a nice try though." She smiled. "It's about time he died."

Logan looked over at Raven, he could see the rage in her face, but she said nothing. Which was scarier? He thought.

Rubia looked at Star next. "How is your husband these days, my dear?"

Star was not so calm her fingers started to glow a light blue, she shot what looked like lightning directly into Rubia's face. It knocked her back but that was it.

Rubia looked at Star and smiled. "That hurt, my dear, but I understand."

A green flash hit Star and she dropped. Logan's magic surrounded him, and his armour was now covering his body. He drew his sword and shield. Logan knelt to see if Star was alive, he felt for a pulse. She had one but barely. He closed his eyes and focussed his power, silver flowed from his hand and Star opened her eyes.

Logan looked at her. "Just stay down." She looked at him and nodded.

Logan stepped forward and looked at Rubia, his eyes were completely silver again. Midra her general took a step back as he had fought this human once and had no wish to do so again.

Rubia laughed. "Well, look at this. Moonrion took her time with you! So much power. Just like in my throne room. And what has she received? A warrior who uses his heart more than his brain."

Logan looked at her. "At least I have a heart, bitch."

"Oh, Logan, they are so overrated, think of all the things you have done since you have been here! Always wanting to be the hero, never thinking it through, just running to help anyone who needed it. And for what? It almost cost you your life, for these weak Elves who run at the first sight of trouble." Rubia continued. "Thousands of Elves and only three stand by you. And this one, Raven, hates you and cares little if you live or die."

Raven stepped forward. "Do not speak for me, you know nothing." She spit on the ground.

"Oh, I know what is in your heart, my dear, me killing your parents, your grandfather dying. Your parents were weak fools, if Dark Owl had not stepped in, you would be almost as powerful as me by now. Isn't that what you want, Raven? Power!" Rubia smiled. "I can give it to you, show you things these Elves could not even begin to understand."

Raven looked at her. "If becoming anything like you means more power you can keep it, bitch." Raven fired a quick shot of green light, this time it took Rubia off her feet.

Logan knew Rubia was going to kill her. Rubia rose to her feet, you could see the side of her face was burned. Although once she got her bearings back it healed. She looked at Raven, Logan rolled and rose his shield and deflected a powerful blast.

Logan stood up and looked at her. "That is enough Rubia, why have you come here?"

She looked at the human. "Well, you've made threats against myself and my soldiers and even killed some. I am tired of the threats, so I wanted you to make them directly to me."

Logan sneered. "I told your assassin and your other abominations if they came back here, I would kill them and you. And it looks like you cannot follow directions very well. For I see you have brought one of those abominations with you."

She smiled. "You underestimate me."

Logan's sneer turned into a dangerous smile. "If you're so powerful, let's end this now, you and me, right here right now, unless you're not ready."

Hawk looked at Logan. "No, Logan, not here, please!"

Rubia sent another green flash towards Hawk, it was met with a blue light that surrounded Hawk's body he was knocked back but unharmed.

Rubia smiled. "Hmm, another powerful Mage! Interesting, Hawk, is it? I had heard you were powerful."

Hawk looked at her. "We will finish this but not today, and not in the centre of my town."

Rubia spoke harshly. "Listen here, acting Elder. I will do as I please when I please."

Hawk smiled at her. "And the only thing standing between you and Logan is me, so be careful, bitch."

Logan was tired of this, he started walking towards Rubia and he was going to kill her, or she would kill him. He was just about in striking distance when he raised his sword. Within seconds, Sarah stood in front of Rubia.

Logan stopped dead in his tracks and slowly walked back a few steps. "So much for all of your power, you coward." Rubia smirked. "My dear Logan, she was so easy to find, she is the only being in Silver Moon that does not have magic. What's wrong hero, cat got your tongue?"

Logan's armour began to pulsate. Hawk looked up to the sky and the clouds cleared from the moon and it seemed to be shining directly onto him.

Logan looked at Rubia. "If you harm a hair on her head, I swear I will destroy you and anything that gets in my way."

Hawk didn't think Rubia would be crazy enough to bring Sarah into this.

Rubia herself had looked at the moon. Rubia looked at Logan. "Back up or I will kill her."

He backed up. Logan heard a voice in his head. *"Strike the ground."*

Logan shook his head and then backed up and with all his power he punched the ground. The impact was immense, a huge crack with a red light went directly towards Sarah. She looked horrified, but as soon as the red light hit her, she was standing behind Logan. Rubia was furious and surprised.

Logan looked at her. "You never should've involved Sarah in this."

Logan moved like a flash and took Midra's head, his body dropped still spurting blood. He moved towards her; his sword flashed. Rubia blocked the strike with her Bow staff, the impact knocked down Hawk and the others. Rubia spun back to ready herself for another strike. Logan kept moving towards her with a fury even she had never felt before.

Hawk looked at Logan. "Logan, stop, please, there will be another day."

Logan stopped. Rubia looked at him with hatred. She put her bow staff in front of her. She pointed to the moon.

"On the next blue moon, I will be back, and you and I will finish this, human, and know this, I will release my entire army upon this town, and they will kill all of you and your families and children. None will be spared." Logan smiled. "I will be on the Plains waiting for you, coward." With a flash of black she was gone.

Logan helped Star back to her feet, she tried to smile but she was very weak. Logan's armour swirled away again.

Raven came over to help Logan with Star.

Hawk looked at them. "We need to get back. I need to look at my books to see when the next blue moon will rise."

Logan looked worried, he still had so much to learn about Silver Moon, for all he knew, they could only have days. He hoped that was not the case.

CHAPTER 32
THE LOSS OF AN ELDER

They made it back to the Tree of Power. Hawk could not believe no one had died. He knew the only reason they were alive was due to Logan's abilities. As he had noticed when Rubia had blocked Logan's strike with her staff, her arms had buckled ever so slightly. She broke off the fight as she was not sure she would survive another strike like that. He decided to keep this to himself.

Lilly came through the door. She looked at Sarah. "Oh, thank Moonrion you're OK. I had no idea what would happen after you disappeared."

Logan looked at Lilly. "The cowardly bitch used her as a shield."

Lilly looked at Logan. "Not much of a surprise there."

Hawk nodded, and asked Logan. "How did you know to strike the ground to bring Sarah back to you?"

Logan looked at Hawk. "I heard a voice in my head."

Hawk was not really all that surprised, when it came to Logan and his power, he never knew what was going to happen.

Logan had remembered what Moonrion had said to him. '*You're never alone, Logan.*' He smiled at the thought of the beautiful Pegasus.

Hawk looked at Star. "How are you feeling?"

She smiled. "I am tired and a little sore, but whatever

Logan did to me seems to be continuing to help."

Logan smiled. "I could not let Petal grow up an orphan."

Star shook her head. "I owe you, again."

"You owe me nothing, Petal is my little friend!"

Star laughed. "This is true."

Logan looked at Hawk. "So, how long do we have until this next blue moon?"

"I am not sure yet," Hawk answered. Hawk looked at everyone. "Excuse me, I need to get a few things from my lab. Will you assist me, Logan?"

Logan looked at him. "Of course."

They both headed down the stairs into Hawk's classroom and lab.

Logan looked at Hawk. "So, what are we looking for?"

"My journal, some moon phase charts and a map of Silver Moon."

"I hope this blue moon is not for a while," Logan replied.

Hawk nodded. "I am hoping so as well."

Logan frowned. "We need to have a funeral for Dark Owl."

Hawk nodded. "I know, but for now we need to worry about the living." Logan said nothing more on the subject. Hawk looked at Logan with a worried look. "I need to talk to you about something."

Logan looked at him. "OK, shoot."

Hawk really did not want to talk about this, but he knew he had to. He cleared his throat and began. "Logan, you have done a lot for us and I thank you, even tonight you saved Star and Raven's lives. And I think of you as a friend and brother, but with this battle coming to its conclusion there is something I need to tell you." Logan was listening. "You may never be able to return to the Earth realm. I do not know what will happen when all this ends. I don't know if you will retain your magic if you kill Rubia."

"If? Thanks for the confidence!"

Hawk looked at him. "You must not underestimate her; she has been alive longer than your oldest ancestor. And she will come at you with everything she has. I have faith you can beat her but who knows what will happen, we thought we killed her once and now we are paying for that assumption. Logan, what I am trying to really get at is, if you do kill her and you retain your power, you will need to stay here. And this is going to be hard for you to hear, now that you possess our power you may begin to age like us. And Sarah will not."

Logan sat down at one of the desks. "I've never even thought of that. I mean, I can handle staying here. But losing Sarah and being alone for so long after she has gone, I don't know if that is something I can do."

Hawk looked at the pain in his friend's face. "Logan, I could be wrong, you may lose your magic if you kill Rubia."

Logan nodded. "Thank you for telling me. I know it must have been difficult. It's a lot to take in, but we have other problems, let's get back to it please."

Hawk nodded. "Let's get everything so I can look over all of this." Hawk and Logan returned upstairs.

Logan grabbed Sarah and pulled her close and kissed her. She looked at him. "What was that for?"

He smiled. "Just because. And when Rubia had you it reminded me of how precious life was."

Hawk started to lay charts all over the table and took his journal out.

Lilly looked at Hawk. "We need to put Dark Owl to rest."

Hawk nodded. "Now that I have all this, we must set up the pyre and arrange for all the Elves to attend. Ring the bell please, Raven, so everyone knows they can return."

For the first time that Logan could remember she did exactly as she was told. It took a bit of time to get to the bell, but Raven had reached it and sent out the call. Hawk knew it would take some time to round everyone up.

He looked at Lilly. "We will put him in his armour from the first war."

They brought the body into the common area and set to work putting their Elder in his armour. It was morbid watching them as they put armour on a dead Elf. Logan looked and just figured this was another tradition he did not fully understand.

Raven had come back just as they were finishing. She had never seen her grandfather in his Battle Mage armour, it was a sight to behold! It was silver and purple, and the helmet had two large owl wings on it.

"Tell the Elves to meet at the pyre."

Raven looked at them. "Shadow is already doing so; he took the news pretty hard."

Hawk nodded, for they all new Shadow had fought with him in the first war. They heard another bell.

Raven nodded. "They are ready. I will carry him."

Logan was not sure how she could lift him with all that armour on. He figured she would use magic of some sort. And a few moments later Dark Owl's body began to glow a light green and his body rose from the ground. It carried him down the stairs and as they all stood beside it, he was in a lying position. The Elves were lined up all the way to the pyre and as they passed, they began following them. Once they reached the pyre, his body was gently set atop of it. They decided

235

Raven would address the Elves as she was the last of his bloodline.

She stood strong and began. "My Dear Elves of Eclipse, today is a sad day for all, as we must put to rest our Elder and leader Dark Owl. He was a hero of the first war although he always told me he was just lucky. As he was a wise and humble Elf. But now is not the time for tears. As we have a beast at our door. Now is the time for all Moon Elves to cry out that we will no longer be afraid, we will fight, and we will win." She looked at them. "This is all I will say as we still have the beast to deal with. May our Elder sit with Moonrion, for he is finally home."

Peregrine lit his arrow and fired it into the pyre. The Elves watched as the arrow struck the body and with a flash their Elder was gone. Raven ran towards the Tree of Power. The rest of the Elves threw purple roses and other flowers and began to head home.

There was no celebrating tonight as the Moon Elves had nothing to celebrate with a dead Elder and Rubia still alive. Logan and Sarah held hands all the way back. Logan looked at her, he smiled, ever since they had come to Silver Moon things between them had been so good. Now knowing he may outlive her by hundreds of years was an unbearable thought. He tried not to think about it and tried to be in the moment. They all returned to Dark Owl's home which felt cold and empty now.

Raven was in her Grandfathers room; she had been so strong during the ceremony. Now she was crying quietly. They all left her as they knew she would need time. Hawk started to go through his journal and was looking at the Lunar charts, Logan was watching him, he walked over to Hawk and lightly took him by the arm.

"You need some rest, my friend, we all do, we will figure this out tomorrow."

Hawk looked at him and stopped. "Logan, I need to figure this out."

Logan looked at him. "And we will tomorrow. You need to rest."

Lilly came over and took Logan's place. Hawk looked at her and knew there was no sense in arguing with her.

"We will meet back here tomorrow night and figure this out."

With that everyone went to their quarters. Logan needed a shower which they had attached to their room. It was all wood as well, even the taps and shower head.

He smiled at Sarah. "Do you want to join me?"

She smiled back. "Of course, but we must be quiet, Star is in the other room."

They both undressed and Sarah could not help noticing how much muscle mass Logan had put on. She did not know if it was the magic, or the armour and she really did not care as she got to enjoy the view. They held each other in the shower for a long time. The water was said to come from the tree itself. After their shower they made love. Logan was so passionate Sarah was not sure where all of this was coming from and she cared little as she liked this side of him. They held each other; Logan was playing with her hair which she loved.

"Logan."

"Yes, love."

"What does it feel like when you're in that armour?"

He thought about it for a moment. "I feel invincible.

Stronger, faster, and smarter, like having unlimited knowledge of fighting techniques and magic."

She smiled. "Is it hard to control?"

"Sometimes, although it seems the more I use it the more in control I am."

Sarah looked worried. "That must be something, having all that power."

Logan nodded. He looked into her eyes. "What is wrong, love?"

She pulled him close. "I just know how you are, Logan, you have always wanted to be able to save people, I mean you almost died for Aura and I love you for it, but I need you too, Logan, and I don't want you to fight Rubia."

Logan smiled. "I don't want to fight her either, but she hasn't given me much of a choice."

Sarah looked at Logan with desperation. "We could run and hide; the Forest Elves want to meet you. We could hide there and bring the other Elves with us."

"I can't run and hide, Sarah, this was a task given to me and I have to see it through."

She sighed. "I know. I just wish you hadn't read so many comic books when you were a kid, what if she finds your kryptonite."

He smiled at her. "She already has, Sarah, and you know it's you. And you will be nowhere near the fight." He moved some of the hair on her face and kissed her. "No more worries tonight, let's just enjoy this and get some sleep."

She kissed him back and laid on his chest they were asleep in moments.

CHAPTER 33
THE COUNTDOWN BEGINS

Logan woke up feeling better than he had in a while. He looked at Sarah still asleep, he felt love and sadness at the same time. He hoped he lost his power after this. Although living hundreds of years had some appeal to it, if he could not do it with Sarah then he would sacrifice this power in a second. He heard a small knock on the door, he got out of bed without disturbing Sarah. He opened the door with just pants on, Raven stood in the door, she looked at his body for a moment as she had never seen a human's body before.

She still had a coldness to her. "May I speak with you, please?"

Logan frowned and thought to himself. 'This should be fun.'

They were standing at the round table. She looked at him. "Listen, I know I have been horrible to you and Sarah. And for this I am sorry, you saved my life without any hesitation, you also healed Star, I was so mad and after Sarah punched me, I even had thoughts of leaving and seeking out Rubia. Fortunately, a friend pointed me in a different direction and my grandfather believed in Moonrion's decision and I will too. So, can we start over?"

Logan smiled at her. "Sarah hit you?"

Raven looked at him. "Yes but I deserved it."

Logan looked at Raven. "Of course, we can start over, I

know that must have been difficult for you! And I understand that we are outsiders."

Raven smiled. "You have become family to many here and now you can add one more."

The front door opened, it was Hawk, he was looking at Raven and Logan on opposite sides of the table. "Am I interrupting something?"

Raven shook her head. "No, we were just finishing."

Hawk and Lilly walked in followed by Star and Petal. Petal ran up to Logan, he picked her up and she hugged him.

"Thank you for making Rubia leave."

He set her down. "No problem, kiddo."

She looked at him. "Hey, I am older than you!" They laughed.

Star looked at her daughter. "Remember, honey, humans age differently than you."

"I know, that's why Logan's so big for his age, and Sarah too."

Hawk looked at Logan. "I figured out last night that we have around three cycles."

Logan gave Hawk a confused look. "I thought you were supposed to rest last night. And how long are three cycles?"

Hawk smiled. "I did sleep. I already had the blue moon timing written in my notes. And three cycles would be roughly three months in your time, give or take a few days."

Logan smiled. "This is good news; we have time to get something set up. This is assuming she keeps her word on the timeline."

"So, Logan, what were you thinking? You said you wanted to turn the forest into a death trap."

Logan nodded. "Do we have a map I can see?"

Hawk opened the map to Silver Moon. Logan looked at the map and finally found Eclipse. He looked at what he had to work with and smiled. Rubia's army had to go through the woods, there was nowhere to bypass them which meant they could make traps everywhere. Logan looked up and started pointing to different spots on the map explaining his basic idea with pitfalls with sharpened sticks and where they could place dead falls and snares.

Hawk looked at him. "Where did you learn all of this?"

"Well, before my dad passed, he was into survival training. I was only young then. And the rest, mostly from watching movies and reading historical novels."

Hawk smacked his head. "Movies."

The rest of the Elves were confused. Lilly asked, "What's a movie?"

Hawk looked at her. "It's hard to explain. It's something humans watch for entertainment basically."

Logan looked at Hawk. "Hey, a lot of movies are based on real events, and besides, I am the barbarian here, remember. I come from a race constantly at war."

Hawk could not argue with that. "So, do you think this will keep them out?"

Logan looked at him. "Well, it will keep the first couple waves out, but not all of them."

Hawk sighed. "So, what will we do after that?"

Logan looked at the Elves, he knew they would not like this idea.

"We will evacuate the town, and once the rest enter, we blow the town."

All the Elves looked at him like he was insane. Hawk looked at him. "You want us to blow up our whole town? OK, first, where would all of us go after this? And second, this is our home, Logan."

Logan nodded. "Yes, a town that can be rebuilt, whereas Elven lives cannot be."

Sarah walked into the room still groggy. "Sorry I slept in, what is going on?"

Hawk started to laugh sarcastically. "Oh, nothing, your mate here just wants to blow up our whole town."

Sarah looked at Logan. "Um, Logan, what the fuck, have you lost your mind?"

He looked at her and re explained the plan. "Do you even have explosives here?" asked Sarah.

Hawk looked at her. "Yes, we have some Dwarven charges, we use them to clear out rock."

Hawk looked at them. "But we are not using them."

Logan sighed. "Fine, I will train hundreds of Elves on how to use swords in three months so they can be slaughtered."

Hawk looked at Logan and he knew it was impossible to teach all the Elves how to use swords and shields in three months. He also knew he was not blowing up their town.

"OK, Logan, trapping the forest is a good idea, blowing up the town, not so much."

"Well, if anyone has any other ideas, I am listening."

Star pointed to the Brimard mountains. "What if we ask the Dwarves and the Forest Elves for help? The Dwarves still have a strong army, and they love a good fight."

Hawk shook his head. "Even if we used a portal to get there, I doubt they will help us, and the Forest Elves will keep their land safe, but you know how they feel about this already."

Sarah looked at Hawk. "Jade wanted to meet Logan, it was part of our deal for the dragon saliva."

Logan looked at them. "Wouldn't it be easier to ask for shelter than warriors?"

Hawk looked at him. "We are not blowing up the town."

"OK, what do you suggest then?"

Hawk thought for a moment. "If you kill Rubia quickly then her army will return to their original form."

Logan looked at Hawk. "That's a shit idea. How many of you will die while I am fighting her?"

Hawk thought for a moment. "None. we will evacuate the town and ask for shelter with the Dwarves and Forest Elves, because you are right, Logan, it is easier to ask for shelter than warriors."

Logan nodded. "OK, and if she kills me?"

Hawk frowned. "If she kills you, she will have her town, just not the Elves she wanted. She will not attack the Dwarves head on, just getting up the mountain itself she would lose a large amount of Snakaras as she picked the wrong creatures for the job as it's freezing up there."

"What if she uses a portal?" Logan asked.

Hawk nodded. "She could use a portal, but not even she is powerful enough to do it all at once. And once the Snakaras came through the portal they would have an army of angry Dwarves to deal with. And the Dwarves would slaughter them."

Logan smiled at the thought of that. "OK, what about the Forest Elves?" Logan asked.

Hawk smiled. "No way would she be able to open a portal in that forest. Jade would shut it down before Rubia even had a chance to send one Snakara."

"OK, this whole idea only works if the Forest Elves and Dwarves agree to it, what if they say no?"

Hawk sighed. "Then we blow the town!"

Everyone looked at each other.

Logan broke the silence. "Looks like we have some asses to kiss."

"First, we start setting the traps throughout the forest. Then Logan and I will go, as Logan put it, 'Kiss some asses.'" Hawk sighed.

CHAPTER 34
RUBIA'S PREPARATIONS

Rubia had returned to her lair minus her general. She cared little about that; she could summon a new King Cobra at any time from the Earth realm. She had decided not to, she would just use Sucuri and Malay to lead her army. As the two of them alone had breached the Elves forest and made it into town. She had given the Elves until the blue moon, she wanted them to have time to think about their demise. Without the human they had no chance of victory, she would take care of him. He was immensely powerful, he had almost broke through her block back in Eclipse. She still had many tricks for him up her sleeve and she would not underestimate him again.

She called upon Malay and Sucuri and gave them their timeline to have her army ready. She reminded them of Thresher and the price to pay for failure. She was not worried, her Snakaras were restless for a fight. She was down some men due to Logan and the Elves. Even some of her Snakaras who got too close to the Forest Elves forest had been brought down by their archers. She still had a large army which would have little problem crushing the Elves. She also knew that the Forest Elves and Dwarves would not involve themselves in this fight, as she had no intention of attacking them, as her army would suffer huge loses. And she had enough to worry about with the human. She would have to be more cautious than when she had battled Moon Shatter as her sarcophagus could not be used again. She had cheated death once and she was not sure she would be able to do so again.

She had been looking through her spells and books to see if there were any other way to perhaps cheat death again. It was not looking promising, although she had time. And she had planned to bring a battalion of Snakaras with her to perhaps tire the human to give her an edge. If the human thought she would fight fair than he had learnt nothing. Moonrion had made him powerful, showing Rubia that even the Goddess was against her. Now she knew that Moonrion could not directly interfere, but she had given this human power that not even she understood. She would be ready, if she could not beat him in a physical battle then she would attack him psychologically and bring him to his knees. She smiled, she had new armour to make, she turned and walked to her inner sanctuary and began to make her plans. She was trying to find a way to perhaps attach her soul to her new armour.

'One step at a time,' she thought to herself. Her armour would need to be light but strong as she had seen how fast this human moves. She had a design in mind, and she would enchant the armour with every evil ability she knew. She played with the thought of a cape, but she quickly dismissed the idea as it may prove to be a disadvantage in combat. She would however be adding wings to her armour. It would not allow her to fly permanently or at a great height. But it would give her the ability to jump higher and move in the air for short bursts. Which was something not even the human could do, or at least she had not seen him perform anything like it. She smiled; her sketch was coming together nicely. Now she would just have a few things she would need to collect to start her creation.

CHAPTER 35
LOGAN AND THE FOREST ELVES

Logan had been teaching the Elves about dead falls and digging holes with sharpened sticks and every other trick Logan could think of. The Elves thought it was genius and they had been working hard, and they learned very quickly. Peregrine gave him a daily update and he was quite proud of the work the Elves were doing. Logan himself was impressed at how fast they were moving but when you are in threat of being slaughtered it was a good motivator. Logan was practising his sword techniques as this was a new daily occurrence. He knew he would have to be in great shape and his technique would need to be perfect for his fight. He always practised with his shirt off as he would get hot, and it made him focus better as some of the thrusts and parries at quick speed if not done correctly could cause him to cut himself which was a painful lesson and a quick teacher.

Sarah came down to watch him practising, she had to admit she cared little about the sword practise she just liked looking at his muscled body sweat. And Petal watched him almost daily. Sarah frowned as she noticed a few female Elves had become interested as well.

'Oh well,' she thought. She could not blame them.

She called Logan, he continued his technique and then looked up to Sarah who threw him a towel. He poured some cold water over his body and dried off quickly he grabbed Sarah and picked her up and gave her a kiss.

She laughed. "You're needed upstairs, Hawk wants to talk to you." He kissed her again, she smiled during the kiss. "Behave, there are children around."

Petal sighed. "I've seen people kiss before, jeez."

Logan smiled. "Yeah, Sarah, jeez!"

"Just get upstairs," Sarah replied.

Logan made his way to the top of the Tree of Power to find Hawk at his normal spot these days, standing over the table with books and maps.

Logan looked at him. "What's up, boss?"

Hawk looked up. "We are going to the Forest Elves today."

Logan smiled. "Just when I thought we were going to have a boring day."

Hawk nodded. "Please follow my lead carefully, the Forest Elves can be jumpy, and I don't feel like getting an arrow in the ass." Logan smiled. "We will take two Thyrions and we will be there by nightfall."

"Oh yeah, I forgot about the Thyrions, you said you have a stable with these creatures." Logan was excited to see the beasts.

Hawk nodded. "Have you ever ridden a horse in the Earth realm?"

Logan frowned. "Yes and I was bucked off onto my ass."

Hawk smiled at the image. "Well, I guess you will just have to learn quickly."

"I guess so," replied Logan. He asked Hawk. "Are they calm?"

Hawk looked at him. "To be honest, they can be quite

aggressive, let's just hope they are in a good mood."

Logan looked at Hawk. "You're loving this, aren't you?

Hawk laughed. It was the first time Logan had heard him laugh in a while, it was nice to hear. "Maybe a little."

Logan laughed as well and asked when they were leaving.

Hawk looked up. "We will head to the stables now. You can have first pick." Hawk smiled.

They grabbed a few small things; Logan grabbed his sword and shield.

Hawk looked at him. "I am not sure you should bring those."

Logan looked at him. "You never know what we might run into."

Hawk thought about it. "I guess you're right. Let's go."

They started to walk through town, Hawk leading the way until they finally came to a building that looked and smelt like a stable. They walked in. Lilly and Star were putting saddles on the Thyrions. Logan looked at the beautiful creatures, they looked like a cross between a Clydesdale horse and a large ram, they had two large horns that curled back and were jet black. The two being saddled were different colours, one was so black it almost looked purple in the right light, and the other one was silver.

Lilly looked at Logan. "We both thought you would appreciate the silver one."

Logan nodded. "It is beautiful, they both are." Both Thyrions shook their heads as if they understood the compliment. "Can they understand us?" Logan asked.

Hawk smiled. "They are highly intelligent but no, they cannot directly understand us. They are sensitive to magic though, and they can tell the difference between good and evil.

So, you should be fine," replied Hawk.

Logan looked at how big they were and sighed. 'That is a long fall,' he thought to himself.

They were done with the saddles. Hawk looked over. "Let's get going." He smiled again.

Logan nodded his head. "OK."

He got on the stool and put his foot in the stirrup and pulled himself up. Grabbing the horn quickly, he settled into the saddle, he felt like a fish out of water. Star and Lilly giggled a little at the sight of Logan getting on. Logan looked over and watched as Hawk jumped into the saddle like a pro.

Hawk smiled at him. "Show off." Logan smirked.

Hawk got them moving at a slow trot through town which was good because Logan was still trying to figure a few things out. They made their way through the trees in the forest with Peregrine showing them where to stay away from.

They cleared the trees, Hawk looked over at Logan. "Are you ready?"

Logan looked over at him. "No, but let's get this over with."

Hawk gave his Thyrion a small kick on the side and the next thing Logan knew both were going full tilt, his eyes watered. The Thyrions were faster than Logan was expecting, the ground was going by in a blur of speed, he almost called upon his armour just in case. His hands hurt he was holding on so tightly. The Thyrions seemed to have unlimited stamina as they never lost any speed and the next thing Logan knew, Hawk was slowing them down.

"What's wrong?" Logan asked.

Hawk said nothing and jumped off his saddle. "We walk from here."

Logan could not believe they were already near their destination. Hawk looked up. "Heads up." A volley of arrows was flying down towards them. Logan grabbed his shield and sword, the first volley he blocked with his shield the second he cut through with his sword.

Hawk looked at him. "Now who's showing off."

Logan just looked at him. "I was just practising."

Hawk put his hands over his mouth and yelled. "We are here to speak with your Elder, this is Logan, the human she wanted to meet."

They waited, Logan noticed they were not being shot at anymore which, seemed like a good start.

A voice came back from the Forest Elves. "She will see you. No funny business, Moon Elf."

Logan looked at Hawk. "What's that all about?"

Hawk frowned. "Long story."

Logan dropped it. The Forest Elves looked different than the Moon Elves, they were tan as opposed to the very white skinned Moon Elves. They also had ears more like the Elves that Logan's books back home had portrayed, pointing straight up.

The Forest Elf looked at Logan. "I am Jaguar."

Logan smiled. "And I am Logan."

Jaguar looked at Logan. "OK, human Logan, no weapons are permitted."

Logan looked at him. "I am sorry, but these weapons can only be carried by me."

Jaguar stared him down for a moment. "How did you cut our arrows from the sky with a sword?"

Logan looked back at him. "Lots of practise."

Jaguar nodded as he was a warrior himself and asked

nothing more on the subject.

"OK, human Logan. I will allow the weapons into the Forest but only halfway, they will be safe here."

Logan agreed to the terms, they were walking in the Forest, Logan could not believe it. It looked more like a rain forest than the coniferous and broad-leaved deciduous forests the Moon Elves lived in. Logan was surprised that he could not see any other Elves in the forest.

He looked at Hawk. "Where are the other Elves?"

Hawk smiled. "They are all around us. In this forest they are virtually invisible, it's one of their most unique abilities."

Jaguar smiled. "The Moon Elf is right! Do not worry, human Logan, they will not harm you unless you give them a reason to." Jaguar looked at Logan again. "OK, this is about halfway, please put your weapons down."

Logan did as he was instructed, and they continued to follow Jaguar. They finally came to what looked like a dome from the tree roots with an opening in the front of it. Jaguar waved them towards the dome, they both followed him in.

Jaguar looked at his Elder. "Jade, this is human Logan and the Moon Elf."

Logan thought the introduction sounded like a bad band name. She smiled at them, she had light green hair and large green eyes that were like a cat, Logan noticed Jaguars eyes were cat like as well, just a different colour.

She looked at Jaguar. "Please return to your post." Jaguar left the dome. She motioned for them to sit, she looked at both for a few moments before she said anything. "I see Sarah has kept both parts of the bargain now."

Logan looked at her. "What was her first part?"

Jade pointed to a red lock of hair which had been wrapped

with a leaf, it looked beautiful.

Logan smiled. "She does have beautiful hair."

Jade smiled. "Yes, she does, and now I meet the powerful Logan," she replied. "You are quite tall, like the Plains People." She looked at him differently and Logan felt like she was looking directly into his soul. She smiled, as if thinking something to herself. "How did you like our forest, Logan?"

He looked at her. "It's beautiful and if I may say so, you are as well."

She smiled. "A charmer I see." She looked at Hawk and a sadness filled her eyes. "I am sorry for your loss, Dark Owl was a wise and kind Elf, his absence is a great loss to all of Silver Moon."

Hawk nodded and thanked her for the kind words. She kept her attention on Hawk. "You are quite young to be an Elder, if you ever need advice please know you are welcome."

Hawk smiled at her. "Could you get rid of Rubia for us?"

Jade smiled. "You know our thoughts on Rubia, and besides, Moonrion has already chosen someone for that job." She turned her attention back to Logan. "This must've been hard for you, a human, a new realm, meeting races you thought were only in books, and now you have been tasked with protecting and saving them."

Logan nodded. "It was difficult at first, all I wanted to do was leave."

Jade looked at him. "And how do you feel now, Logan?"

He thought about it. "I won't lie, there are still days where I want to leave. But I have made friends here and now, I cannot allow Rubia to kill them, not to mention she almost killed me and used the love of my life as a shield, so we also have some unfinished business of our own."

253

Jade listened and asked another question. "Why do you think these powers were given to you?"

Logan thought about it. "I have been asking myself that very question since day one. I was somewhat of a loser back in my realm. I had a lot of depression and anxiety and I was a drunk, I honestly just wanted to be left alone to die."

Jade looked at him sadly. "Yes, you humans have destroyed your planet and now there is no magic. It's sad to watch your kind, for I see people like you and Sarah and how good you can be and the love you could express. If you had these powers in your realm would you use it to help your kind?"

Logan nodded. "In a heartbeat, but unfortunately I feel it's too late for humans."

Jaded looked at him sadly again. "You could be right, Logan, but enough of humans, let me ask you another question. Do you fear Rubia?"

Logan looked at her, his eyes flashed silver. "I do not fear her. I fear what will happen if I fail."

"Ah!" Jade smiled. "You must not underestimate her. She will not only attack your body, but she will also attack your mind. She will use every fear and every wrongdoing that you have ever done, against you."

Logan looked at Jade. "Well, I wasn't expecting a fair fight. And I have made peace with death long ago. So, let her do her worst. I won't stop fighting while there is air in my lungs."

Jade smiled. "I see a good soul in you, Logan. You risk yourself without hesitation and you cherish life, just don't let her darken that soul with hatred." She looked at both. "So, your Elves need shelter."

Logan and Hawk looked at each other. Hawk asked, "How did you know that?"

She smiled. "When you get to be my age, you become an expert in reading people."

Logan looked at her. "Please, we ask for no warriors or for any of you to get involved."

She thought for a moment. "You say we will not be involved but if we take refugees we are directly involved."

Logan sighed. "You are right, but please help them. I will do anything you wish."

She smiled. "Logan, I want nothing from you. But because Sarah kept her word to me, we will take in as many Moon Elves as we can."

Logan smiled. "Thank you so much. I will make this up to you somehow."

Jade smiled. "I know you will."

Logan had one more question for her. "What is the Jaded arrow?"

She smiled. "I tell you what, Logan, if you live through this, I will tell you."

He smiled and nodded. "Deal."

Jade looked at Hawk. "We will need ten days to be ready for your people."

Logan looked at Jade. "Will Rubia be able to feel the Elves moving?"

Jade looked at him. "Not if I do not wish her to, she cannot feel my power."

"How is that possible?" Logan looked at her.

She smiled. "Have you ever had someone turn the lights on in a room when you have been in the darkness for a while, well it's kind of like that."

'That makes sense,' thought Logan.

Jade looked at Hawk. "Could you give Logan and I a few moments alone please, it won't take too long." Hawk looked at her stood up and headed out of the dome. She looked at Logan very seriously. "Logan, I know you have been through many things. Especially when that venom was running through your veins. Rubia fears your physicality, but she knows you have many fears and doubts, and she will play on all of them. Do you remember anything from when you were so close to death?"

Logan looked towards the ground. "Well, to be honest, I saw Moonrion, but I am sure that was just a hallucination, she said I was in purgatory and my soul must choose which way it wanted to go."

Jade looked at him still very seriously. "What did you see in purgatory?"

Logan shrugged. "There was nothing, just trees. No animals, nothing, and that's when Moonrion told me where I was and then all I felt was an indescribable pain and burning."

Jade looked at him. "So why do you think when you were in purgatory, there was nothing?"

Logan shrugged. "I have no idea."

Jade took his hand. "For those souls who go to purgatory, they are shown their greatest fear. And now we know yours."

Logan looked at her and thought for a moment. "I think I understand, so my greatest fear is being alone."

Jade gave him a light slap on the hand. "Exactly, so at least you can prepare for that. Logan, what are you holding back?"

He pulled his hand away. "I don't care to speak of it."

Jade nodded and pushed no further. Logan looked at her and he sighed and told her everything about his horrible dream.

No judgement crossed her face, she looked at him as if she had expected something like this.

Jade took Logan's hand again. "I am sorry you had such a horrible dream, Logan. But know this, there is a good chance she knows of this dream and she will tempt you with this power. As the blue moon gets closer, I am sure you will have more nightmares, as she will strike your mind before the fights even begins."

Logan did not like the sounds of that. "How can she invade my dreams?"

Jade looked at him. "Logan, every time she is near, you can feel it and so can she, you have a psychic link as you are two sides of the same coin."

Logan nodded, it made sense. "Is there a way I can block her?"

Jade smiled. "Perhaps. I would try to focus on the good things before you fall asleep."

"I will be OK, Jade. I have Sarah by my side at night, and not even she can taint that."

"You are a quick learner, Logan." Jade smiled. "Your love for her runs deep and that can be mightier than any sword or shield, hold on to it."

Logan's face darkened. "I am afraid when this battle is over and I win, if this power stays within me, Hawk told me I may start aging like an Elf."

Jade looked at him. "Hawk is not wrong, it could happen, and you fear Sarah will still age like a human?"

Logan put his face into his hands. "I don't want to live hundreds of years without her."

Jade thought of how short human lives could be, and she felt sorrow for Logan's dilemma. "Logan, none of us can escape death, it comes for all one day, but have faith, remember you are in Silver Moon, the air is cleaner, the land is not polluted, she may live much longer than you think."

Logan looked up and smiled. "I suppose, could I use my magic to keep her alive longer?"

Jade looked at him. "No, Logan, that would not be natural and if you went down that road you would be no better than Rubia, have faith, Logan, for Moonrion is a wise Goddess and I am sure she has thought of this. Now remember what we've talked about and remember what I said about love, for it may be the strongest power you have, Logan." She hugged him. "All things will work themselves out one way or another."

Logan smiled. "Thank you, Jade, for all of your wisdom and kindness."

She smiled as well. "Don't be a stranger, young man."

With that Logan got up and went to find Hawk and Jaguar who were talking outside the dome.

"You ready?" asked Hawk. Logan nodded.

They headed back to the centre of the forest to retrieve Logan's weapons. And then they headed to the front of the forest where their Thyrions were waiting.

Jaguar looked at Logan. "Human Logan, you are a great warrior. I hope to see you again."

Logan smiled. "The feeling is mutual, Jaguar." With that the Forest Elf disappeared into the forest.

"Well, that went well," smiled Logan.

Hawk nodded. "It did. I guess we owe Sarah for that."

Logan noticed Hawk did not seem incredibly happy. "What's going on with you?"

He shrugged. "I am just hoping we are not killed by the Dwarves."

Logan looked at him. "I guess things will not be so easy in Brimard."

Hawk nodded. "That's quite an understatement but we have no choice, we must get back to Eclipse, we will use a portal to the mountains."

Getting back up on his Thyrion was difficult for Logan but eventually he got it. They travelled quickly. Too quickly for Logan's liking but they were soon back in Eclipse. They took both Thyrions back to the stables.

Logan looked at Hawk. "I am exhausted."

Hawk agreed. "I am as well, we will get some rest and I will begin the portal tomorrow, it will take one night to complete." Logan nodded.

They both headed back to the Tree of Power. They made their way up the stairs, both a little sore from their ride.

Lilly, Sarah and Raven were drinking wine together when they both walked in. The three smiled at them, Logan was still getting used to Raven smiling at him.

Sarah gave him a hug. "How did it go, babe?"

He looked over at Hawk, he smiled, and Logan answered her. "They have agreed to help us. You made quite the impression."

Hawk looked at Sarah. "Yes, one of the main reasons Jade said yes was you keeping your word."

Lilly jumped into Hawk's arms. "This is excellent news, thank Moonrion."

Hawk looked at her. "Our greatest task is not over yet; the Dwarves will not be so easy to persuade."

Lilly kissed his forehead. "Just enjoy this one victory and worry about that when the time comes."

Hawk smiled. "You are right."

Logan looked at Hawk. "I am going to turn in, I am exhausted."

Hawk looked at Lilly and Raven. "Let's let Logan rest, and I need it as well."

All three said their good nights and left. Sarah and Logan went into their room. As soon as they entered the room Logan spun Sarah and kissed her, picking her up off the ground. His passion surged through them. Sarah had been caught off guard. They ripped each other's clothes off, and Logan picked her up again and gently set her in the bed. They made love like they never had before Logan's magic circling around the whole room. Sarah had noticed how much stronger Logan had become but he was able to control it perfectly. They rolled off each other both laughing.

Sarah looked at him. "What brought that on?"

"I missed you." He kissed her gently.

She played with his chest hair. "I love you, Logan."

He smiled. "I love you, too."

He held her closely and stroked her hair. He thought of what Jade had told him. And if love was a weapon, he may be a challenge for Moonrion herself, he smiled to himself and they both fell asleep in each other's arms.

CHAPTER 36
UNWANTED GUESTS

Logan woke up to see Sarah standing with a blanket wrapped around her. She was looking out the window.

He smiled. "A penny for your thoughts."

She turned around and smiled. Logan stood up and hugged her from behind.

"I just miss the sun sometimes. I mean, they only have four hours, and we are usually asleep."

He kissed her neck. "I miss it too, babe, but if we have each other we'll be OK."

She leaned into him. "You promise?"

Logan turned her around. "I promise you, babe. I will be here to take care of you."

She smiled. "You can't promise that! You have a bitch from hell to battle remember."

He kissed her again. "'Have faith, Sarah."

She nodded. "You sound like the Elves now."

"I know, but I feel it, Sarah, our love will get us through."

She hugged him close. "Logan, this isn't some comic book or one of your novels, this is real, and you know good doesn't always win."

"Well, that's OK because I am great, not simply good."

She laughed. "You're such an idiot."

He looked at her. "Yeah, but an idiot with the most beautiful girlfriend in Silver Moon."

She smiled. "I can't argue with that."

They heard the front door open. Logan thought to himself, "Dammit, Hawk, way to ruin the moment."

They started getting dressed and Logan walked into the common room where the War table was. He had just decided to call it that.

He looked at Hawk. "Evening."

Hawk nodded. "Evening."

Lilly came in moments later. "Hello, Logan, where is Sarah?"

Logan smiled. "Just getting dressed." Hawk was sorting some small bottles, and he had a large book that looked ancient. "So, you had mentioned this was going to take a full night to prepare."

Hawk nodded not saying anything. Logan did not want to interrupt so he decided he would find Peregrine and see how the Elves were making out with the traps. He headed down the stairs and entered the forest.

He found Peregrine and Shadow discussing where to put another pit. The Plains People were a great help due to their strength.

Shadow noticed Logan first. "Ah, Logan, good to see you! You are looking well; I see the training is paying off."

He nodded. "Thanks, Shadow, but I still feel small next to you."

Shadow laughed. It was always nice to hear someone laugh with everything that was going on. Peregrine looked at him. "Logan, we are making good time." He was showing him all of the traps on the map.

"Excellent, you have done a great job."

Peregrine smiled. "Thorn and I also added a new trap we

came up with. We found some crossbows and have them rigged with trip wires."

Logan smiled back. "That's great, I wouldn't want to be walking into this forest."

Peregrine nodded back. "Me neither."

They started walking through the forest to get a look at the traps. Logan got a look at the crossbow traps and he was impressed, they looked like a terrible way to go. They finally finished the maze of death.

Logan looked at Peregrine. "Just be careful, I do not want anyone getting hurt."

Peregrine nodded. "Star has placed a magical barrier into the forest for all the children."

Logan smiled. "I am glad to hear that, we all know how curious children can be."

Shadow nodded. "You are right, my young Wolves are always a handful."

Logan patted them both on the back. "Excellent work, gentlemen. I am going to check in with Hawk."

He waved and headed back to see what Hawk was up to. He walked in the door and Hawk was still at the war table.

He looked up. "Ah, Logan, sorry for before. I was concentrating on something."

Logan noticed the book was now open. He walked over and looked at the writing in the book. At first he could not read it. He focused and the words changed to English, but it still made no sense.

Hawk smiled. "If you tried to translate this into English with your magic, it still wouldn't make sense to you. It's an old Elven dialect we only use to cast spells. Even we Elven Mages must learn to read it and this dialect is particularly tricky."

Logan looked at it again. "It looks like it's read up and down, not side to side."

Hawk was impressed. "You are correct."

"It's like some Asian cultures on Earth, they read that way."

Hawk kept reading but spoke. "Yes, I had learnt that in some of my studies on the Earth realm."

"What is this for anyways?" Logan asked.

"It's a shielding spell that will protect me when we come out of the portal for several minutes."

Logan frowned. "Surely the Dwarves are not that hateful of Elves."

Hawk kept reading but answered. "I'll put it into Earth terms, better safe than sorry, besides, we don't all have magic armour."

Logan nodded. "Fair enough."

Hawk was deep in concentration and the women had gone for a walk. So, he decided he would go and practise his sword techniques. He went downstairs to his regular spot took off his black t-shirt Lilly had made for him. He started with his basic thrusts and parries and soon he was whirling his blade from hand to hand in front of him so fast the sword looked bladeless. He stopped quickly and turned, performing a back handed block and a quick parry, everyone knew to stay far away from him when he practised with his sword.

He had not been at it long when he heard a woman yell. "Hey, sexy."

It did not break his concentration, and he finished the back thrust he had started. He stopped and smiled after he was done. He walked up to Sarah.

She had a sparkle in her eye. "You know I practised martial arts most of my life and watching you with that sword is like a beautiful dance."

He smiled. "I'll take that as a compliment, Sensei."

She laughed. "Get cleaned up you big lug but kiss me first." He kissed her on the lips and forehead.

She ran up the stairs and Logan enjoyed the view. Logan got cleaned up, put his shirt back on and headed upstairs.

Hawk was talking with Lilly and he had closed the book he had been deciphering. Sarah was smiling when he walked in.

Hawk turned around. "We are good to go for tomorrow night."

Logan smiled. "So, you figured out the spell."

Hawk looked at him. "Yes, it's all worked out, the spell was the easy part, trust me."

Logan looked at Hawk. "We'll be fine, Hawk."

Lilly looked at Logan. "Logan, the Dwarves are quite different than we Elves, they will not be anything like the Forest Elves."

Logan nodded. "So, I have been told." Sarah gave Logan a worried look. Logan looked at everyone.

"We will go to the Dwarves and if they say no, we will leave. I am sure the Dwarves are not even close to the evil that is knocking on our door, can we agree on that?" They all nodded except for Sarah who had never seen a Dwarf. "Well then, shall we get ready for tomorrow night? Logan, you will need your weapons this time."

Logan looked at Hawk. "I will not kill any Dwarves; they are not our enemy."

Hawk frowned. "They may not give you a choice."

Logan nodded. "Let's just pray it does not come to that tomorrow night."

Hawk looked at him. "Just be well rested. Raven and Lilly will be in charge while I am gone."

Lilly looked at Logan. "I showed Sarah our guest house today and I would like you to move in there once you have returned, instead of that cramped room."

Logan looked at Lilly. "I don't think we can accept such a gift; we are OK here."

Sarah looked at him. "You barely fit in that room and your feet hang off the side of the bed, we are taking the guest house."

Logan knew better than to argue and smiled. "You are too kind to us, Lilly."

Lilly hugged him. "It's we who should be thanking you, Logan."

He nodded. He said good night to all and headed towards the room, he wanted to rest and think.

He was laying in the bed with his hands behind his head. Sarah came into the room and laid down next to him. He wrapped his arms around her and started playing with her hair.

She looked up at him. "What's wrong, Logan?"

He smiled. "What makes you think something is wrong?" She smiled and he knew it was a dumb question. "I am just hoping tomorrow does not lead to a fight."

Sarah smiled at him and kissed him gently. "I guess that's up to the Dwarves, there is nothing wrong with defending yourself."

He sighed. "No, I guess not, just get some sleep and hold me."

He slept without any dreams which he was thankful for,

he been expecting them to start by now. Sarah and Logan both woke up at the same time they looked at each other and Logan pulled her close and kissed her forehead. They heard Hawk and Lilly come in, Logan put his black armour clothes on for he was sure he would need it tonight. Logan walked out of the room and Raven was with Hawk and Lilly.

Logan looked at her. "So, you're the boss until we get back."

She smiled. "Something like that."

Hawk looked at Logan. "We need to leave right away, go see Sarah then we shall go."

Logan turned and Sarah was behind him; he kissed her. "I love you."

She smiled. "Take it easy on the Dwarves." He nodded.

He motioned to Hawk that he was ready. Hawk kissed Lilly on the forehead, and they headed towards the door.

Lilly called out. "Take care of him, Logan!"

Logan turned, smiled and walked out the door.

Hawk was talking all the way down the stairs. "Now, Dwarves have no Elder, they have a King and Queen; they don't use magic like we do. They use it in their forges to add different abilities to their weapons themselves. So, don't be surprised if a Dwarf swings his axe and it has fire coming from the blade or lightning things like this."

Logan looked at Hawk. "Hell of a time for a lesson."

Hawk shrugged. "sorry, I was busy last night."

Logan looked at him. "Let's just get this done." Hawk nodded.

They arrived at the round structure where he had come through from Earth. Hawk started to cast the spell; Logan was getting himself ready for his second portal trip as the first one was not a good one. Soon there was a blue portal in front of them.

Logan looked at Hawk. "I will go first."

Logan jumped into the portal; Hawk waited a moment so he would not bang into Logan. Hawk closed his eyes and went through the portal.

Logan felt a huge rush forward, it felt like a giant hand had grabbed him and was pulling him at an incredible velocity. And then he stopped dead, he fell to the ground but recovered quickly. Hawk was soon beside him standing perfectly still. Logan really wanted to know how he did that. They were soon standing in front of a stone wall with two huge doors. Which were wide open.

Logan looked at Hawk. "Looks like they're not expecting any company."

They moved forward slowly, that's when two Dwarven guards noticed them. They both had some sort of horn around their necks which they blew, it made a huge noise in the mountains.

"No sense in taking the silent approach now." Logan grabbed his sword and shield.

The Dwarves were in armour from head to toe, it was beautifully made, Logan noticed.

"You are trespassing on the Land of King Ember, turn back or prepare for battle."

Logan called out. "We need to speak with your King, please."

"The King does not need to speak with an Elf and whatever you are, be gone!"

Logan sighed. "I am afraid we cannot do that."

The guard looked at him. "Then you choose death."

The two guards began to run towards them. Logan had his sword and shield out ready for the Dwarves. His armour swirled around him in its regular silver and black colour. He thought maybe that would stop the Dwarves, it did not. Logan focused his magic into his shield, he waited for the Dwarves to get close, and he released a large blast from the shield, it knocked both Dwarves back a fair distance. They were both laying on their backs, they both got back up not sure what to do. They blew their horns again and more Dwarves came running to their aid. They also wore a lot of armour; Logan was in a defensive position looking for any areas that were left open. There was not a lot, but he did see places he could strike without killing any of them.

There was ten of them now, and they worked in perfect unison, they moved in a triangle formation making them harder to hit, with each Dwarf positioning their shields to the side. Logan thought quickly and went for the Dwarf in the front, he ran forward and kicked the Dwarf directly in the chest who went down hard. Logan rolled over his body and now stood behind the Dwarves. Hawk used a spell, and a bolt of lightning struck the ground beside the Dwarves. They broke formation and went after Hawk. Logan moved quickly and overtook all the Dwarves. He ran past two and nicked them both on the jugular, both stopped, thinking they were dead, but the cuts were superficial. He continued this technique on all ten Dwarves sending the message that if I wanted you dead you would be. They had slowed their attack, wary of Logan. His next attack was to cut between their shoulder armour and gauntlets. He was just about ready to launch his attack when they heard a loud and powerful voice.

"Enough!" All the dwarves stood at attention.

Hawk looked at Logan. "Whatever happens, follow my lead."

Logan relaxed his stance. Their King wore armour as well, although his had a large red cape flowing behind him. All the Dwarves had light red hair, it was quite different from Sarah's, and beards of many different varieties.

The King was close now and he did not look happy. "You have injured my men."

Logan nodded. "I could've killed them all."

"Aye, you made your point, lad. What do you and this Moon Elf want?"

Hawk looked at him. "We seek your wisdom and guidance, your majesty."

He looked at Hawk. "Wisdom, huh! Well, you've come to the wrong place, we are warriors, not philosophers, and quit ass kissing, Elf."

Logan looked at the King. "Listen, my name is Logan and we have come to talk, that's all."

The Dwarf looked at him. "I am King Ember of the Brimard Dwarves."

Logan smiled. "Nice to meet you."

The King looked at him. "You have struck my curiosity boy with your skill of the blade; we will go to my chambers. I am freezing my balls off out here."

And with that they all started to head to the King's chambers, they made their way through the huge doors. There were stone buildings everywhere, the architecture was unique and very well made. No wonder Rubia did not want to attack the Dwarves, Logan couldn't see one without some sort of armour and the mountain top was a fortress. Logan still had his armour on as the Dwarves followed them very closely, and all of them were armed. They made their way to what looked like a castle built directly into the mountain. A statue of a large Pegasus was in what Logan figured to be the centre of the town. They made their way up the stairs of the castle which had two large steel doors and two guards with deadly looking lances. They went inside where they had tapestries and stone heads of all the Dwarven kings. There was art on all the walls, most of which depicted a battle scene and one with a silver dragon on it. They walked on a red carpet which seemed to be on most of the floors. Logan was looking at everything, it was incredible and even though everything was made of stone the place felt warm and welcoming. They finally made it to the throne room. The Dwarves were much shorter than Logan, but they were very muscular and the way they could swing such large weapons was a testament to this.

King Ember went to his throne and sat down, the Queen entered the room, she was not as stout as the men and she had long red hair, similar to the males, she was much thinner than the males. She was still much broader than the Elven women he had seen, she was wearing an armoured style dress with a cape like the King. Logan wondered if there was one Dwarf who did not wear some sort of armour.

King Ember spoke. "This is my Queen, Azurite." Hawk went down to one knee as did the Dwarves; Logan followed suit. The Queen nodded and they all rose again. The King introduced Logan, he looked towards Hawk. "And I did not get your name, Elf."

"It's Hawk, your highness."

"Well, you have used a portal and have injured my men, so my uninvited guests, let us talk, what do you want?" The King looked at Logan. "Can you remove your helmet so I can see your face?"

Logan focused and his armour swirled itself off him. The Dwarves gasped for two reasons; one was the armour the other was the fact he was human. The King and Queen looked at each other in surprise.

The King looked angrily at Hawk. "What is a fucking human doing in this realm? He is not one of your Plains People, he's too short, so answer me, Elf."

Hawk looked at the King. "He was given a gift from Moonrion herself as Rubia has returned."

The King looked at Logan. "Humans, an entire race of shit heads."

Logan stood up straight and replied. "I can't really say I disagree with you, your Highness. Although there are some of us who are intelligent good people."

The King looked at him. "Intelligent, you say." He laughed.

Logan was starting to get pissed. "Well, this one broke down your battle tactics in a few moments, and I am sure I am the youngest here."

The King stopped laughing. He looked hard at Logan. "Yes, it would seem you did. Your sword and shield, I have not seen them since the war, they still look brand new."

Logan looked at them. "Yes, they are beautiful and deadly, the sword is perfectly balanced, and the shield design and abilities are remarkable. They must have been made by Moonrion for Moon Shatter during the war."

King Ember smiled. "Well, yes and no. I crafted both of those weapons with my bare hands and with the steel of the Goddess." The King looked at Logan. "Yes, it was my finest work, and I am glad you appreciate them."

Logan looked at the King. "They have saved my ass a few times."

The King laughed. "Perhaps you're not a shithead after all. And I see Moonrion has given you some help as well."

Logan looked at the King. "Yes, your highness."

He nodded and looked at Hawk. "Now, what's this talk of Rubia being alive. I saw Moon Shatter run his sword through her chest myself."

"She must have found a way to preserve her body as one was never found."

King Ember looked at Hawk. "Fucking Moon Elves always playing with magic they shouldn't be." Hawk said nothing. The King continued. "You'll not see a single warrior from me, Elf, and I know she would never come up here, the cowardly bitch. Does she still use Snakaras?" the King asked.

Hawk looked at him. "Yes, she has a large army of them."

King Ember nodded. "Ugly clumsy warriors, and dumb too! I told Dark Owl not to disband his army after the war, but he was a dreamer that one, thinking the peace would last, where we Dwarves know you must always be ready for the next fight."

Hawk looked at him. "May I ask why your people helped us in the first war?"

King Ember laughed. "I got caught with my dick in my hand."

Hawk looked at him. "Excuse me?"

"Well, I was down at the bottom of the mountain doing some hunting when I set my weapons down to take a piss, I had no idea that a huge brown bear was coming up right for me. Now if I was facing the beast with weapons in hand, I would've welcomed a good fight. Your Dark Owl was gathering herbs and plants for his potions. He saw the bear coming for me and he used some sort of spell as the bear made a sound of pain and started running the other way. I almost shit myself as it could've killed me. I thanked him and owed him my life and we Dwarves take that very seriously. So, he called upon myself and my Army to help with the fight, so owing him my life we fought together, it's Dwarven code."

Hawk understood, Dwarves always repaid their debts, even if it meant death.

Queen Azurite looked at Logan. "I am curious how a human became mixed up in all of this?" Her voice was almost musical compared to the King.

"Well, it's a long story. I was in my own realm and I was given this gift by Moonrion to help the Elves in their battle, and here I am."

She smiled at him. "That must've been difficult for you."

Logan looked at her. "Yes, your Highness, it was at first now I feel like I am helping my own people."

"So, you, a human, will risk your life for these Elves?"

Logan smiled. "Yes, even if that means dying."

She thought for a moment. "Perhaps there is more to you humans than we have given you credit for."

Logan smiled. "No, the King is right, most are shitheads." King Ember laughed and slapped his knee. Logan looked at the King. "We are not here to ask for warriors. What we seek is sanctuary for some Elves while I battle Rubia."

King Ember looked at him. "Well, Logan, the problem is I am bored, I need some entertainment. I'll make you a deal, if you can beat my best warrior, I will give the Elves sanctuary." The Queen looked over with a disapproving look but said nothing. "Only one rule, no shield, for I know what it can do, and it gives you an unfair advantage."

Logan thought about it. "I agree. Here is my shield."

Two Dwarves tried to take the shield only to find they couldn't lift it.

King Ember smiled. "Leave it there lads, as Logan is the only one who can hold it." The King looked approvingly. "You hear that, lads, we have a challenger." The Dwarves all cheered.

"When will this happen?" asked Hawk.

The King thought about it. "It'll take everyone a couple of hours to fill the arena. So, you have two hours." Hawk nodded.

Logan looked at the King. "Who is your champion?"

He smiled. "Her name is Tundra, and she has never been beaten."

Logan looked at him. "Her!"

"Yes," answered the King. "And if you have a problem fighting a woman you might get that out of your head for she has bested every male Dwarf she has fought."

Logan frowned. "Is this to the death?"

The King laughed. "Don't be so dramatic, human, you fight until one can no longer continue, no one will be dying." Logan was relieved to hear that. "You may head to the arena, we shall see how good you really are, Logan."

Hawk and Logan started to walk out when Hawk asked, "Where is the arena?"

The King winked. "Don't worry, you can't miss it."

Hawk looked at Logan and shrugged.

They walked out of the castle. Hawk looked at Logan very seriously. "I think the Dwarves have underestimated you. Make the fight a good and close match. If you win too quickly the Dwarf fighting will lose face and we don't want that. Remember the Dwarves are masterful tacticians and powerful fighters, and if this Tundra has beaten all these other Dwarves, she must be exceptionally good, Dwarves practice every day."

Logan nodded. "I understand, I will keep it close. I guess we should get going."

They both started walking, following the crowd as they had blown another horn. They heard some Dwarves talking and Hawk overheard that this Tundra is the Kings daughter.

Hawk elbowed Logan. "Did you hear that?"

Logan looked at Hawk. "What does it matter who she is?"

Hawk looked at him. "Maybe make it a draw!"

Logan shook his head. "No, we stick to the original plan. I will not fake a draw, and do you think this Tundra will let it end in a draw?"

Hawk sighed. "No, I guess not, just take it easy."

Logan looked at him. "Just breathe, Hawk. I got this! Worse case I lose, and we have to figure something else out." Logan smirked and Hawk knew he did not plan on losing.

They were getting close to the Arena, it was a massive square, Dwarves were coming from every direction. Logan thought the Arena would be round like the pictures he had seen in Rome on Earth.

As they got closer to the Arena a Dwarf approached them. "Are you the one they call Logan?"

Logan looked at him. "Yes I am."

The Dwarf looked Logan up and down. Logan was much taller than the Dwarves at six foot two and with all his sword practising he was well muscled.

The Dwarf smiled at him. "Are you sure you still want to do this, lad?"

Logan looked down at the Dwarf. "Just show me where to wait."

The Dwarf turned around and started towards the arena. Logan heard the Dwarf call him 'A suicidal shit for brains.' He said nothing, his mind was on the duel that was to come. Hawk was not worried about Logan winning. He was worried about his temper. Although Hawk had to admit Logan had become much more disciplined with his daily training.

They entered a side room that had a second door as well, the Dwarf pointed. "That is the door you will come out of when you hear the horn blow." Logan nodded that he understood. The Dwarf went out the door, he looked at Logan. "Good luck, you're going to need it."

Logan just smiled and sat on the bench in the middle of the room. He had his eyes closed and Hawk left him to whatever he was doing. He stood up shortly after.

Hawk looked at him. "What was that?"

"I was just getting my bearings," Logan replied.

He picked up his sword and started to warm up for the fight. Hawk was watching Logan and he now feared for this young Dwarf. He had a hard time even seeing the blade. Logan and Hawk heard a loud horn!

"Looks like it's time," smiled Hawk.

Logan smiled. "I guess so, let's get this over with."

Logan and Hawk went through the door and it led to one long hall with a huge door at the end. Now this reminded Logan of the old Roman movies he had seen. His adrenaline was pumping through his body. He heard the King tell the Dwarves they had a challenger. The Dwarves all cheered; the sound was deafening. He was not sure if they would introduce him first or this Tundra. He got his answer quickly.

"Now shall we meet our challenger." They all booed and threw out other profanities. "Or do you want your Champion to come into the arena first?"

They all cheered to the point that Hawk and Logan covered their ears as the sound reverberated through the stone. Logan heard a large door open, and the crowd again roared in approval.

The King shouted. "Here she is, Tundra!"

Logan was unphased by any of this, after seeing Rubia's evil it would take more than Dwarves to rattle him.

The King now made his voice more sinister. "And here, my fellow Dwarves, is Logan the Shithead!" The Dwarves laughed.

Logan was starting to get a little pissed at the disrespect he was receiving, maybe he would just go across the arena and embarrass this Tundra.

Hawk saw the look in his eyes. "Remember, Logan, do not embarrass the Dwarf, she is the King's daughter."

Logan nodded. "I remember, although I would like to teach these Dwarves a lesson in humility."

Hawk grabbed his shoulder. "I know, so would I. But if you do that we may not get out of here!"

The door opened and Logan walked out, the crowd booed and called him every name in the book. Even some he did not understand. One Dwarf called him a 'Whore's son!' He looked at the Dwarf and pointed his sword directly at him and the Dwarf sat down quickly and said no more.

The King watched as Logan walked into the arena. His armour was beautifully made, it was bright silver with black accents. The King was not sure he had made a good choice, he had read of humans' capacity for violence, and if he fought

278

like Moon Shatter this would be his daughter's greatest opponent.

Hawk thought Logan was going to kill the Dwarf that called him a 'Whore's son.' The Dwarf knew nothing of Logan's history and how his mother had passed, he let out a sigh of relief when Logan just pointed his sword at him. Logan looked across the arena to see his opponent. She was dressed in white and blue armour; it was stunning, and she had a helmet that had long blue hair of some kind coming out of the top that went down her back. Logan admired the craftsmanship of the armour but cared little as he was focusing on the battle.

She was a lot shorter than Logan which would make things more difficult for him, as he was used to fighting things the same size or bigger than him. She carried a large single bladed axe with a pike on top of it, it had a blue crystal in the handle and a small tuft of the same blue hair as her helmet in the pommel. The King stood up, Tundra went down to one knee, Logan followed suit.

"Fighters rise." Logan stood up; the King looked at both combatants. "Salute!"

Tundra pointed her weapon towards Logan who returned the gesture. The tension in the arena was like nothing Logan had ever felt.

The King put up his arm up; he then dropped it and called out, "Begin."

Logan wasn't sure what this Dwarf was capable of, but he had little time to think as she ran directly at him. He braced himself. She brought her axe up and stopped dead and threw it directly at Logan. He rolled to the right and it just barely missed him. He remembered the King saying this was not to the death, although that throw would've caused a terrible wound if he had been hit.

Tundra ran, she tucked and rolled much quicker than he thought a Dwarf could move and retrieved her axe. She slammed the axe into the ground turning it to ice. Logan was not prepared for it and fell on his ass, the crowd cheered. She slid across the ice. Logan waited until she got closer once her leg was in striking distance, he swept her legs out from under her hard. The crowd booed. She recovered quickly and swung her axe where Logan used to be, he was surprised at the strength in which the axe hit the ground, ice shattered everywhere.

Logan was not happy that he had gone down. If she wanted to use a magical weapon, he was fine with that. He now knew what the blue stone did within the weapon, Hawk had warned him they used magic in their weapon making. Tundra swung her axe and it fired what looked like an ice dagger. His eyes turned silver and he punched the ice projectile out of the air.

If Tundra was surprised, she did not show it, she came at Logan with a barrage of swings and slashes, he blocked and parried them easily and now he was behind her he kicked her in the back. He did not use his full strength as that would have been the end of the fight. She stumbled but did not go down, she turned and cried out in primal rage. She attacked out of anger, Logan simply side stepped the attack. She turned and tried to hit him with the pike on top of the axe, he blocked the strike again with ease.

He decided it was time to see how her defence was, he brought his sword up, he faked right and swung the sword to her left, she almost missed the block from the quick attack. Logan performed a quick fade and dodged another swing. He went to a front guard and attacked with a barrage of swings and slashes. He began to move faster and faster, rolling the sword handle from hand to hand he knew the Dwarf could not keep this pace up much longer. Tundra knew she was in trouble; it was like he was everywhere at once. She rolled out of the way to try to get a rest. The King looked on, knowing his daughter had met her match, no one had ever lasted this long against her.

Logan knew she needed a rest, he had no idea how long they had been fighting for, he was zoned out. She came at him again with swings that Logan could've blocked with his eyes closed. She was making mistakes due to fatigue. He decided it was time to finish the battle, he went back to front guard, he thrusted forward, she blocked, he spun around, and his blade was on her neck where her armour did not cover.

Tundra knew she had been bested, had this been a real battle she would no longer have a head. She went down to one knee the crowd was dead silent. Logan guessed going to one knee for Dwarves meant 'Uncle!'

Logan removed his blade from her neck and tried to help her up; she batted his hand away. She stood up and took off her helmet, she had long red hair, which was covered in sweat, she ran her hand through it. She was not what Logan was expecting at all, she was definitely a Dwarf with a round face, she had light blue eyes which were looking dead into his dark blue eyes, all the books he had read mostly described Dwarves as short fat and ugly. She was short and broad but definitely not ugly. She stuck out her arm, Logan stuck his out.

She grabbed his whole forearm. "Well fought, human."

He smiled. "You too, you are a mighty warrior, and my ass will hurt for a week."

She smiled. "Thank you, Logan. Sorry about your ass." She laughed.

The King stood up. "And our winner is, Logan." Everyone clapped half heartily.

Logan walked with Tundra, still arm in arm. He raised both and called out. "To Tundra and Logan, the shithead!"

The crowd laughed and stood up and clapped and cheered. Hawk could not believe it, Logan had a way with people, he had to admit. The King and Queen arose, and everyone went to one knee.

The King looked at his people. "And tonight, we feast." The crowd continued to cheer.

Logan walked towards Hawk who was smiling. "Well played, sir." Logan looked like he barely broke a sweat. Hawk looked at him. "You OK?" He smiled.

Logan nodded. "Yeah, I am OK, my tail bone just hurts a little, the ice caught me off guard!"

Hawk chuckled. "I did warn you about their weapons."

Logan smiled. "Yes you did, and I need to make sure I don't make a mistake like that against Rubia, or it will be a quick fight for her."

Hawk looked at him. "How much of your power were you actually using?"

Logan looked at him. "None really, except when I punched that ice dagger, I didn't want to freak the Dwarves out or have them say I cheated by using magic."

Hawk smiled. "See you're not a shithead, that was smart, and it looked good."

Logan allowed his armour to swirl away and smiled at Hawk. "So now what happens?"

Hawk shrugged. "We eat and get drunk basically."

Logan smiled, he could use some food and a good time.

Logan got cleaned up, he figured he would wear his armour for the feast as the King had called it. Logan called upon it again, it shined a beautiful silver, he wanted to see what else he could make this armour do. He focused his magic and a black cape flowed from the back, he smiled, now he looked dressy and badass.

Hawk walked in and looked at Logan. "I see you've been testing your armour. The cape does add a touch of class to it."

Logan nodded. "Yes it would seem this armour is fully loaded."

Hawk looked towards the door. "It's time to go, the banquet is going to start."

They both headed towards the castle all the Dwarves had polished their armour, some of the female Dwarves wore dresses, some wore armour and others wore something in between. Hawk had a simple black suit on.

Logan looked. "You need to teach me the spell for clothes sometime."

Hawk smiled. "It's a basic spell, but I will teach you one day. For now, let's get in there as you are the guest of honour."

Logan stopped dead in his tracks. "Guest of honour, what does that entail?" asked Logan. "I don't like being the centre of attention."

Hawk smirked. "Says the guy who stood in the centre of an arena and called himself a shithead!"

Logan looked at him. "That was totally different, this is some fancy banquet and I know none of their customs."

Hawk laughed. "You'll sit near the King and Queen and the Princess and eat food and drink and that's pretty much it."

Logan nodded. "OK, I can handle that."

They entered the castle; Dwarves were patting him on the back and praising him. Logan made it through the crowd and was shown to the banquet hall. It was huge with the longest and widest table he had ever seen. It again had paintings on the walls and tapestries everywhere. Logan looked at the food, it covered the whole table. They had multiple roasted pigs and other meats, fruit and lots of what he guessed was Dwarven Mead.

The King was at the head of the table, he waved for Logan and Hawk to come forward. They walked to the front of the table where they were shown to their seats. The King had the same armour he had on when they had met him. The Queen and Princess had dresses on with no armour. Logan bowed to the ladies and sat down; the King gave him a strong punch in the chest.

"You did well today, lad, and I must say you did it in a very honourable way." He laughed. "Logan the shithead, not the best name for a warrior, though."

Logan smiled. "I guess you're right, your Highness."

The King laughed. "Just call me Ember, you've earned it."

The Queen smiled at him. "I should be mad at you, young man, for winning but as my husband has said, you did it with great humility, you may call me Azurite, a great warrior with a sense of humour is hard to find," she smiled.

Logan had noticed Tundra had been looking at him, he turned to her, she blushed. Logan asked how she was feeling.

"Well," she answered, "my left leg is sore from that leg sweep to be honest. I suppose it's better than a sore ass though, am I right, Sir Shithead?"

Logan laughed and she raised her mug, they smashed them together. "Now let's see if you can drink as well as you can fight." She chugged down her mug in seconds.

Logan followed suit, the Dwarven mead was strong, and it reminded him of a stout like Guinness back in the Earth realm, only it was smoother.

The King patted Logan on the back. "Well done, my boy. Dwarven mead is the drink of the Goddess herself."

Logan could not imagine a silver Pegasus drinking mead out of a mug, he smiled to himself. They began to eat, and Logan had roasted pig and venison. It was all cooked perfectly.

Tundra looked at him. "So, Logan, how do you plan to defeat Rubia? I've heard she is a ruthless evil bitch."

Logan frowned. "She is all of that, for sure. And how do I plan on beating her? I am not sure. With heart and steel, I suppose."

The King looked at him. "Well answered, lad. Tundra, I don't want that name mentioned at my table again tonight."

She looked at him. "Sorry father. This is a night of celebration and I do not wish to dwell on that evil bitch."

They continued to drink and eat when Tundra asked Logan if he was a warrior back in the Earth realm.

Logan looked at her. "No, Tundra, I was not a warrior, that all took place when I came to this realm. To be honest when all of this first happened, I wanted nothing to do with it. I did not even know that Elves and Dwarves were real except in books and many of the other things I have seen."

Azurite looked at Logan. "And now you feast with us, so what do you think of us Dwarves?"

Logan smiled. "You might not like the answer."

Azurite smiled. "I will take my chances."

"To be honest, you are a strong people who come off as pricks at first. Now I know that you are an honourable people just protecting your own, which I respect. And I do like the fact you allow women warriors."

Azurite smiled. "Yes, we are not the damsels in distress kind of women."

King Ember nodded. "What they lack in overall strength they make up for in speed and wisdom, some of the best warriors we have are our women folk."

"Well, if they fight like Tundra, I wouldn't want to cross any of them." Tundra blushed again.

Hawk smiled as Logan was oblivious that this Tundra might have a little crush on him.

Ember looked at Logan. "It's too bad you're not a Dwarf, Logan, for by winning today you would have won the right to request my daughters' hand in marriage."

Now Logan blushed. "I wasn't aware of that."

Ember smiled at Logan. "That is another reason why Tundra is so dangerous. All the men she fights are not thinking with the right head and they get easily outsmarted."

Logan laughed. "It seems that regardless of the race, men are men."

Ember laughed. "It would seem so, Logan." Ember looked at Hawk. "So, when should we be expecting our Elven refugees?"

Hawk looked at Ember. "I leave that to you; we have until the blue moon."

The King nodded. "Well then, we might as well get started right away. Give us three days and tell your people not to be alarmed for I will be doubling my guards at the gates. Once all of your people are here, we will seal off Brimard just in case Rubia decides to become suicidal and tries to pay us a visit."

Logan looked at King Ember. "Thank you for this, if you

ever need my sword, I will happily stand with you and your people."

Ember smiled. "Thank you, lad, and I hope the day never comes where that is necessary." Logan nodded in agreeance.

Logan looked at Ember. "You were in the first war; is there any advice you can give me?"

Ember looked at him with sad eyes. "Just know this, Logan, do not expect a fair fight and remember don't let her get inside your head, just fight and keep her busy so she has little time to cast spells."

Tundra looked at her father. "I thought we weren't speaking of her anymore."

Logan nodded. "Sorry, Tundra. I was just seeking some wisdom."

Out of nowhere a flute and harp started playing Tundra looked at Logan. "Will you dance with me, Logan?"

"I don't really know how."

She smiled. "I will lead, do not worry."

Logan stood up and Tundra took his hand and they headed to what Logan figured was the dance floor. Tundra put her hand on Logan's back and they both held hands out in front, and they danced forward and then side to side. It was the way classy people danced in the Earth realm and Logan was far from classy. He felt like an idiot but soon the song was over, and they bowed to each other and headed back to the table.

Tundra smiled. "Thank you, Logan, although you should stick to fighting."

Azurite laughed at her daughter. "Be kind, it was Logan's first time, and he does not know our dances, he tried." Logan blushed.

King Ember laughed. "Don't worry, Logan, great warriors

are always bad dancers."

Azurite looked at her husband. "He's right about that, Logan, this one still steps on my toes."

They continued to eat and drink until the sun came up. But like all good things it had to end, and the Dwarves started to clear out.

Logan and Hawk were both given quarters within the castle. Logan and Hawk were both quite drunk and their beds felt great after a long night, although without Sarah Logan had a hard time falling asleep. Eventually though the mead won.

He was awoken by a knock on the door. It was Hawk.

"Time to get going, we still have lots of work to do."

Logan stood and stretched and followed Hawk down some stairs. He did not remember the way back at all from the previous night. Hawk on the other hand seemed to find the entrance with ease. The King, Queen and Princess were waiting for them.

King Ember looked at Hawk. "We will treat your people as our own."

Hawk smiled. "Thank you, King Ember and Queen Azurite."

King Ember looked at Logan. "Just make sure the bitch is really dead this time." Logan nodded. The King patted his shoulder.

Queen Azurite hugged both Hawk and Logan. "Good luck."

Tundra looked at Logan. "Will you and Hawk be visiting us again?"

Logan looked grim. "I cannot make any promises as I may not survive this battle. If I do, I promise to return."

Tundra smiled. "Good. I want a rematch."

Logan smiled. "You got it!"

Hawk looked at Logan. "C'mon, Logan, time to go."

They were heading towards the doors when King Ember grabbed Logan by the shoulder. "Remember, lad, a good warrior uses his mind first and his weapon second."

Logan nodded. "Thank you, Ember."

"Just try not to die." Was the last thing the King said.

Hawk and Logan headed back to where the portal had been. Hawk began the spell the portal quickly opened this time, they both stepped through back to Eclipse.

CHAPTER 37
RUBIA'S FINAL PREPARATIONS

Rubia's armour was finally coming together, although she did not have the help of a Goddess, but there were many dark arts that worked fine. She used blood magic from her own soldiers to make the chest piece which, through her power, was as strong as any steel. She knew it would not withstand a direct strike from Logan, but she never planned to let him get that close. The wings were the most challenging task. They resembled the wings of a gargoyle; they were jet black and could be tucked behind her to be almost invisible. She wanted them to be a psychological advantage, a dark surprise if you will. She smiled, she had used some old armour from her armoury for the legs and had strengthened them with more blood magic. For her helmet she had used the skull of a Moon Elf, she had distorted its looks, it was jet black, and the face piece had fangs and looked like a demon from the dark realms.

There were many evil realms she could draw magic from, even the one the humans called hell. She smiled, it was not under their feet, although it was a real realm and was a place not even she had the courage to visit. Many of the humans' beliefs were half right and half wrong when it came to true evil and Gods and Goddesses. She smiled, although Logan would learn all this the hard way. She knew if it came to a fair fight, she could not beat this human. Moonrion had made sure of that, his power was not to be underestimated. She would rely on attacks of the mind. As she knew all humans had a darkness to them whether they liked it or not.

Her armour was deep crimson red and black, and she had to admit it was deadly looking. She smiled; things were coming together nicely. She had also added two secret blades into her Bo staff, she tested the switch and both blades flipped outwards in perfect timing. She had tried to attach her soul to the armour, but all her attempts had failed. It seemed cheating death was a one-time only spell. She was trying to come up with a secondary fail safe. She hated Moonrion for bringing forth this human, everything would have been so easy without him. Oh well, she still needed something as a back-up plan if she were going to die, she wanted to know the Elves would still perish.

She started looking at some of her more powerful summoning spells. She looked at all the books on her large shelves and one stood out to her. It was a black book with gold writing on it. She looked at it and with some hesitation and pulled it off the shelf. The book was covered in cobwebs and dust, she gave it a light wipe with her hand. She looked at the book and carefully opened it as the book was older than anyone truly knew. It was a book for summoning demons, and not just any demons, the evillest of all the demons in all the different realms. Even she was wary of the book, she held in her hand for she knew that no one had ever dared to use it in this realm. She was going through the book, which in some realms was called a Grimoire, looking at pictures of some of the demons, they drew fear even into her twisted and evil mind.

She looked at the spells and she knew she could perform some of them but what she did not know was if she summoned the demon, would she have the power to control it. If she summoned one that she could not control, it might kill her before she even had time to destroy the Elves. She also knew she must be careful as Moonrion would not directly intervene with the battle against Logan. Although, she may disrupt her plans if she summoned a demon that did not belong in this realm. Goddesses frowned on such actions, bringing snakes from another realm was one thing, summoning a powerful demon was on a whole other level.

She found a page with a demon on it that looked promising. It was jet black, stood upright and had long fangs with two large horns coming from what seemed to be its shoulders and large clawed hands. The book said they were intelligent and immensely powerful and could take many forms. The book also said the demon did not have one name as they gave themselves their names according to the book, the last one summoned was called Slain.

She needed to think on this but if it were intelligent, perhaps she could work out a deal with it, although she needed to rest before she tried anything of this level. It was going to be interesting, if she could convince this demon to help her, things might turn out vastly different.

After some rest she returned to her work, she had decided that she would try the summoning spell. If the demon did not cooperate, she would simply send it back to where it came from. She opened her Grimoire and found the page of the demon she was seeking. She would have to be careful not to make any mistakes, for it may be her last, and the Elves would win by default. She gathered all the things necessary to begin the spell. She cut her hand with her magical dagger and began the drawing of the symbols; she would need to hold the demon in place while she tried to make her deal with the beast. She had everything she needed to begin the ritual. She healed her hand and began the spell.

The room went pitch black and became quite cold. She could see her breath. She continued with the spell to its finality. After she opened her eyes there was nothing standing in the circle she had made. She thought perhaps she had missed something; she turned to the book and checked the spell and she had made no mistakes. She turned around and was surprised for standing in front of her was the demon. Her shield spell was working, and the creature was encircled in an orange light.

The demon looked exactly as it had in the book, jet black with red eyes. It paced back and forth looking at her the way a predator looks at its prey.

It looked at her. *'Why have you summoned me to this place.'*

She looked at the demon. "I would like to make a deal with you."

The demon laughed, it was a horrible sound like the cries of thousands of men, women and children. The demon looked at her. *'In order to make a deal you must have something this one wants.'* It smiled showing its long fangs and sharp teeth.

Rubia knew this was all an act to intimidate her. She smiled back. "Would my soul be enough for you?"

The demon stopped pacing and looked at her. *'Why would I need something this one already has thousands of?'*

Rubia thought for a moment. "Surely none of the souls you possess have the power that I would bring to you."

The demon smiled. *'I have many powerful souls. I am a destroyer of realms, your every nightmare, even the demons in the realm of hell do not wish to cross paths with me, witch.'*

Rubia was starting to think this was a bad idea. "You would have all my powers and could rule this realm."

The demon had restarted its pacing. *'I feel too much good*

in this realm, this I do not like, witch.'

"Ah but you could destroy this goodness." Rubia smiled.

The Demon smiled. *'If we wanted to rule this realm, we would not need your help in doing so.'* The demon stuck its claw into the orange shield holding him. Rubia had to refocus her magic. The Demon laughed again. *'We can feel you weakening, be careful, witch, for if your shield fails, I promise my first act in this realm will be to tear you apart.'*

Rubia was getting tired of this but the demon was right, the longer she held the shield the more tired she became. Rubia tried one more time. "OK, Demon. I want to know your name and if you agree to my terms."

The Demon hissed. *'I have been called many things but if you must know my name is Horde and I do not wish to be in this realm or to help you, witch.'*

Rubia had wasted her time, she began the spell to send the Demon back to wherever it came from. It made a horrible shrieking sound and began to disappear; its body was sucked down a dark hole. The Demon, who had called himself Horde, stuck one of its clawed hands up and one of those claws were ripped off and stuck into the stone where the symbols had been drawn in blood and the Demon was gone, as if it had never been.

Rubia sighed if she died this time it looked like it was permanent. She knew all had to meet death one day, even her if the Moon Elves died with her, she could accept this fate. And besides, she did not plan on losing to Logan anyways. She truly fucking hated that man. She would destroy his mind and even if she lost, he would live a life of pain and suffering, she would make sure of that.

Malay and Sucuri came into her spell room all they could smell was sulphur. They both looked at their Queen. "We are ready to strike."

Rubia smiled, if only the demon could be so easily manipulated. She thought of looking for a different demon, but she needed to save her power for the battle with the human.

She looked at her large Snakaras and smiled. "Excellent work."

She thought of attacking earlier than the blue moon but she knew after summoning the demon she needed rest and regardless of how many Elves died, Logan would come for her and she was not completely ready.

She dismissed both Snakaras and headed towards her bookshelf and took a spell book which was entitled Magical Telepathy. She walked towards her throne room completely missing the single claw that had been torn from the demon's hand.

CHAPTER 38
PREPARATIONS

Logan and Hawk returned through the portal. Logan almost kept his balance but still fell.

He looked up at Hawk. "Why is it you never fall?"

Hawk smiled. "Portal jumping takes a little getting used to, but you're getting better. C'mon we still have lots of work to do."

Logan got up and they headed back to the Tree of Power. They walked into the common room and the only person who was there was Raven.

She smiled at both. "Well, it's good to see the Dwarves didn't kill you."

Hawk smiled back at her. "Yes, we faired quite well. Where are Lilly and Sarah?"

Raven looked at Logan. "They are getting the guest house ready. It's a surprise, Logan, as they thought you would be longer, so act surprised."

He smiled at Raven. "Will do."

They both decided to stay with Raven until the women returned.

Logan looked at both. "I am going to take a little rest; it's been an eventful couple of days."

Logan walked into the room and took his clothes off and laid down he fell asleep quickly.

Logan rolled over and there was Rubia lying next to him

naked. She smiled at him. "Hello, Logan. I've come one more time to see if I cannot change your mind in joining me." She was skin to skin with him. "It seems one part of you wants to spend time with me."

Logan's anger was at an all-time high as his own body had betrayed him, he knew it meant nothing as he had noticed before she was beautiful, and they were lying naked and awfully close together.

He looked at her with fury in his eyes. "This isn't real and the only thing that has happened is a biological reaction, nothing more."

She smiled at him again. "Logan, you can rule this land with an iron fist. You can have me as your lover and I will never leave you alone, for if you do start aging like us you will live hundreds of years after Sarah is dead and in the ground."

Logan smiled evilly. "For someone who is supposed to be so wise and powerful. You're a slow learner. The only love you will receive from me is the love of my sword taking your head, bitch."

Rubia frowned. "Fine, die with the rest of them."

Logan was now standing on the Plains, there was lightning hitting the ground all around him, in front of him stood Rubia with one of her large Snakaras. She had Sarah on her knees, Logan went to run forward but he could not move. He watched as Rubia slit her throat. Logan screamed out, although he still could not move. He watched as the large Snakara started to swallow his love whole. He almost exploded with rage.

He woke to find his hand wrapped around Sarah's throat he immediately let go. He was covered in sweat; the bed was soaked. Sarah looked at him with fear in her eyes.

Logan wiped his forehead; he looked at Sarah. "I am so sorry, are you OK?"

She nodded. "I am OK, you had just grabbed me, but what would have happened if you hadn't woken up when you did?"

Hawk had walked in behind Sarah. "He could've killed you."

Logan looked at Hawk there was a fury he had not seen in Logan's eyes before.

"I would never hurt Sarah, you know this."

Hawk looked at him sadly. "Logan, I know you would never hurt Sarah intentionally but now that Rubia has opened your telepathic connection we must watch you carefully when you sleep. For we have no idea what could happen, you might even have magical outbursts. From now on you will need someone with magical training to watch as you sleep for everyone's safety. We will figure it out, my friend, and you also must sleep alone."

Sarah helped him out of bed and dried him off, he was shaking. She hugged him. "Do not feel bad, babe, it was not you."

He lifted her chin and a small amount of silver travelled through her body and took all the pain away. She smiled.

He kissed her. "I missed you."

She hugged him tighter, he could feel a tear going down her cheek. "When will this hell end?"

He looked down with silver eyes. "Soon, my love, I promise."

Logan got dressed and headed to the war table, he looked at Hawk. "Are you sure I have to sleep alone, maybe if Sarah was beside me, I wouldn't have had the dream?"

Hawk looked at Logan. "It's a little more complex than

just a dream, Logan, it's a direct link between the two of you."

Logan thought about it. "So, I could use it against her as well?"

Hawk nodded. "In theory, but she cares for nothing, how do you scare someone with no soul? She feels nothing, Logan."

Logan thought on this for a moment. "You're wrong, Hawk, she fears defeat and death."

Hawk frowned. "Don't get into a psychological fight with her, trust me. I will consult my books and see if we cannot block this link. Besides, we need to start planning the evacuation of the town."

Logan frowned. "I know." He looked at everyone in the room.

Raven smiled at him. "So how was the meeting with the Dwarves?"

Logan looked at Raven who had a large smile on her face. "What?" he asked.

Raven looked at him. "We were just wondering how your ass was." The women all started laughing, even Hawk was laughing a little.

Logan looked at all of them. "Yes Tundra knocked me on my ass, ha-ha! But without me you wouldn't have any help from the Dwarves."

Lilly stopped laughing wiping tears from her eyes. "No, Logan, we are grateful, we know how big a pain in the ass it must have been."

They were all roaring now, even Logan was laughing. Sarah came up behind him and hugged him, she was still laughing but he knew this was going to be the last laugh most of them would have until after the battle was over, so he enjoyed it with everyone. Soon after everyone calmed down, they had to return to the harsh reality of the plan to move all the Elves. Logan also had a new plan for the Dwarven charges.

Logan looked at Hawk. "So, what's the plan for moving your people?"

Hawk looked at Logan. "We are going to do this in two large groups and one small third group."

Raven spoke up. "Where is the small third group going?"

Shadow walked into the room. "I will take a small group of Elves with me to my people, I've been gone too long and when this battle starts, I will need to be with them."

Hawk looked at Shadow. "Thank you, Shadow, we will figure out a way to thank your people."

Shadow nodded. "How about everyone just survives this nightmare, and that will be all we ask for."

Lilly looked at Logan. "I still cannot believe you managed to get the Dwarves to help us."

Hawk smiled. "He and King Ember really hit it off, even Queen Azurite took a liking to him. It's a good thing he isn't a Dwarf, or he might be getting married right now."

Sarah punched him in the arm. "What the hell does that mean?"

Logan looked at her and smiled. "The Dwarf I fought was named Tundra. And it turned out Tundra was a female and the Princess, and King Ember informed me no one had beaten his daughter and if I were a Dwarf, I would have the right to ask for her hand in marriage."

Sarah looked at him. "Wow, really?"

Lilly looked at Sarah. "Dwarven women are mighty warriors and train the same as the males."

Sarah looked at Logan. "Always the charmer."

Logan smiled. "Well at least they are going to help us now, and I don't know why you think the Dwarves are cold hearted. I genuinely think they are a good race of people."

Hawk looked at Logan. "It's not that, it's just they are stubborn, and King Ember is very protective of his people and he blames us for all of this mess."

Logan understood the King's concerns. "Well, we have their help now, so let's get things going."

Hawk looked at the map. "We will have two main groups, one will be led by Star and Raven, the other will be led by Sarah and Lilly. I will stay back for as long as I can, and Shadow will take the third small group. Star and Raven, you will be going to the Dwarves, Sarah and Lilly you will be going to the Forest Elves, Shadow will take the rest to the Plains den."

Logan looked at Hawk, it seemed like a good idea.

Hawk looked up. "What were your new plans for the Dwarven charges?"

Logan smiled. "We are not going to blow up the town, we are going to set them at the border with trip wires."

Hawk looked at Logan. "That would definitely thin their numbers."

Logan smiled. "And they will still have to deal with the forest. How powerful are these Dwarven mines?"

Hawk looked at Logan. "Well, they blow through rock like it was glass. How many do you plan on using?"

Logan looked at him. "How many do you have?"

"Four I believe, maybe six."

Logan nodded. "OK, we will use them all."

Hawk looked at Logan like he was crazy. "Logan, that's a lot, the blast wave would be quite large."

He thought for a moment. "Will the explosion effect any of our people?"

Hawk did some measurements on the map. "It looks like we should be OK."

Logan looked at the map and marked where he wanted to place them and how far apart for maximum damage. Logan nodded. "Hopefully, the explosion will catch Rubia off her guard as well. It may be the quick distraction that I need to land a killing blow."

Hawk looked at Logan. "Well, I cannot believe we managed to get this far."

Logan smiled at the thought of Rubia's army being blown to bits.

Lilly looked at Hawk. "Are we going to have a town meeting?"

Hawk shook his head. "We don't have time, start spreading the word, any Elves who give you a hard time, just inform them they can stay and fight Rubia's army by themselves." Hawk looked at Logan. "How are you feeling about the battle with Rubia?"

Logan had hatred in his eyes, which went slightly silver. "I would go now if I could."

Hawk smiled. "Patience, my friend, the night of the battle will be here before you know it." Logan nodded.

Sarah looked at Hawk. "I will be sleeping in the same bed with Logan until the evacuation."

Hawk looked at her. "I cannot allow that, Sarah, it's too dangerous."

She looked at Hawk sternly. "Hawk, I may not know Rubia's abilities, and frankly I don't care. I will be staying with him; I will take care of him and perhaps with us together we can stop this bitches link with Logan."

Hawk knew there was no sense in arguing with her. Logan turned and looked at her. "Sarah, what if I hurt you? I already grabbed you by the throat."

She kissed him lightly on the lips. "And as soon as you did you woke up. I don't think that was a coincidence, not even her evil can taint how much I love you, Logan, and I know not even she has the power to make you hurt me."

He smiled. "I love you, Sarah."

He kissed her forehead and looked at her, a tear fell down his face, he still had not told her about his magic and his aging, and he could not imagine life without her.

She looked at him and wiped his tear away. "What's wrong, Logan?"

He smiled. "Nothing. I just got caught up in the moment."

Hawk and Lilly looked at each other for they knew Logan had not told Sarah about what might happen with his gifts. Lilly stepped out of the room for a moment as it broke her heart thinking of what Logan must be going through. Although they could be wrong, Hawk did not think it was likely.

Logan looked at Sarah. "I need to go talk to Peregrine about the Dwarven charges and get in some sword practice. I'll be back soon, love."

Hawk said nothing as he knew Logan needed to go and clear his head, he would talk to him later.

Sarah looked at him and gave him a big hug. "OK, just be careful you don't blow yourself up."

Hawk smiled. "Don't worry, Sarah, the charges are quite safe."

Logan went down the stairs to look for Peregrine, he would need his help with the charges as he forgot to ask what the hell they looked like. He made his way towards the tree line. Peregrine and Thorn were looking at the map Hawk had given them. Logan walked up to them to see what was going on.

Thorn looked up. "Ah, Logan, good to see you. Peregrine and I were just checking the map to see if there was anywhere else we could set up traps."

Logan smiled. "I have a new idea." They both looked at him. "We are going to use the Dwarven charges at the border."

They both looked at him with concern on their faces. Peregrine thought about it. "Logan, you do realize Dwarven mines are extremely powerful!"

Logan smiled. "Don't worry, Hawk has done the calculations and it would not hurt any of us. He even calculated the blast wave and thinks we should be OK."

Thorn looked at Logan. "He thinks?"

"Look, it may be dangerous but so is what is coming and think of what it will do to their numbers, and that is before they even hit the forest."

They both looked at each other and wrapped up the map they had been looking at. The three of them headed towards the armoury. Logan let the two Elves enter first as they knew what the mines looked like. It did not take long to find them; they were square and almost looked like plastique he had seen in movies back in the Earth realm. They had a strange symbol on the top of them, after Logan focused his magic, he learned it was just an explosive symbol. They looked heavy but after Logan picked one up, he was surprised, they were quite light. He took two and Peregrine and Thorn each took one. They walked back to the tree line; the border was quite a bit further away.

Logan looked at the Elves, he had another idea. "We will make a fire line and the three of us will be at the end to set them up."

They looked at each other and Logan explained what he meant. They both nodded. Thorn let out a loud whistle and Elves started to appear from the tree line. They started to line up in one long formation and Logan, Peregrine and Thorn headed to the border. Logan smiled, this was going to work better than he had thought, there were enough Elves to pass the explosives down to each place he had marked on the map.

It took all night and when the sun was coming up, they had just finished planting the last charge. They were all tired, and they headed to their homes to get some rest. Logan headed back to the Tree of Power and climbed the stairs. He walked in and Sarah was the only one waiting for him.

She looked at him and smiled. "Everyone else is sleeping, do you want to just sleep here or head to the guest house?"

He looked at her and smiled. "Let's head to the guest house as I have not seen it yet." They walked down the stairs and Logan followed Sarah hand in hand.

She smiled. "Did you ever think we would have a home together?"

Logan smiled at her. "I thought about it daily, but I never thought it would ever happen."

She smiled. "You thought about it every day, even when I had basically stopped calling?"

Logan looked at her. "I always wanted to be with you, Sarah, but unfortunately, I kept drinking and fucking things up."

She looked at him. "Well now you are the man I always knew you were."

Logan looked upset. "Yeah, I just wish I could fix the sins of my past."

She nodded. "You have made up for those sins and more with me and you have helped so many people, Logan. You have saved lives and at the cost of almost losing yours."

He nodded and smiled. "Now I just have to fight pure evil and survive."

They had arrived at the guest house it was beautiful! It was carved into a huge tree as all the Elves homes were. Sarah opened the door and pulled him inside. Logan looked around, it was much bigger than it looked from the outside, it reminded him of the log cabins he had seen on TV. It had everything they needed, all the furniture was carefully carved from the wood of the tree and then covered with soft looking cushions and deer skin blankets.

Sarah looked at him. "The bathroom is that way, you are filthy, go shower and I will show you the bedroom after that."

Logan stripped down and stepped into the shower, there were no taps anywhere. A few moments later the water started, and it was at a perfect temperature. Logan washed his body and let the water calm his sore muscles. He found a towel and dried off, he wrapped it around his waist, he opened the door.

Sarah was there waiting for him; she took his towel off slowly and smiled. "You will not need this where we are heading."

She pulled him into the bedroom which had a large bed in it. He kissed her softly and picked her up, she kissed him back, she kissed his neck, he set her down, she laid him down on the bed and climbed on top of him. She guided him inside of her, she laid down to kiss his chest and sat up, they moved together in a perfect rhythm. They both eventually began to move faster and faster until they both finished together. Sarah laid on his chest for a while and then rolled off him. He looked at her but said nothing as he did not want to wreck the moment.

She cuddled up to him and kissed his cheek. "Logan, what is bothering you?"

He looked down at her. "What do you mean, babe?"

She looked at him. "I know you and there is something you're not telling me."

He sighed, he thought about it all and looked at her with those beautiful eyes. "I just wish we could stay like this, and it didn't take all of this for me to get my shit together." He looked at her a tear ran down his cheek. "Sarah, I have wanted to tell you this for a while. Hawk thinks after this is all over and I keep my powers I will age like the Elves."

She looked at him, now she had tears in her eyes. "So, you will live a long time after I have died?"

Logan nodded. "Yes, I am sorry I didn't tell you sooner, it's just I can't imagine my life without you."

She looked at him and kissed his forehead. "Oh, Logan, babe. I didn't know you were carrying this around, let's not let it ruin this right now. We will figure something out after all this is over with."

He smiled. "I didn't think you would take this information so well."

She touched his face. "Logan, I am a nurse, you don't think I haven't had this cross my mind, we have all seen your power and although I don't totally understand it, I have seen what it has done to your body already. You're as muscular as Shadow is now. But like I said, let's be in the moment."

He pulled her close. "You always were smarter than me."

Logan slept without any nightmares.

They both woke up together, they stayed cuddled up in bed for a while before they got up. Logan thought about the battle that was quickly approaching. It was hard to keep control of his anger after all Rubia had done, he closed his eyes and focused on calming himself. He opened his eyes and Sarah was looking at him.

She laid her head on his chest. "Are you thinking of the fight?"

He looked down at her; he smiled but said nothing. They decided it was time to head to Raven's and see what was awaiting them this evening. They held hands and took their time walking, both noticing the trees had started to change colours, the red and purple leaves of the black oaks were not as vibrant. Logan and Sarah had been through so much, they never even thought to ask about the seasons in Silver Moon.

Logan smiled, he had not felt this happy in a long time, maybe ever. He looked at how beautiful everything was here. He finally had Sarah in his life, and they loved each other more than ever, they were like two teenagers again. He finally had everything he had ever wanted. Of course, all he had to do was fight pure evil to the death to keep it. This seemed to be Logan's luck for much of his life. He smiled, at least this time he would be able to do something about it. He let it go and enjoyed the walk.

Eventually they made it to their destination and headed up the stairs. It was a full house this evening, Hawk was standing in the centre of what Logan had nicknamed the war table. They all looked up when he and Sarah walked in.

"Nice of you to join us." Hawk smiled.

Logan looked at him. "Hey, I already know what I must do fight an evil bitch and win."

They all looked at him with sad eyes and smiled. Petal ran up to Logan and she gave him a hug.

He picked her up. "Hello little one, how are you?" She had tears in her eyes, she was trying her best with little success to stop them. Logan looked at her and smiled. "What's wrong, Petal?"

She snuggled into his shoulder. "I don't want you to fight Rubia. Just come with us where she can't get you like Mommy and me."

He smiled. "Petal, look at me." She did as he said. "I know this has been an extremely hard time for you, child, and if I could go with you I would, but I must fight Rubia so she can never hurt anyone again, and as soon as I have done that, we can all be safe."

She looked at him and nodded. She reached into her pocket and took a small necklace out with a silver Pegasus charm on it. She smiled. "Here, this will protect you."

He took the necklace and gave Petal a kiss on the forehead. "Thank you, Petal." He set her down.

Star looked at Petal. "Go and play in the other room, love, we have some things to discuss, OK?"

She headed to Raven's room and under her breath they all heard her say, "I wish this fucking bitch would just go away."

Everyone immediately looked at Sarah who blushed. "OK! I will work on my language." Logan started laughing! Everyone laughed.

Hawk smiled. "I have to say, I agree with Petal."

Even Star laughed, it lightened the mood a little. Unfortunately, they had to get back to work.

Hawk looked at Peregrine. "Are the woods ready for the attack?"

Peregrine nodded. "We have traps everywhere. We have left only one small trail for Shadow and the Elves to take; and our people heading to the Forest Elves."

Hawk nodded. "Excellent work, I would like you and Thorn to take all the archers you trained and go with the group heading to the Forest Elves as they will be more exposed."

Peregrine nodded. "I will begin rounding everyone up now." With that, Peregrine headed towards the door, he stopped and looked at Logan. "Thank you for all of this, Logan, you are OK for a human." Logan smiled. "Good luck, my friend." And with that he was gone.

Hawk looked back at the map. "Lilly and Sarah, you will be taking our people to the Forest Elves, you will need to keep everyone quiet and in single file. Move as quickly as you can."

Sarah looked at Hawk. "Why not just use another portal?"

Hawk smiled. "I wish I could, but one portal we can get away with, but with two Rubia might figure out we are up to something." Sarah smiled, it made sense. Hawk continued. "Once you are with the Forest Elves, do exactly as Jade says as we are their guests." He looked at Raven and Star. "You will all be using the portal, make sure you spread everyone out a few at a time or we will have a pile of Elves on the other side and injuries we don't need."

Star smiled. "Thanks boss, but Raven and I aren't rookies."

He smiled. "I know, it's all our other people I am worried about, most of them have never used a portal."

Logan looked at Hawk. "How many days until the blue moon?"

He looked at Logan. "It will rise in three night's from now."

Logan sighed. "We are cutting this close."

Hawk nodded. "Very."

The planning continued and soon everyone knew their duties. Logan looked out one of the windows and there were Elves already getting ready.

Petal came out of Raven's room. "Is it time to go meet the Dwarves yet, Momma?"

Star smiled. "Yes, very soon love." Petal had a huge smile on her face. Star looked at the rest of them. "She has never seen a Dwarf before, so she is excited to meet them."

Raven looked at the little girl. "I haven't seen a Dwarf since I was your age."

Petal went back to Raven's room. They all looked at Logan who had the hardest task of all.

Hawk looked at him. "How are you feeling?"

Logan shrugged. "I feel fine, I just have no idea how this will play out. The only thing I know for sure is she won't fight fair; I'll just have to trust my skill and Moonrion and fight with everything I have."

Star looked at Logan. "Just be careful of the psychological attacks, if things get dark in your mind try to remember the good things. Like Sarah, and Petal as she loves you, Logan, we all do. And you will need that to fight her as much as your sword and shield."

Logan blushed, he had been told this multiple times in different ways, he hoped he was ready. "Thank you, I will remember, and I feel the same way. I would like the rest of tonight to be with Sarah alone."

Hawk nodded. "We are ready. Sarah, you and Lilly will leave first thing tomorrow evening."

They both nodded and Logan and Sarah headed back to

the guest house to have the night together.

As soon as they entered the house and Sarah closed the door she dropped to her knees and started crying. Logan reached down and hugged her tight and picked her up and set her on the couch. She took his face in her hands looking at him as if she were never going to see him again. He ran his hand through her hair and smiled she laid her head on his shoulder still crying. He said nothing and let her get it out of her system.

She looked up at him. "I don't know if I am strong enough for all of this."

Logan smiled at her. "You're the strongest woman I have ever met. You can do this, and you will have Lilly."

She shook her head. "I never would have dreamt something like this would happen to us."

He smiled. "That's an understatement. I never thought I would be responsible for trying to save a race, back in our realm I couldn't even save myself. Now here we sit, you are leading the Elves to safety and me fighting pure evil."

Logan really did not know what else to say so he picked her up and they laid in bed together just looking into each other's eyes, stroking and cuddling each other.

Logan looked at her. "Remember, our love will be with me and not even she can destroy that."

She smiled and kissed him they made love through the night until they were both exhausted and fell asleep in each other's arms. Logan heard Rubia's voice in his head that night.

'Enjoy your last night with your bitch!'

Logan shot up. Sarah was there she laid him back down and rubbed his chest. "Bad dream?"

He nodded. "Sort of, although this time it was just her voice."

Sarah did not ask what she had said to Logan as it was not important, and she did not want to let her ruin their time together. Logan sighed, glad that she did not ask, he decided that he would try this psychic link.

'We shall see if you fight as well as you talk, bitch!'

He smiled, he figured two could play this game. He closed his eyes and held Sarah close as the clock was ticking, and he had no idea how long it would be before he would see her again or at all.

The sun was coming up which meant they had about four hours left together. It has always been said that sunrises were beautiful but for Logan this one only reminded him of fire and death. Sarah was still snuggled into him asleep. She stirred and opened her eyes. She looked at the window and looked at the sun coming up, by her reaction she was not happy to see it either. She looked at Logan and wondered why he had to be the one chosen for this job or duty whatever. Deep down she was still pissed that the Elves were running and not standing beside him. She also knew this is what Logan had fought so hard to accomplish and he had succeeded, although this did not surprise her. Logan, even at his worst on Earth, always had a way with people and his smile could disarm almost anyone.

She was worried that if anything happened to Logan, she would never forgive the Elves for their cowardice. Some had stood by him and fought but she knew without Logan these Elves would already be dead. She said nothing to Logan as he thought this was his fight and he was doing the right thing. She just wished he did not have this hero complex. She knew after his parent's accident when he was just a boy, he bounced around the system and reading comic books and Fantasy fiction novels were his only escape. Unfortunately, this was no book and heroes did not always win in real life, as she had said to him before. Logan looked down at her and kissed her cheek.

"Are you OK?"

She looked up at him and smiled. "Not really, I never thought I would find a sunrise so ominous."

Logan nodded. "I thought the exact same thing."

Four hours from now they would be separated until all of this was over. She smiled at him not knowing what to say she never thought she would be dating the saviour of a race.

He looked and smiled at her. "Look at me, love." She looked at him. "I know this is the hardest and craziest thing that perhaps any human couple has had to endure but I must do this, and not just for the Elves but for myself."

She sighed. "I know I am being selfish but sometimes I wish this had never happened."

He smiled. "I know love, some days I have those feelings too. Although if this had not happened, I would not have had this time with you, and we would never be where we are now. I would still just be a drunk bartender and I do not want to go back to that and if I die at least I had some time with you which is fine by me."

She smiled. "I would call you cheesy, but I understand what you mean."

Logan laughed. "Let's just enjoy these few hours."

They were in the middle of making love when there was a frantic knock on the door. Logan could not believe this was happening, he wrapped a blanket around himself and headed towards the door.

It was Hawk, he looked worried. "I am sorry, Logan, but Lilly and Sarah have to start the journey to the Forest Elves." Hawk looked at Logan and could tell he was a little more than pissed.

Logan ran his fingers through his hair. "Why what's happening now?"

Hawk looked at him. "Peregrine noticed torches and fires being set just a few miles away from the Forest."

Logan nodded. "I will tell Sarah; she will meet Lilly as soon as she is dressed."

Hawk looked at Logan. "I am terribly sorry, Logan."

He nodded. "It's not your fault, Hawk."

With that he closed the door and headed back to the bedroom. Sarah looked at him and she knew by his face it had not been good news.

He sighed. "You and Lilly must get ready now to leave."

Her face went red. "What? Why! For fuck sakes it's always something!"

Logan understood her anger for he was not impressed either. He looked at her. "Peregrine noticed that Rubia's army is closer to the Forest Elves location than we previously anticipated."

She put her head up and sighed. "Of course, they are." They both started to get dressed Sarah looked at Logan. "Why did I become an Elven leader?"

Logan smiled. "Hey, at least you don't have to fight with blue balls."

They both started laughing. She looked at Logan. "You're such a dumbass!"

He smiled. "I know, but we better get out there, Hawk looked like he was going to have an aneurysm."

She got dressed in her new traveling gear which had a camouflage spell on it, Lilly had made them of course. The clothes looked pretty much the same as hiking clothes back in the Earth realm.

They headed towards the Tree of Power which none of them would see for a while. There were Elves lined up everywhere. Logan just hoped they would all make it to the Forest in time, he wondered if he should go with them. They finally made it to the front of the line where Lilly was standing with Hawk and Peregrine. Lilly's clothes were almost the same as Sarah's.

Lilly smiled at Sarah. "I am sorry we have to leave early but we don't want to run into Rubia's army." Sarah could not argue with that.

Logan looked at Hawk. "Should I go with them?"

He frowned. "I wish I could send you, but I might need you to watch my back while I get the portal ready." Logan understood but he still did not like it.

Lilly looked at Sarah. "Are you ready for this?"

She sighed. "No, but I guess we better get going." Sarah turned to Logan, she took his hands with tears in her eyes, she kissed him. He picked her up and he looked into her beautiful green eyes as he was not sure he would see them again.

"I'll be OK, this is not goodbye, it's a see you later."

She smiled. "Please come back to me."

He smiled. "I will, love."

Although in his mind he was not so sure, he set her down and looked over to see Hawk and Lilly saying their goodbyes. Peregrine let out a loud whistle, Thorn was with him and around fifty Elves with bows. Logan looked at them, he guessed the archers were better than no protection at all. Lilly took Sarah by the hand and they both headed to the front of the line. And slowly the Elves began to move forward.

Logan walked over to Hawk. "At this pace I am worried

they won't make it."

Hawk frowned. "They will speed up once they have cleared the forest, they only have one path with all our traps."

Shadow approached Hawk and Logan. "We will be going after this group has cleared."

Aura came over to Logan and kissed him on the cheek. "Thank you for saving my life, Logan. I can never repay you."

Logan looked at her. "You can pay me back by having a good life and taking care of this big guy here."

Shadow smiled and walked over to Logan and stuck out his arm. Logan gripped his arm and smiled. Shadow looked him in the eyes. "You would've been one hell of a wolf, I wish you well, Brother, know that our hearts and souls go with you."

Logan nodded. "Thank you, Shadow, take care of your people, perhaps one day I can meet them all."

Shadow smiled. "I would like that." With that they headed back to the Elves they were taking with them. Eventually half of the Elves had cleared the forest.

Logan looked at Hawk. "So, when are we opening the portal?"

"Right now."

Logan looked to see Star and Raven coming down the stairs and the other half of the Elves coming towards the tree. Petal was just a little behind them. She ran up to see Logan who picked her up.

He smiled. "Hello, my little friend, are you ready to meet the Dwarves?" She nodded but said nothing, she was upset. Logan looked at her. "What's wrong, Petal?"

"I am worried that when you beat Rubia, you and Sarah will go back to your own Realm and I'll never see you again."

Logan looked at her. "Well, we shall see after all this is

over, OK?"

She nodded. "OK." He set her down and she headed back to her mother. He looked at Hawk. "Let's get started, my friend."

Hawk looked miserable. "Star is going to assist me, so it won't take as long."

Logan nodded and moved out of the way so Hawk and Star could start the spell. Hawk was right, with the two of them it was much quicker and soon the portal was open. Raven and Star both walked up to Logan.

Star hugged him tightly. "Come back to us and may Moonrion shine down on you." She turned and with that her and Petal stepped through the portal.

Raven looked at him and smiled. "We have come a long way, Logan. I still don't know if you're brave or stupid, I guess we shall see. Good luck and do me a favour, don't lose." She turned and headed through the portal.

Hawk was slowly guiding Elves through the portal and within a few hours the town was empty. Hawk looked at Logan. "I was thinking I would stay and help you."

Logan walked towards Hawk and hugged him and stepped back and pushed him into the portal. The portal closed behind him and Logan was standing in a completely empty town. He walked up the stairs, he picked up his sword and shield and headed towards the stream where he had first seen Moonrion, he dipped his hand in the stream and wiped some across his forehead. He did not know if this would help or not, but it comforted him a little.

He looked up at the large blue moon. "Well, Moonrion. I guess this is the main event, please watch over everyone and give me the strength to be victorious."

He headed out to find a spot for his final battle with Rubia.

CHAPTER 39
THE FINAL BATTLE

Lilly and Sarah kept the Moon Elves moving as quickly as possible, the archers keeping a keen eye on fires that seemed to be getting closer. At their current pace, Sarah was very worried they would not have all the Elves in the forest by the time they crossed paths with Rubia's army. Lilly looked at her and by the look on her face she was thinking the same thing. Peregrine was getting frustrated with his people. He was pushing them to move faster, telling parents to carry their children.

He ordered half of his archers to help with the children. "We need to move, Elves, unless you want to come face to face with Rubia's army." He hated using scare tactics on his people, but it was the only thing that he could think of. And it seemed to be working, they were moving a little quicker.

The fires were getting closer, Thorn ran up to Peregrine. "We are not going to get everyone in on time, Rubia's army is advancing to quickly." Peregrine ran over to Lilly and Sarah; he relayed the information while they were still moving.

Sarah looked at Lilly. "What do we do?"

She thought quickly, the Elves at the front of the line were almost at the forest entrance.

She looked at Peregrine. "Move all the children to the front of the line and then the women." Peregrine nodded.

Sarah looked at Lilly. "If anything happens, you make

sure all the Elves get in the forest."

Lilly looked at her confused. "Sarah, we are all going to make it in, we just need to hurry."

Sarah nodded and smiled. "I am just saying, if things go south, don't worry about me, I can handle myself."

Lilly and Sarah quickly moved the women and children to the front of the line, they had almost reached the front of the Forest. Lilly and Sarah started to get the children organised, most of them were terrified. Sarah felt bad for the little Elves, but she knew they had to get them into that Forest. The front of the line was only a few minutes away, but they had over a mile of Elves to get inside. The torch fires were getting closer, and they could hear the march of the Snakaras, they had picked up their pace.

Sarah looked at the torch fire, she looked at Peregrine. "Are they in range for your archers?"

He looked towards the torches. "Not quite, but very soon they will be."

Sarah looked at Lilly. "Should we use the archers to try and slow them down?"

Lilly looked at Sarah and then Peregrine, she was not sure what to do. "We could end up just making them move faster if they started getting pelted with arrows."

Peregrine nodded. "That's definitely a possibility or they might back off I give it a fifty-fifty chance."

Lilly thought quickly. "Let's keep moving, I don't think we should provoke them just yet."

The front of the line was at the forest entrance. Jaguar was waiting for them. He smiled. "Hello, human Sarah."

She smiled. "Hello, Jaguar."

He looked at Lilly. "We will talk later, there is no time

now, we must get moving, come."

They started sending the women and children into the Forest. One male Elf started running for the Forest entrance. Sarah saw the Elf; she ran up behind him and hooked his ankle with her foot.

She stood over him and grabbed him by the collar. "What was it you didn't understand about women and children first? Try that again and you will be left out here to fend for yourself."

He re-joined the line but not before he got a slap in the back of the head from Thorn. Sarah ran back to the front of the line to help Lilly and Jaguar. They had about half of the Elves in the Forest when Rubia's army cleared the ridge, the other Elves where in plain view. The army was led by the two huge Snakaras, they all started hissing and the foot soldiers started to rattle in rhythm. Sarah looked at Lilly, they knew some of the Elves were not going to make it in.

Thorn looked at his fellow Elves, the only word that came from him was, "Move!"

He readied his bow. One of the large Snakaras raised a sword in the air and with a terrible cry dropped it. The soldiers began to run directly towards them.

Sarah looked at the hideous creatures coming for them and thought to herself, 'Well, we're fucked.'

Jaguar looked at what was coming, he whistled loudly and kept moving the Elves into the Forest. Lilly heard it before Sarah did, it was a strange sound, like a whooshing in the air. She looked up and with the blue moon she could see thousands of arrows flying towards the advancing army. Sarah looked over to see Lilly looking up when she too saw all the arrows. The advancing Snakara army began to drop left and right.

Thorn had begun firing his bow as had Peregrine and some of their other archers. Lilly and Sarah kept moving Elves instead of watching the battle. Rubia's army had lost a lot of warriors in a small amount of time.

The large Snakara called off the attack. "Our destination is Eclipse, there will be another time for these Elves."

The army changed direction towards Eclipse. Peregrine smiled; they had no idea the shit storm they were walking into.

Lilly and Sarah finally got all the Elves into the Forest, Lilly and Sarah with the archers were the last in. Sarah gasped when they were all inside, a huge orange shield blocked the entire opening.

Jaguar looked at them. "Jade does not take chances; you are all safe now."

Sarah frowned and looked out towards the moon. "Yes, we are all safe, except for Logan."

***

King Ember and Queen Azurite were waiting for a portal to open as they knew the Moon Elves would be arriving at any time. They had set-up for as many Elves as they could, as they did not have the room that the Forest Elves did except for the tunnels in the mountains which were too dangerous if you did not know your way around. Tundra joined them in her full armour.

King Ember looked at his daughter. "The portal is bringing us Moon Elves, not an army."

She looked over at her father. "You're the one who told me to be ready at all times."

The King smiled, she was right, he had taught her that. A

322

few minutes later a large portal opened in front of the Dwarves main walls and doors. The first three Elves who came through were two women and a child. One had jet black hair which the King knew was rare in Elven women, the other woman had the females usual silver hair, as did the child. They slowly walked toward the Dwarves, once they were close enough, they introduced themselves as Star and Raven and the child was named Petal.

The King and Queen smiled. "I am King Ember this is Queen Azurite and our Daughter Princess Tundra."

The little Elven girl gasped when he mentioned Tundra's name. She walked over and looked up at her. "You're the mighty Tundra who fought Logan, wow!"

Tundra removed her helmet and looked at Petal. "I am. What is your name, young one?"

"I am Petal, and I am going to be a woman warrior as well when I grow up."

King Ember laughed. "I like this one."

Star smiled. "Thank you, she has been excited to meet your kind as this is her first time seeing a Dwarf."

King Ember smiled. "Well, hopefully the next time we meet it will be under better circumstances." Raven and Star both agreed on that.

All the Elves had made it through the portal, the last Elf that came through rolled across the ground and slowly got up. Star looked over to see that it was Hawk, which was strange as he usually came through portals very gracefully. He stood up and brushed himself off and headed over to Star, Raven and Petal. Hawk was terribly angry.

Star looked at him. "What happened to you?"

He looked at her. "Logan and I were saying our goodbyes

and he gave me a hug and I was going to offer my help when he pushed me into the portal."

Star smiled. "Sounds like Logan."

Hawk looked at King Ember. "Your Highness."

The King looked at Hawk. "Let's get your people behind the wall and get everyone situated."

Tundra looked at her father. "Surely we can send one unit to help Logan, I will lead it."

King Ember shook his head. "This is Logan's fight, and we would most likely just be in his way, and if you knew Rubia, you'd be much less eager to get involved." The King smiled at his daughter. "Let's get the Elves behind the wall and lockdown the doors and wait this out."

She did as she was told and started to help the Elves move along to the doors.

Hawk looked at Star and Raven. "I wonder how Lilly and Sarah made out."

Star looked at Hawk. "They will be OK, Hawk."

He smiled. "I reached out with my magic and I have felt nothing from Lilly which most likely means she is already in the Forest." Hawk was still thinking about Logan having to do this alone and it broke his heart. He headed towards the doors as well, he looked at the portal as it closed.

***

Logan headed towards the Plains and found a suitable place for the final battle. It had a few places that rose a little higher than the rest of the terrain, which he could use to his advantage. He sat on a stone and waited for Rubia as he knew she could feel exactly where he was. He wondered if all the Elves had made it to their destinations safely. He knew Sarah was OK as he would have felt it if something had happened to her. He wished Moonrion had visited him before this final battle but honestly, what would she say that he did not already know? He had made a few modifications to his armour; his mouth area was now covered as he did not want another scratch from Rubia. He had made the mouth covering look like two rows of sharp teeth like the Samurai masks of old. The blue moon was so bright you could see everything. Logan looked at how beautiful this realm was. Out of nowhere he heard the howling of wolves and he smiled, he wondered if Shadow was saying good luck in his people's true form.

It had almost been a full day before Rubia showed herself. Finally, Logan could see torch lights coming over the ridge. Shortly after that he could see Rubia with a small battalion of Snakaras behind her. Logan did not expect a fair fight anyways, so this was no surprise at all. The armour she was wearing, however, was somewhat of a surprise, it was blood red and had two gargoyle like wings on the back.

'Great,' Logan thought to himself, 'now this bitch could fly.' Oh well, he now knew what his first two targets were going to be. He imagined, with her armour being blood red, it was most likely made from blood itself as he knew how twisted she was. Rubia was now close enough that they could talk to each other.

Logan called upon his armour and looked at Rubia. "That's close enough."

She smiled and stopped, she looked at Logan's armour, it seemed he had learned his lesson from her scratch as now there was no exposed skin, only sharp looking teeth. She had to admit he did look formidable, but it was all for nothing as he was going to die here tonight. She looked at him and threw him something wrapped in cloth.

He opened it. It was Sarah's head. At first his rage went through the roof, but he knew this was not real. He closed his eyes and threw it back at Rubia hard enough that it knocked her back. She looked down to see her own face.

She laughed. "It would seem you have learned a few new tricks since our last meeting."

Logan was still pissed but he had to keep a clear head as he knew more tricks would be on their way. Logan looked at the Snakaras. "It seems you've brought me some warmup."

She smiled. "I figured they would tire you some." Logan looked at the Snakaras who were too stupid to run. Rubia looked at Logan. "Last chance to join me, Logan."

Logan looked at her. "No, Rubia, this is your last chance, call off your attack and I will kill you quickly."

She laughed. "Oh, Logan, you actually think you have a chance, interesting I have been alive longer than your ancestors."

Logan nodded. "That may be true, but you think you're an original, special, you're a fucking cliché, the "Evil Queen" it's a story I've read many times, and who gave you the tittle of Queen, or did you just make that up too? You forget I am human; we have many like you back in my realm, all chasing power with no cares of who they hurt in the process and violence is our forte."

He must have struck a nerve, she looked at him. "I grow tired of this, kill him!"

The Snakaras moved in toward Logan, he brought up his sword and shield and ran directly through the centre of the attacking party, he was now behind them, Snakaras dropped on the left and right side of the centre path he had now cleared. It had happened so quickly that some who dropped did not even know they had been cut, like a razor. Logan attacked them from the back, his sword thrusting and slashing, he was moving so quickly the Snakaras did not even have time to block his attacks.

Rubia watched as Logan went through her creations so quickly, she had a hard time seeing him amongst the slaughter. She fired a green bolt of lightning from her hand, it did not hit him directly, but it struck the ground next to him and he was knocked off his feet. Snakaras were on top of him, hacking and slashing. Logan's armour was holding up just fine, he barely felt any of the blows, he brought his shield over his head and focused his power and blew most of the Snakaras flying, some of the closer ones having their necks broken from the upwards power.

Logan returned to his feet. Rubia fired another shot which he deflected with his shield, he tucked and rolled running his sword into the belly of another enemy. He decided he was done with these Snakaras, he picked up his pace, starting his deadly dance of power and steel. Heads flew and Snakara after Snakara fell to the ground until the entire battalion was destroyed. Rubia looked at Logan as he cleaned the blood and scales off his sword.

"Impressive, I see someone has been practising."

He walked over until they were almost face to face. "Now it's just you and me."

He stepped back, Rubia magically called upon her bow staff, she pushed a button on the staff and two blades revealed themselves on both ends. Logan was unimpressed, she let her wings stretch out now, they looked impressive. Logan watched her body language, he saw her move her left leg back, he readied himself.

She jumped up in the air and brought her bow staff down with the blade on the end acting more like a spear. Logan blocked the attack with his shield and rolled to the right. Her wings allowed her to fly and move quickly but Logan noticed she could not fly extremely high and that they were more for speed than height. Logan ran towards her, he jumped and delivered a mighty overhead strike which she easily blocked, and that's exactly what Logan had wanted as the strike was to bring her closer to the ground. He threw a sidekick into her stomach which she buckled from and flew to the ground. Her armour protected her from some of the blow, but Logan knew she had felt that. She recovered quicker than he was expecting though, she came at him twirling her staff. Logan fended off the attack and spun around sweeping her legs as he did. She was up quickly again.

Logan looked at her. "That's twice!" He smiled.

He put his shield down as he wanted more mobility with his sword. She stopped and looked at Logan thinking of her next attack, she fired another green bolt of lightning he blocked it with his sword, it still knocked him off his feet. He shook his head, that he felt.

She smiled. "What's wrong, Logan, did that hurt? It will be nothing compared to what I do to Sarah, perhaps I will give all my Snakaras male genitalia so she can be raped all day."

Logan sprung forward, he hacked and slashed with such ferocity that Rubia was worried that perhaps she should have kept her mouth shut. She was tiring from all the blocking; she flew back to give herself some room. Just as Logan was going to continue his attack there was a massive explosion off in the direction of Eclipse, both Rubia and Logan looked in the direction of the explosion.

Logan smiled, they worked. He looked at Rubia. "If you're wondering what that was, it's your army being decimated by Dwarven mines."

She looked at him with hatred in her eyes. "It matters little, Logan, my army is too large, there will still be enough to kill all the Elves remaining in the town."

Logan smiled. "Oh, I forgot to tell you, no one is home. Didn't you, in all your wisdom, know there are no Elves in Eclipse?"

She felt out with her magic and could feel nothing in the town. She looked at Logan, she screamed! She attacked Logan and hatred was getting the best of her, this was his plan. He blocked another strike and flipped in the air over her head and with two quick strikes both wings now lay on the ground, she turned and screamed. Logan was not sure if it was out of pain or anger or both, the scream was so powerful it knocked Logan onto his back. He stood back up.

"You stupid human, when I finish with you, I will destroy the Elves and the Dwarves, I will bathe in their blood."

She quickly fired something blue from her hand, it hit Logan directly in the head. He screamed and dropped to the ground as everything terrible that had ever happened to him was flashing through his mind. He was seeing Sarah being raped and all of his friends dead and Rubia pouring their blood over her body, he saw himself drinking and being drunk and all the horrible things he had ever said to Sarah in a drunken rage.

Rubia watched as Logan held his head, he sounded like an angry animal. She started to see his armour flickering as he could not focus. Her mind attack was working, eventually Logan's armour was completely gone. Rubia focused her magic and fired dark red fire from her hands, it completely engulfed Logan. Logan's visions stopped quickly, he looked around, he was engulfed in some sort of red fire, he was hot and sweating but for some reason the fire was not killing him, even without his armour.

Rubia stopped the fire attack, she could not believe what her eyes were seeing. Logan was crouched, his clothes were completely burned off his body, he was naked, there was steam rising from his skin, he should have been nothing but ash. He struggled forward and picked up his sword, if he was going to die, he was not going to do it on his knees, he forced himself to his feet. He fell back onto his knees, the fire had not killed him, but it had weakened him greatly, he decided to save his energy for one more strike.

Rubia smiled and walked over to where he kneeled. She stood over him like a predator that was going to deal its death blow.

She picked his head up and looked him in the eyes. "Well, Logan. I'll give you credit, you're full of surprises, it's going to be a pity to kill you, don't worry, I will take care of Sarah for you."

His face changed and his eyes filled with hatred and silver light, he almost looked demonic. She moved back from his face and stood up to deal the killing blow. She raised her bow staff and aimed it for Logan's head, the blade shining in the light of the blue moon. She forced the staff down with all her might, it hit stone.

Logan had been waiting for this, he rolled at the last second, he was still on his knees, she moved quickly to strike again. Logan swung his sword upwards with all his remaining power, his sword broke through the magical staff. He thrust his blade upwards it went through the bottom of Rubia's mouth and came out through the top of her head, he left the blade in as she fell to the ground.

He crawled over to her. "Now you die as you have lived, alone."

There was a bright light and Rubia's body rose. Logan was worried he had not killed her, seconds later she imploded, her body was gone, for a few moments a bright red light and green light sat where her body had been, then it dissipated and there was nothing.

Logan laid on the ground, still naked and exhausted. He couldn't move and he decided this was as good as any place to die.

CHAPTER 40
THE UNKNOWN

It seemed like they had been in the forest forever. Although Sarah knew it had been no more than a couple of days as the sun was now up. She was having a hard time focusing on anything, she sat with her back against a large tree. Jaguar approached and handed her a large leaf with some sort of food on it. It didn't look appetizing, but it smelt delicious, she thanked him, but she did not want to eat.

Jaguar looked at her. "Human Sarah, you must eat to keep your strength up. Logan would not want you to starve yourself."

She looked at him and sighed. "I suppose you're right, thank you, Jaguar, and you can just call me Sarah."

He smiled at her and nodded and left to help feed the other Elves. Sarah looked at the food, she tried to eat and ended up eating all of it, she did not realize how hungry she was. She was still very anxious and worried, wondering what she would do if Logan did not come back. Would she stay in Silver Moon or go back to the Earth realm? She had no answers for these questions.

Lilly walked up to her with some water, she drank some and just kept looking towards the shield that protected the front of the forest.

Lilly knelt beside her, she brushed Sarah's hair out of her face. "He's going to be OK, have faith."

She looked at Lilly. "I have faith in Logan. I always have, even in his darkest moments. I am not so much worried about him dying as he's so damn stubborn. I worry that the Logan that left us, will not be the same Logan who returns."

Lilly was not sure what to say so she said nothing and just sat down beside Sarah and held her hand.

***

Hawk was pacing back and forth in front of the Dwarven castle, his stomach in knots. He jumped when a strong hand touched his shoulder. Hawk turned to see King Ember standing behind him.

"You're going to wear away the stone of my stair, Elf!" He smiled. "Come, let us go have a drink, you look like you could use one."

Hawk had no objections, they went to the large room and table where he and Logan had enjoyed the feast, which seemed like a lifetime ago. The only people who sat at the table were the royal family, Star and Raven and of course, Petal. Petal was still questioning Tundra about her being a woman warrior.

Star looked to her daughter. "Petal, honey, give Tundra a few minutes to relax."

Tundra looked at Star. "It's OK. I don't mind talking about being a warrior. Just remember, Petal, never let anyone tell you women cannot be warriors." Petal nodded and smiled towards her mother and gave Tundra a break.

King Ember and Hawk entered the large hall, they both took a seat. He asked one of his Dwarves to bring them some mead and wine for their guests. The Dwarf returned with mead and wine and some bread and dried meat. The Dwarf poured mead for Hawk and wine for the women, except for Tundra who preferred mead, and lastly the King.

Petal looked at her mother. "Momma, may I try a small sip of wine?"

Normally Star would have said no way, but it was a unique time and she decided to allow Petal a small amount.

The King raised his glass, everyone at the table followed suit. "To Logan, one of the bravest and most noble men I have had the pleasure of knowing, may he strike down that murderous bitch once and for all."

The King looked at Star. "Uh, sorry. I got caught up in the moment."

Star laughed. "I would not worry about Miss Petal here; she has said worse when it comes to Rubia."

Petal smiled. "Logan's female mate swears a lot."

King Ember laughed. "It sounds like I would like her."

Petal nodded. "She is nice, and she has red hair like yours."

The King smiled. "I did not know humans could grow red hair."

Queen Azurite smiled. "You've only met one."

The King looked at his wife. "Aye, this is true love. You see, ladies, my wife is much smarter than I."

The Queen smirked. "Yes, but this seems to be true of most women."

The women at the table laughed, even the King and Hawk laughed as neither of them had any arguments about that.

Hawk looked at King Ember seriously for a moment. "You were in the first war and fought alongside Moon Shatter, which is common knowledge, but what do you honestly think Logan's chances are?"

Everyone looked towards the King as he was the only one in the room who had been in the first war. He thought about it for a few moments before answering the question. The King looked at everyone. "I don't want to give anyone false hope, but if it came down to a fair fight then Logan would destroy her, his swordsmanship is better than even Moon Shatter's was, but there is not one of us sitting at this table who doesn't know Rubia will not make this a fair fight. She will use every trick she has up her sleeve, let's just hope his mind is as strong as his body."

Hawk sat back in his chair and took a large mouthful of mead which was helping him relax a little.

Petal looked at all the adults, they all looked sad or worried. She was angry. "I don't know why you're all sad or worried, Logan will win, and he will come back. I gave him my necklace and it will protect him even from her."

Star looked at her daughter and smiled. "Look at me, Petal, you know that Logan may not return."

Petal looked at her mother defiantly. "You can all think what you want, but I know Logan is coming back!"

Hawk looked at Petal and wished he were young again and had that blind faith as he could use it now. They continued to drink and talk until the sun was starting to come up as none of them would be able to sleep.

Out of nowhere Hawk was hit with a force that was like a punch to the chest, Star and Raven felt it also. The Dwarves looked at the three of them, confused as to what just happened.

"It's over." Was all Hawk said.

King Ember looked at him. "What do you mean, did Logan kill her or she him?"

Hawk closed his eyes. "I am trying to figure that out, but

something is blocking me." Hawk looked grim. "I cannot get a reading of anything."

***

Logan was still laying on the ground looking up into the sky knowing he had won, and all the Elves and Sarah would be OK. He smiled. But he also knew this would be his final resting place. His eyes closed when he felt a gentle nudge on his shoulder.

'Logan, open your eyes!' He did as was instructed. Tears rolled down his cheeks as what he was seeing had to be an angel. *'Logan it's me, Moonrion!'*

Logan shook his head. "You are not Moonrion, she is a Pegasus!"

Moonrion smiled, *'Logan, this is my Elven form that very few have seen.'*

He looked at her more closely. "You're beautiful!"

She smiled. *'Thank you.'*

She put her hand on his forehead and within moments he could feel his power returning and all his pain eased.

Logan shook his head and sat up. "Wow, thanks for the recharge, boss!"

Moonrion smiled, *'It seems Rubia has not stripped you of your sense of humour. I am proud of you, Logan, you have done what most would have called impossible.'*

He looked at her. "What happens now?"

Moonrion looked at him. *'That depends on you, Logan.'*

He looked around. "Well, do you want me to stay in Silver Moon?"

She smiled again. *'Like I said, that is a choice you must*

make.'

Logan looked at her. "I want to stay here, but I do have a condition."

Moonrion asked. *'And what is your condition?'*

Logan frowned. "Hawk had mentioned that if I stay here I will begin to age like the Elves, and if that is true, I want Sarah to be able to have this gift as well. I do not want to be alone for hundreds of years."

Moonrion looked at Logan. *'That is all? Oh Logan, of course I will grant this for you, but you must remember that even Elves die at different times, not even I can stop death. So, you must understand nothing with life can be promised. But she will now age like my Elves.'* She stood up. *'Kneel!'* Logan did as he was instructed. *'I, Moonrion, Goddess of Silver Moon and Keeper of the realm, Knight thee Logan Coyle as Guardian of the realm and of all life within it.'*

She touched each shoulder with her blade. She then presented him with a new sword, it was similar in shape to the blade he had now, with a slight curve at the top of the blade. He looked at the design, the guard looked like a crescent moon, the handle was blue, and the pommel was the head of a Pegasus, the blade seemed to glow like the moon itself.

Moonrion smiled. *'Present your old sword.'* He did as he was asked. She took the sword and it disappeared. He swung the new blade, it was a little heavier, but it felt perfect in his hands. Moonrion looked at him. *'This is a God blade, it will protect you and will cut through anything, take care of it, Logan!'*

He smiled. "I give you my word. What happened to the other sword?"

She nodded. *'It's back with Moon Shatter.'*

Logan just looked at the Goddess. "Thank him for me."

'You have already thanked him by destroying Rubia, his soul can move on.'

Logan thought for a moment and asked one last question. "Can we keep all of this between us? I don't want any titles or being called Sir; I just want to be Logan. I am dreading going back to the Elves and Sarah and the Dwarves and being called a hero and all that. I only did this because I thought it was right, not for titles."

The Goddess smiled. *'Always the humble one, do not worry, your title will be known only by me.'* She looked at him. *'Now go to Sarah and enjoy your victory! And Logan, I will always be here when you need me. Take care, Sir Logan!'*

And with that she was gone.

***

Logan was back to his normal self and he was elated that Moonrion had granted him his one wish. Now Sarah would age like he did, the new sword was a nice touch as well. He started to run towards the Forest Elves land. He was moving at an impossible speed for a normal human and he had barely even got his heart going yet.

It was nightfall when Logan arrived at the Forest opening, only to find there was a giant orange shield of some kind. Jade must have put it up after the Moon Elves were safely inside. He walked towards the shield, he reached his hand towards the shield and hesitated after thinking about what had happened the last time his hand had touched something magical. He decided to call upon his armour, he moved forward and decided he would just walk through. He moved forward and went through the shield and as soon as he was on the other side the shield disappeared.

Jaguar jumped down from a tree, Logan's hand went directly to his sword.

Jaguar put his hands up. "It's just me, Jaguar!" He had a worried look in his eyes.

Logan removed his hand from his sword. "Sorry, Jaguar, my friend. I guess I am still a little jumpy."

Jaguar looked at Logan. "So, Rubia is dead." Jaguar smiled. "Follow me."

Logan followed Jaguar as both races of Elves were rising and whispering different things as Logan walked by, it was hard to understand all of it due to the two different dialects. Jaguar brought Logan to where Sarah and Lilly had fallen asleep. Seeing Sarah was like a dream, she was so beautiful when she slept, he almost did not want to wake her. He sat beside her and tucked a piece of her hair behind her ear. She stirred and opened her eyes; she did not realise Logan was sitting right beside her at first. She was about to go back to sleep when from beside her she heard the most soothing voice and knew instantly who it belonged to.

"Hey, babe, you come here often?"

She looked over and sitting beside her was Logan. "Logan, is that really you?" She pinched her skin.

She jumped onto his lap and put her head on his shoulder, she was crying. It was a happy cry though, she took his face into her hands and they locked eyes, both had tears in them. She kissed him gently and looked into his dark blue eyes. She still had his face in her hands, and she started moving it to the right and left and checking his body.

Logan smiled. "I am fine, love."

Sarah smiled. "I just thought I would never see you again, this still feels like a dream."

Logan laughed. "Thanks for having faith in me, love."

She looked at him. "I had faith that you would kill her, I just didn't know if the same Logan would return, I was worried she would destroy your mind."

Logan frowned. "The bitch certainly tried; can we change the subject? I do not wish to talk about it right now."

Sarah smiled. "Of course, babe."

Lilly had just woken up and looked over and could not believe her eyes, there right in front of her was Sarah sitting in Logan's lap.

She jumped up. "Logan, is that really you, are you OK?"

He looked at her. "Yes, Lilly, it's me, and yes I am the best I have ever been."

She ran over and hugged them both much tighter than Logan thought she had the strength to do. She also looked over his body checking for any wounds.

Logan smiled; it must be their maternal instincts. "I am fine, Lilly, fit as a fiddle."

She looked at him. "I didn't think this was possible. I expected a bloody broken warrior."

Logan smiled. "It's amazing what faith can accomplish in this realm." And that was the only thing he said on the matter.

The Elves began to cheer now that word had spread. This was the part that Logan had been dreading, the cheers and chanting of his name.

He looked at Sarah. "I am just going to thank Jade."

Sarah grabbed his hand. "These people are all alive because of you. You are their hero."

He looked at Sarah. "I don't want to be a hero; I am just

an ordinary man who was put in an extra ordinary situation. I just want to be with you and have some peace and quiet."

She smiled. "I know, Logan, but stand up and give them a wave and then go and see Jade. I will wait for you here."

Logan stood up and smiled and waved to all the cheering Elves who had now started chanting his name. Peregrine and Thorn smiled at him and nodded, and he nodded back knowing this meant more to him than any words they could've said to him. Logan headed to Jade's home; he was about to knock when Jade told him to come in.

She looked at him. "I see the reluctant hero has returned, and yes, before you say anything, I know you don't want to be called a hero."

He nodded. "And you are wise as always."

She smiled. "Logan, you are going to have to get used to being looked up to by the Elves, think of all the lives you have saved! You have done what most thought was impossible, something an entire army failed at doing. You are the protector of this realm now and with it comes heavy responsibilities."

Logan looked at her in shock. "How do you know I am not going back to the Earth realm?"

Jade looked at him. "Oh, Logan, you wear your heart on your sleeve and I know you will be staying, that's quite the new sword."

Logan smiled; he did not think he could get anything past Jade when it came to knowledge. He looked at her. "I am staying, and I will protect the realm and I hope I can visit you for knowledge and advice from time to time."

Jade looked at Logan. "You are always welcome here, Logan, as it's now as much your land as it is us Elves."

Logan smiled. "Thank you for your help, but I still have

work to do getting all the Moon Elves home."

She smiled. "Go to Sarah and help the Elves, I hope to see you again soon."

Logan looked at her. "You will, once this all calms down."

Logan walked to where Sarah and Lilly were waiting for him.

Sarah put her arm around his waist. "So now what?"

"Let's get the Moon Elves back to Eclipse and go from there."

Lilly gave him a kiss on both of his cheeks. "Thank you, Logan. I will get everyone organised."

A short time later the Moon Elves were ready to make the trek back.

CHAPTER 41
HOME COMING

Hawk woke in the chair he had been sitting in. He reached out with his magic, he could feel a large amount of magic, he woke the others who had also fallen asleep. Everyone woke up groggy and confused.

Raven and Star both looked at Hawk who smiled. "Can you feel it?"

They both closed their eyes and when they opened them, they looked at Hawk. "Rubia is dead, and Logan is with the Forest Elves."

Hawk nodded. "Yes, that's what I thought. I just wanted both of you to confirm it to make sure I was not going crazy."

Petal looked at all the adults. "So does that mean Logan beat Rubia?"

Star looked at her daughter. "Yes, love, it would seem he has won the battle."

Petal smiled and looked at all of them with a 'I told you so' look on her face.

'The faith of children in their innocence is amazing,' thought Hawk to himself.

They all smiled. Hawk was filled with so many emotions, Logan had actually pulled it off, he knew Logan was powerful and stubborn, but he had been worried how his mind would hold up, to be honest they still didn't know if Logan were mentally Ok or if he would be changed.

King Ember looked at the Elves. "It would seem Moonrion knows how to pick them. The shithead pulled it off," laughed the King.

Petal gave the King a dirty look as she did not understand why the King would insult the man who saved them. Her mother told her she would explain later, and it was not an insult, it was a joke between Logan and the King. Petal looked at her mother, she knew Logan was funny, so the joke made sense.

Hawk looked at the King. "It looks like we will not be in your hair for as long as we thought." Hawk stood up and looked at Star. "We need to open the portal. I need to go back and see what kind of damage Rubia's army did to our town."

Raven looked at him. "The three of us will go and make sure it is safe."

Hawk agreed, Star looked at the King. "Do you mind looking after Petal while we are away?"

Tundra smiled. "I'll take her with me and show her my battle axe and what it can do."

Petal looked at her mother. "I'll be OK, Momma, I'll be careful, and I really want to see what Tundra's axe can do!"

Star looked at Tundra and her daughter. "Thank you, Tundra." With that, the three Elves headed to where the original portal had been.

The three of them focused their magic to reopen it. With the power of three the portal opened within minutes. Hawk was impressed by Raven's control; he was worried they would be going into Eclipse and it would be decimated but unfortunately the only way to find out was to go and look. He hoped he was wrong, they stepped through the portal.

Once they arrived in Eclipse the first thing that hit them

was the smell, it was terrible. It smelt of burnt and rotting flesh. Raven thought of Shadow's lecture and threw up. Hawk was close to doing the same. He quickly used a sensory spell so he could no longer smell anything. They walked slowly and carefully towards the Tree of Power. There was armour lying on the ground and under some of it were the Diamond back rattlesnakes used by Rubia as her main foot soldiers.

Star and Hawk used fire spells to kill them as they continued to move slowly forward. They reached the Tree of Power and looked across the town and were surprised to see almost nothing in the town was different besides all the empty armour. Hawk smiled, he guessed between the Dwarven mines and all their traps, very few Snakaras had made it to the city. And he wondered if the Forest Elves had killed some on the way by their land. And finally, once Logan had killed Rubia, all her abominations had returned to their original serpent form. They had some cleaning up to do but their town had survived the invasion.

All three came together and hugged each other. Hawk spoke. "Thank Moonrion and Logan, I can't believe we pulled this off."

They heard a noise in the trees, all three jumped back and prepared attack spells. Two large wolves walked towards them and then the usual flash and standing in front of them was Shadow and Aura.

Hawk smiled at Shadow. "It's good to see you, my friend."

Shadow smiled back. "We came to see what kind of shape the town was in, and if it was safe to start bringing your people back, they are definitely not made for Plains living."

Hawk laughed. "No, they definitely were not, but it looks

like you can start bringing them back."

Shadow looked around the town, he was surprised the Dwarven mines had not damaged anything as they had heard the explosion from their den. They heard more commotion in the woods along the only safe passage they had left for now. Lilly, Sarah and Logan came through the trees and behind them Elves started to flow into their town.

Lilly ran to Hawk, he picked her up and spun her around and kissed her repeatedly. She laughed through her tears, although they had only been apart a couple of days it had seemed like forever. Hawk also did not know how close they had come to disaster. Hawk set Lilly down and looked at Logan and Sarah, he smiled, the Elves were all patting Logan on the back and praising his name.

Logan walked forward to Hawk. "I am sorry I pushed you through the portal, but I couldn't have you doing anything stupid."

Hawk was so happy to see everyone he had almost forgotten about it. "Yeah but I understand, and it looks like you managed OK without me."

Raven walked over to Logan and gave him a small hug. "Not bad for a human." They smiled at each other and Raven even gave Sarah a small hug.

Shadow and Aura were next in line to thank Logan. Logan looked at Shadow. He smiled. "If you would have asked me if one man could destroy Rubia, I would have deemed them mad. Although, I guess you're not exactly normal, you have done more for me and Silver Moon than words can say, if you ever need me, I will always have your back, my friend."

Aura said nothing but she did hug Logan so tightly it felt like she was going to break his back. She let him go and smiled, nothing needed to be said, her eyes said enough.

Shadow looked at Aura. "Let's go and bring the Moon Elves home." With that they both headed into the woods, with two flashes they were gone.

Logan looked at Hawk. "I suppose we should go and thank King Ember."

Hawk told them they would be back shortly and they both went through the portal. When they arrived on the other side, Logan nearly fell but he managed to keep his balance this time.

Hawk looked at him. "See, practice."

There were Elves beyond the Dwarves wall as the King had started to get them ready when he had heard Logan had been victorious. The royal family was in front, with Tundra holding Petal who she set down as she started to run to Logan.

Logan picked her up, he handed her the necklace she had given him. "Thank you, Petal, this helped save my life."

She smiled and looked at him like she already knew it had. She asked him if Rubia was really gone and if they were all safe.

Logan smiled. "Yes, Petal, you're safe now."

King Ember walked up to Logan. "Ah, Logan, it's good to see you in one-piece, lad! I am still not sure if you are one of the bravest men I have ever met or fucking crazy!"

Logan laughed. "Honestly, I think it's a little of both."

The King smiled. "I guess I can't call you shithead anymore."

Logan laughed. "How about this, only you can."

The King smiled and stepped back. Queen Azurite looked at Logan. "Well done young man, you will always be welcome here. I hope you will revisit us soon after you have settled, I would like to hear of the battle."

347

Logan smiled. "It might be a while before I can talk about that nightmare, but when I am, I will tell you." She smiled in understanding.

Tundra walked up to him. "Well, at least now I can say I fought and lived against the guy who destroyed Rubia, by the way, you are not getting out of that rematch." She hugged him and stepped back.

With that, Hawk and Logan began to let the Elves go through the portal. Logan nodded at the King and walked through the portal. He kept his balance this time.

Sarah and Lilly were waiting by the portal. Sarah ran to Logan as soon as she saw him, she hugged him and kissed his forehead. "Can we go home now?"

He looked at her. "That depends on where you define home now."

She looked at him. "What do you mean?"

He looked at her. "I've been given the job of protecting this realm and all life in it."

She looked down. "Oh. That sounds important, so you will age like the Elves now?"

He smiled. "Yes, love, and don't worry, so do you now."

She looked up. "How can you know that?"

"Being the protector of the realm has a few perks that come with it."

She smiled at him. "What makes you think I want to put up with your ass for that long?"

He laughed. "Well, in this realm who knows, it might not be as long as you think."

She smirked at him. "I guess I can handle being the woman who is with the protector of the realm, normally I would be pissed you didn't check with me on all this first, but

I get to live much longer and be with you, so I'll let it slide this time."

Logan let out a sigh of relief. "I was worried you would want to go back to the Earth realm."

"I have friends here now and after all we have been through, I could never go back."

He smiled. "I know the feeling."

As he saw Hawk walking towards them. "One more meeting at the 'War Table'."

Logan smiled. "Let's go!"

Star now had Petal in her arms, the little one was almost getting too big to be picked up. Star, Petal, Raven, Lilly, Sarah, Hawk and Logan went up the stairs. They were all happy they could all finally have some peace.

Logan looked at Hawk. "I have one question about my battle with Rubia. She engulfed me in red fire and my armour was not protecting me at the time, how am I not dead?"

Hawk looked at Raven and Star. Hawk shook his head. "That's not possible, Logan. Red fire is as strong as Dragon's fire."

Sarah looked at everyone, being a nurse, she threw out a random thought. "Could it be a side effect of the Dragon saliva Logan was given?"

You could almost see the lightbulb go on over Hawk's head. "Of course, I guess all the myths are true."

"What myth?" Logan asked.

"Well, it's said if you survive having Dragon saliva run through your body, it makes you immune to fire. Most do not survive, there has been a few who tried over the centuries, all of them died."

Logan shrugged. "Just blind luck then."

"Not exactly, if you had never gone to save Aura and had not been poisoned, we would never have used the saliva. I guess you going to save her in turn saved your own life."

Logan smiled. "So, in the end, Rubia screwed herself."

Hawk smiled. "It would seem so. Well, we all need rest so let us organise the clean up tomorrow night."

No one argued with Hawk on that point, everyone was more exhausted than they realised, everyone said goodnight.

Hawk looked at Logan. "Oh, I forgot one more thing, we need to go to Rubia's lair and see if she left anything behind that could be dangerous and gather her books."

Logan nodded. "Let's rest and worry about that later, my friend."

Logan and Sarah headed back to their home, they showered together and headed to bed, they held each other, they did not say anything, enjoying the peace of not having to worry about Rubia anymore. Logan thought about all the lives lost and sacrifices people had made and about the battle and he decided to clear his mind and let himself fall asleep with Sarah in his arms. Sarah snuggled into him and for the first time in his life he was truly at peace.

Back in Rubia's lair there was not much now that she was gone, just some books and a summoning circle with a single Demon claw in it.

Manufactured by Amazon.ca
Bolton, ON